TALES IN TIME

EDITED BY PETER CROWTHER

tales in time edited by / peter crowther

cover illustration / larry s. friedman

book design / michelle prahler

White Wolf Publishing
780 Park North Boulevard, Suite 100
Clarkston, GA 30021
www.white-wolf.com

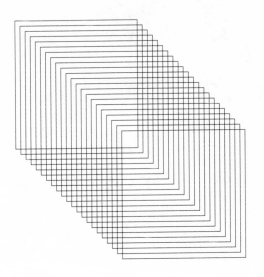

TABLE OF CONTENTS

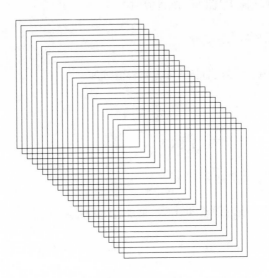

FOREWORD

BY PETER CROWTHER

Time...

Convicts serve it, bored people kill it, bums waste it and busy people try to make it. There's even a few who try to *bend* it...or, at least, they dream up ways that *other* folks might bend it. People like the thirteen writers in this book.

Putting together this collection has been a true labor of love.

There were so many possible stories but, frankly, just not enough space.

Thus the tales that appear here are intensely personal choices and there are inevitably going to be others that some readers feel should also have been included. Well, if this book proves to be popular, then maybe there'll be a second volume. Let us know...and let us know which stories *you* wanted to see again.

Meanwhile, turn the page and find a ghost that walks only when it rains, an old bureau that serves as a mailbox to (and *from!*) another era, a sightseeing tour to the age of the dinosaurs, a lonely astronaut trying to get home and a small boy who can tune into the *strangest* programmes on his radio. Oh, yes...and there are a couple of time machines, too.

My warmest thanks go to John Clute, co-Editor of *The Encyclopedia of Science Fiction*, for his introduction; *New Worlds* editor David Garnett and *Interzone* editor David Pringle for helping me track down copies of a couple of difficult tales; and Stewart Wieck, White Wolf's head honcho, for suggesting we do the book in the first place. And, of course, thanks too to all the wonderful writers whose work once again sees print...hey, who says there's no such thing as time travel!?

Relax and enjoy...believe me, you're in for the *times* of your life!

Peter Crowther
Harrogate, England
November 1996

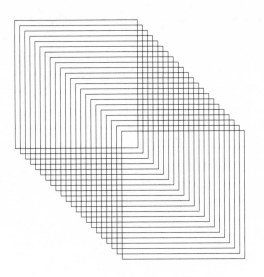

TIME AND THE HUMAN CONDITION

AN INTRODUCTION BY JOHN CLUTE

Then, *now* and *soon*: three words that govern our lives.

Like it or not, the human animal is obsessed with Time. We disguise our preoccupation by engaging ourselves in a variety of interests—politics, sports, entertainment, work…all the various elements that color our existence—but the reality is that even through it all, we experience an underlying anxiety about the nature of Time: primarily, where has it all gone and how much of it is left?

The air we breathe, the roads we travel…these things we accept without question. But the *time* through which we move baffles and mystifies us, for it poses an intriguing, ungraspable problem. This is the nature of the human condition; it is this ability to question things that makes us special—or perhaps it is our curse.

There is a maxim that states: If we were simple enough to understand ourselves, we'd be too stupid to make sense of what we learned. This applies also, albeit slightly modified, to Time: If Time were simple enough to understand, we'd be unable to understand it.

We certainly have tried.

The Encyclopedia of Time (Garland Publishing, Inc.: 1994), edited by Samuel L. Macey, supplies hundreds of takes on Time over its 700 pages. Entries are grouped under various subjects: Aging, Film, Astronomy, Biology, Geology, History, Horology, Law, Literature, Math, Measurement, Music, Philosophy, Physics, Psychology, Religion, Sociology. Some of these entries are quite substantial, while some are more frivolous; but in the end every one of them generates—for me, at least—a vision of the human spirit mired in its own substance. We are stuck here.

But when we come to the telling of tales and the invention of fictions, maybe the picture changes. Just a little.

It is a central contemporary metaphor about the nature of consciousness that the flow of self within the mind is storylike; that introspection is a kind of narrative. So it follows that those who tell stories in the open—that is, stories told or written down for our delight—will, almost by necessity, confront the problematic elements of Time…if unintentionally.

But science fiction and fantasy authors are a different kettle of fish, as the tales assembled here will eloquently demonstrate.

Before science fiction existed, storytellers were all too aware of their pasts and of the past of the society in which they lived. But there was no concept of a future... of a time yet to come. It was not until the 18th century that any story of any significance was set in an explicit (or even implicit) future time. And only in the 1800s did the civilizations of the West begin fully to respond to the concept of Time as a clock, carrying history along a linear course to utopia...or in some other direction to some other place.

Only then did Time become a road that we could travel upon. Suddenly we were able, in our imaginations, to manipulate our own situations.

We may *have been* someplace...and we may *be going* someplace else; but who's to say we can't go back? And who's to say we have to wait to move ahead? Thus, science fiction provided the metaphor of the time traveler. The arrow of Time had become a traffic signal.

There are, of course, two different kinds of time travel. To our late 20th century taste, the first kind is of only moderate interest.

Time travel into the future, for us, tends to serve as little more than a buggywhip convention usually found in stories half a century old or more, which enables authors to hoist their point-of-view characters into an interesting future time. From this vantage point, they send back to us tales of the marvels (or otherwise) in store. H. G. Wells's *The Time Machine* (1895) escapes triviality on two counts: (1) by being the first story in which a time machine is actually described and (2) by virtue of the huge scope of the tale, the devastating evolutionary perspective unfolded as the Time Traveler lunges farther and farther into the deep future, washing our eyes clean of vanity.

The second kind of time travel, which could not come to full fruit until the first kind had domesticated the concept of Time as a road, is of course time travel into the past. Whether its protagonist is traveling from a future point backward to our own present, or (more commonly) traveling from the present into the past, the story of time travel pastward is the category of science fiction that may be the most challenging, alarming, dangerous and enticing of all.

The first real (though not defining) example of the form, Mark Twain's *A Connecticut Yankee in King Arthur's Court* (1889), may have dodged some of the potential consequences of the Yankee Boss's trip to Arthurian Britain; but few subsequent stories of time travel pastward have been able to ignore the implications of moving into history. Because the past is dangerous. Travelers may be trapped there in a claustrophobia of nescience, and in some stories this happens. More often, though, travelers run the risk of altering the very fabric of being and changing the present or the future from which they came.

Stories of this sort—told by one human to another, each steeped in or aware of their own environment—can seem daring and almost blasphemous. It is as though the plug is being pulled on what makes us human. Our bladders collapse. Like those fish in the aquarium, suddenly removed from the safety and familiarity of our environment, we gasp in the naked sun.

It may be for this reason that so many of the stories of time travel pastward—at least those which we can define as science fiction tales—tend not to concentrate on the vertiginous pleasures of changing the course of being, but to focus instead upon time patrol adventures, where cadres of specialist police time past in order to keep things from changing, to keep the world intact.

The impulse to write this sort of fiction is strong, and has made for some fine, if melancholy, novels, such as Poul Anderson's various Time Patrol tales, or John Crowley's *Great Word of Time* (1991). Less often does this impulse generate good short stories; and no stories of this kind have been included here.

What you will find here is a collection of tales about the human condition: the almost inconceivable loneliness and determination of Tiptree's "The Man Who Walked Home," the gentle passion of Finney's "The Love Letter," and the aching nostalgia of Ellison's "Jeffty is Five."

Elsewhere we have paradoxes galore, from Bradbury's Time Safari adventurers in "A Sound of Thunder" to the bemused scientists in Robinson's "'—and Subsequent Construction,'" taking in along the way two bands of hapless observers, one from the future and one from the past, staring at each other across a battlefield in Kilworth's "On the Watchtower at Platea."

These are not simply tales of someone stepping into a machine and pushing a few buttons to go forward or back. These are stories which only exist—*could* only exist—in the worlds of science fiction.

Some are rough-hewn and brutal, others are tender and touching. They are tales which come as close as possible to achieving the kind of perspective only an alien could ever gain in truth: a clear view of the human animal, dancing in the amber of Time.

John Clute
London,
November 1996

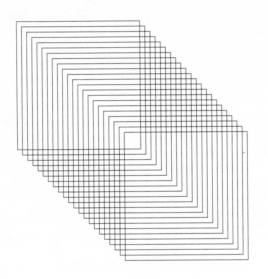

THE VERY SLOW TIME MACHINE

TIME MACHINE

BY IAN WATSON

The Very Slow Time Machine—for convenience: the VSTM[1]—made its first appearance at exactly midday 1 December 1985 in an unoccupied space at the National Physical Laboratory. It signaled its arrival with a loud bang and a squall of expelled air. Dr. Kelvin, who happened to be looking in its direction, reported that the VSTM did not exactly *spring* into existence instantly, but rather expanded very rapidly from a point source, presumably explaining the absence of a more devastating explosion as the VSTM jostled with the air already present in the room. Later, Kelvin declared that what he had actually seen was the *implosion* of the VSTM. Doors were sucked shut by the rush of air, instead of bursting open, after all. However it was a most confused moment—and the confusion persisted, since the occupant of the VSTM (who alone could shed light on its nature) was not only time-reversed with regard to us, but also quite crazy.

One infuriating thing is that the occupant visibly grows saner and more presentable (in his reversed way) the more that time passes. We feel that all the hard work and thought devoted to the enigma of the VSTM is so much energy poured down the entropy sink—because the answer is going to come from him, from inside, not from us; so that we may as well just have bided our time until his condition improved (or, from his point of view, began to degenerate). And in the meantime his arrival distorted and perverted essential research at our laboratory from its course without providing any tangible return for it.

The VSTM was the size of a small station wagon; but it had the shape of a huge lead sulphide, or galena, crystal—which is, in crystallographer's jargon, an octahedron-with-cube formation consisting of eight large hexagonal faces with six smaller square faces filling in the gaps. It perched precariously—but immovably—on the base square, the four lower hexagons bellying up and out towards its waist where four more squares (oblique, vertically) connected with

---

[1] The term V S T M is introduced retrospectively in view of our subsequent understanding of the problem (2019).

the mirror-image upper hemisphere, rising to a square north pole. Indeed it looked like a kind of world globe, lopped and sheered into flat planes: and has remained very much a separate, private world to this day, along with its passenger.

All faces were blank metal except for one equatorial square facing southwards into the main body of the laboratory. This was a window—of glass as thick as that of a deep-ocean diving bell—which could apparently be opened from inside, and only from inside.

The passenger within looked as ragged and tattered as a tramp; as crazy, dirty, woe-begone and tangle-haired as any lunatic in an ancient Bedlam cell. He was apparently very old; or at any rate long solitary confinement in that cell made him seem so. He was pallid, crook-backed, skinny and rotten-toothed. He raved and mumbled soundlessly at our spotlights. Or maybe he only mouthed his ravings and mumbles, since we could hear nothing whatever through the thick glass. When we obtained the services of a lipreader two days later the mad old man seemed to be mouthing mere garbage, a mishmash of sounds. Or was he? Obviously no one could be expected to lip-read backwards; already, from his actions and gestures, Dr. Yang had suggested that the man was time-reversed. So we video-taped the passenger's mouthings and played the tapes backwards for our lip-reader. Well, it was still garbage. Backwards, or forwards, the unfortunate passenger had visibly cracked up. Indeed, one proof of his insanity was that he should be trying to talk to us at all at this late stage of his journey rather than communicate by holding up written messages—as he has now begun to do. (But more of these messages later; they only begin—or, from his point of view, *cease* as he descends further into madness—in the summer of 1989.)

Abandoning hope of enlightenment from him, we set out on the track of scientific explanations. (Fruitlessly. Ruining our other, more important work. Overturning our laboratory projects—and the whole of physics in the process.)

To indicate the way in which we wasted our time, I might record that the first "clue" came from the shape of the VSTM which, as I said, was that of a lead sulphide or galena crystal. Yang emphasized that galena is used as a semiconductor in crystal rectifiers: devices for transforming alternating current into direct current. They set up a much higher resistance to an electric current flowing in one direction than another. Was there an analogy with the current of time? Could the geometry of the VSTM—or the geometry of energies circulating in its metal walls, presumably interlaid with printed circuits—effectively impede the forward flow of time, and reverse it? We had no way to break into the VSTM. Attempts to cut into it proved quite ineffective and were soon discontinued, while X-raying it was foiled, conceivably by lead alloyed in the walls. Sonic scanning provided rough pictures of internal shapes, but nothing as intricate as circuitry; so we had to rely on what we could see of the outward shape, or through the window—and on pure theory.

Yang also stressed that galena rectifiers operate in the same manner as diode valves. Besides transforming the flow of an electric current they can also *demodulate*. They separate information out from a modulated carrier wave—as in a radio or TV set. Were we witnessing, in the VSTM, a machine for separating out "information" in the form of the physical vehicle itself, with its passenger—from a carrier wave stretching back through time? Was the VSTM a solid, tangible analogy of a three-dimensional TV picture, played backwards?

We made many models of VSTMs based on these ideas and tried to send them off into the past, or the future—or anywhere for that matter! They all stayed monotonously present in the laboratory, stubbornly locked to our space and time.

Kelvin, recalling his impression that the VSTM had seemed to expand outward from a point, remarked that this was how three-dimensional beings such as ourselves might well perceive a four-dimensional object first impinging on us. Thus a 4-D sphere would appear as a point and swell into a full sphere then contract again to a point. But a 4-D octahedron-and-cube? According to our maths this shape couldn't have a regular analogue in 4-space, only a simple octahedron could. Besides, what would be the use of a 4-D time machine which shrank to a point at precisely the moment when the passenger needed to mount it? No, the VSTM wasn't a genuine four-dimensional body; though we wasted many weeks running computer programs to describe it as one, and arguing that its passenger was a normal 3-space man imprisoned within a 4-space structure—the discrepancy of one dimension between him and his vehicle effectively isolating him from the rest of the universe so that he could travel hindwards.

That he was indeed traveling hindwards was by now absolutely clear from his feeding habits (i.e. he regurgitated), though his extreme furtiveness about bodily functions coupled with his filthy condition meant that it took several months before we were positive, on these grounds.

All this, in turn, raised another unanswerable question: if the VSTM was indeed travelling backwards through time, precisely where did it *disappear* to, in that instant of its arrival on 1 December 1985? The passenger was hardly on an archaeological jaunt, or he would have tried to climb out.

At long last, on midsummer day 1989, our passenger held up a notice printed on a big plastic eraser slate.

CRAWLING DOWNHILL, SLIDING UPHILL!

He held this up for ten minutes, against the window. The printing was spidery and ragged; so was he.

This could well have been his last lucid moment before the final descent into madness, in despair at the pointlessness of trying to communicate with us. Thereafter it would be *downhill all the way*, we interpreted. Seeing us with all our still eager, still baffled faces, he could only gibber incoherently thenceforth like an enraged monkey at our sheer stupidity.

He didn't communicate for another three months.

When he held up his next (i.e. penultimate) sign, he looked slightly sprucer, a little less crazy (though only comparatively so, having regard to his final mumbling squalor).

THE LONELINESS! BUT LEAVE ME ALONE!
IGNORE ME UNTIL 1995!

We held up signs (to which, we soon realized, his sign was a response):

ARE YOU TRAVELING BACK THROUGH TIME? HOW? WHY?

We would have also dearly loved to ask: WHERE DO YOU DISAPPEAR TO ON DECEMBER 1 1985? But we judged it unwise to ask this most pertinent of all questions in case his disappearance was some sort of disaster, so that we would in effect be foredooming him, accelerating his mental breakdown. Dr. Franklin insisted that this was nonsense; he broke down *anyway*. Still, if we *had* held up that sign, what remorse we would have felt: because we *might* have caused his breakdown and ruined some magnificent undertaking....
We were certain that it had to be a magnificent undertaking to involve such personal sacrifice, such abnegation, such a cutting off of oneself from the rest of the human race. This is about all we were certain of.

(1995)

No progress with our enigma. All our research is dedicated to solving it, but we keep this out of sight of him. While rotas of postgraduate students observe him round the clock, our best brains get on with the real thinking elsewhere in the building. He sits inside his vehicle, less dirty and disheveled now, but monumentally taciturn: a trappist monk under a vow of silence. He spends most of his time re-reading the same dog-eared books, which have fallen to pieces back in our past: Defoe's *Journal of the Plague Year* and *Robinson Crusoe* and Jules Verne's *Journey to the Centre of the Earth*; and listening to what is presumably taped music—which he shreds from the cassettes back in 1989, flinging streamers around his tiny living quarters in a brief mad fiesta (which of course we see as a sudden frenzy of disentangling and repackaging, with maniacal speed and neatness, of tapes which have lain around, trodden underfoot, for years).

Superficially we have ignored him (and he, us) until 1995: assuming that his last sign had some significance. Having got nowhere ourselves, we expect something from him now.

Since he is cleaner, tidier and saner now, in this year of 1995 (not to mention ten years younger) we have a better idea of how old he actually is; thus some clue as to when he might have started his journey.

He must be in his late forties or early fifties—though he aged dreadfully in the last ten years, looking more like seventy or eighty when he reached 1985. Assuming that the future does not hold in store any longevity drugs (in which case he might be a century old, or more!) he should have entered the VSTM sometime between 2010 and 2025. The later date, putting him in his very early twenties if not teens, does rather suggest a "suicide volunteer" who is merely a passenger in the vehicle. The earlier date suggests a more mature researcher who played a major role in the development of the VSTM and was only prepared to test it on his own person. Certainly, now that his madness has abated into a tight, meditative fixity of posture, accompanied by normal activities such as reading, we incline to think of him as a man of moral stature rather than a time-kamikaze; so we put the date of commencement of the journey around 2010 to 2015 (only fifteen to twenty years ahead) when he will be in his thirties. Besides theoretical physics, basic space science has by now been hugely sidetracked by his presence. The lead hope of getting man to the stars was the development of some deep-sleep or refrigeration system. Plainly this does not exist by 2015 or so—or our passenger would be using it. Only a lunatic would voluntarily sit in a tiny compartment for decades on ends, aging and rotting, if he could sleep the time away just as well, and awake as young as the day he set off. On the other hand, his life-support systems seem so impeccable that he can exist for decades within the narrow confines of that vehicle using recycled air, water and solid matter to 100 per cent efficiency. This represents no inconsiderable outlay in research and development—which must have been borrowed from another field, obviously the space sciences. Therefore the astronauts of 2015 or thereabouts require very long-term life support systems capable of sustaining them for years and decades, up and awake. What kind of space travel must they be engaged in, to need these? Well, they can only be going to the stars—the slow way; though not a *very* slow way. Not hundreds of years; but decades. Highly dedicated men must be spending many years cooped up alone in tiny space-craft to reach Alpha Centauri, Tau Ceti, Epsilon Eridani or wherever. If their surroundings are so tiny, then any extra payload costs prohibitively. Now who would contemplate such a journey merely out of curiosity? No one. The notion is ridiculous—*unless* these heroes are carrying something to their destinations which will then link it inexorably and instantaneously with Earth. A tachyon descrambler is the only obvious explanation. They are carrying with them the other end of a tachyon-transmission system for beaming material objects, and even human beings, out to the stars!

So, while one half of physics nowadays grapples with the problems of reverse-time, the other half, funded by most of the money from the space vote, pre-empting the whole previously extant space program, is trying to work out ways to harness and modulate tachyons.

These faster-than-light particles certainly seem to exist; we're fairly certain of that now. The main problem is that the technology for harnessing them is needed *beforehand*, to prove that they do exist and so to work out exactly *how* to harness them.

All these reorientations of science—because of him sitting in his enigmatic vehicle in deliberate alienation from us, reading *Robinson Crusoe*, a strained expression on his face as he slowly approaches his own personal crack-up.

(1996)

If you were locked up in a VSTM for X years, would you want a calendar on permanent display—or not? Would it be consoling or taunting? Obviously his instruments are calibrated—unless it was completely fortuitous that his journey ended on 1 December 1985 at precisely midday! But can he see the calibrations? Or would he prefer to be overtaken suddenly by the end of his journey, rather than have the slow grind of years unwind itself? You see, we are trying to explain why he did not communicate with us in 1995.

Convicts in solitary confinement keep their sanity by scratching five-barred gates of days on the walls with their fingernails; the sense of time passing keeps their spirits up. But on the other hand, tests of time perception carried out on potholers who volunteered to stay below ground for several months on end show that the internal clock lags grossly—by as much as two weeks in a three month period. Our VSTM passenger might gain a reprieve of a year—or five years!—on his total subjective journey time, by ignoring the passing of time. The potholers had no clue to night and day; but then, neither does he! Ever since his arrival, lights have been burning constantly in the laboratory; he has been under constant observation....

He isn't a convict, or he would surely protest, beg to be let out, throw himself on our mercy, give us some clue to the nature of his predicament. Is he the carrier of some fatal disease—a disease so incredibly infectious that it must affect the whole human race unless he were isolated? Which can only be isolated by a time capsule? Which even isolation on the Moon or Mars would not keep from spreading to the human race? He hardly appears to be....

Suppose that he had to be isolated for some very good reason, and suppose that he concurs in his own isolation (which he visibly does, sitting there reading Defoe for the nth time), what demands this unique dissection of one man from the whole continuum of human life and from his own time and space? Medicine, psychiatry, sociology, all the human sciences are being drawn into the problem in the wake of physics and space science. Sitting there doing nothing, he has become a kind of funnel for all the physical and social sciences: a human black hole into which vast energy pours, for a very slight increase in our radius of understanding. That single individual has accumulated as much disruptive potential as a single atom accelerated to the speed of light—which requires all the available energy in the universe to sustain it in its impermissible state.

Meanwhile the orbiting tachyon laboratories report that they are just on the point of uniting quantum mechanics, gravitational theory and relativity; whereupon they will at last "jump" the first high-speed particle packages over the C-barrier into a faster-than-light mode, and back again into our space. But they reported *that* last year—only to have their particle packages "jump back" as antimatter, annihilating five billion dollars' worth of equipment and taking thirty lives. They hadn't jumped into a tachyon mode at all, but had "möbiused" themselves through wormholes in the space-time fabric.

Nevertheless, prisoner of conscience (his own conscience, surely!) or whatever he is, our VSTM passenger seems nobler year by year. As we move away from his terminal madness, increasingly what strikes us is his dedication, his self-sacrifice (for a cause still beyond our comprehension), his Wittgensteinian spirituality. "Take him for all in all, he is a Man. We shall not look upon his like..." Again? We shall look upon his like. Upon the man himself, gaining stature every year! That's the wonderful thing. It's as though Christ, fully exonerated as the Son of God, is uncrucified and his whole life re-enacted before our eyes in full and certain knowledge of his true role. (Except...that this man's role is silence.)

(1997)

Undoubtedly he is a holy man who will suffer mental crucifixion for the sake of some great human project. Now he re-reads Defoe's *Plague Year*, that classic of collective incarceration and the resistance of the human spirit and human organizing ability. Surely the "plague" hint in the title is irrelevant. It's the sheer force of spirit, which beat the Great Plague of London, that is the real keynote of the book.

Our passenger is the object of popular cults by now—a focus for finer feelings. In this way his mere presence has drawn the world's peoples closer together, cultivating respect and dignity, pulling us back from the brink of war, liberating tens of thousands from their concentration camps. These cults extend from purely fashionable manifestations—shirts printed with his face, now neatly shaven in a Vandyke style; rings and worry-beads made from galena crystals— through the architectural (octahedron-and-cube meditation modules) to life-styles themselves: a Zen-like "sitting quietly, doing nothing."

He's Rodin's *Thinker*, the *Belvedere Apollo*, and Michelangelo's *David* rolled into one for our world as the millennium draws to its close. Never have so many copies of Defoe's two books and the Jules Verne been in print before. People memorize them as meditation exercises and recite them as the supremely lucid, rational Western mantras.

The National Physical Laboratory has become a place of pilgrimage, our lawns and grounds a vast camping site—Woodstock and Avalon, Rome and Arlington all in one. About the sheer tattered degradation of his final days less is said; though that has its cultists too, its late twentieth-century anchorites, its Saint Anthonies pole-squatting or cave-immuring themselves in the midst of the urban desert, bringing austere spirituality back to a world which appeared to have lost its soul—though this latter is a fringe phenomenon; the general keynote is nobility, restraint, quiet consideration for others.

And now he holds up a notice.

I IMPLY NOTHING. PAY NO ATTENTION TO MY PRESENCE. KINDLY GET ON DOING YOUR OWN THINGS. I CANNOT EXPLAIN UNTIL 2000.

He holds it up for a whole day, looking not exactly angry, but slightly pained. The whole world, hearing of it, sighs with joy at his modesty, his self-containment, his reticence, his humility. This must be the promised 1995 message, two years late (or two years early; obviously he still has a long way to come). Now he is Oracle; he is the Millennium. This place is Delphi.

The orbiting laboratories run into more difficulties with their tachyon research; but still funds pour into them, private donations too on an unprecedented scale. The world strips itself of excess wealth to strip matter and propel it over the interface between sub-light and trans-light.

The development of closed-cycle living pods for the carriers of those tachyon receivers to the stars is coming along well; a fact which naturally raises the paradoxical question of whether his presence has in fact stimulated the development of the technology by which he himself survives. We at the National Physical Laboratory and at all other such laboratories around the world are convinced that we shall soon make a breakthrough in our understanding of time-reversal—which, intuitively, should connect with that other universal interface in the realm of matter, between our world and the tachyon world—and we feel too, paradoxically, that our current research must surely lead to the development of the VSTM which will then become so opportunely necessary to us, for reasons yet unknown. No one feels they are wasting their time. He is the Future. His presence here vindicates our every effort—even the blindest of blind alleys.

What kind of Messiah must he be, by the time he enters the VSTM? How much charisma, respect, adoration and wonder must he have accrued by his starting point? Why, the whole world will send him off! He will be the focus of so much collective hope and worship that we even start to investigate *Psi* phenomena seriously: the concept of group mental thrust as a hypothesis for his mode of travel—as though he is vectored not through time of 4-space at all but down the waveguide of human will-power and desire.

(2001)

The millennium comes and goes without any revelation. Of course that is predictable; he is lagging by a year or eighteen months. (Obviously he can't see the calibrations on his instruments; it was his choice—that was his way to keep sane on the long haul.)

But finally, now in the autumn of 2001, he holds up a sign, with a certain quiet jubilation:

WILL I LEAVE 1985 SOUND IN WIND & LIMB?

Quiet jubilation, because we have already (from his point of view) held up the sign in answer:

YES! YES!

We're all rooting for him passionately. It isn't really a lie that we tell him. He did leave relatively sound in wind and limb. It was just his mind that was in tatters…. Maybe that is inessential, irrelevant, or he wouldn't have phrased his question to refer merely to his physical body.

He must be approaching his take-off point. He's having a mild fit of tenth-year blues, first decade anxiety, self-doubt; which we clear up for him….

Why doesn't he know what shape he arrived in? Surely that must be a matter of record before he sets off….*No!* Time can not be invariable, determined. Not even the Past. Time is probabilistic. He has refrained from comment for all these years so as not to unpluck the strands of time past and reweave them in another, undesirable way. A tower of strength he has been. *Ein' feste Burg ist unser Zeitganger!* Well, back to the drawing board, and to probabilistic equations for (a) tachyon-scatter out in normal space (b) time-reversal.

A few weeks later he holds up another sign, which must be his promised Delphic revelation:

I AM THE MATRIX OF MAN.

Of course! Of course! He has made himself that over the years. What else?

A matrix is a mold for shaping a cast. And indeed, out of him shapes have been molded increasingly since the late 1990s, such has been his influence.

Was he sent hindwards to save the world from self-slaughter by presenting such a perfect paradigm—which only frayed and tattered in the Eighties when it did not matter any more; when he had already succeeded?

But a matrix is also an array of components for translating from one code into another. So Yang's demodulation of information hypothesis is revived, coupled now with the idea that the VSTM is perhaps a matrix for transmitting the "information" contained in a man across space and time (and the man-transmitter experiments in orbit redouble their efforts); with the corollary (though this could hardly be voiced to the enraptured world at large) that perhaps the passenger was *not there* at all in any real sense; and he had never been; that we merely were witnessing an experiment in the possibility of transmitting a man across the galaxy, performed on a future Earth by future science to test out the degradation factor: the decay of information—mapped from space on to time so that it could be observed by us, their predecessors! Thus the onset of madness (i.e., information decay) in our passenger, timed in years from his starting point, might set a physical limit in *light-years* to the distance to which a man could be beamed (tachyonically?). And this was at once a terrible kick in the teeth to space science—and a great boost. A kick in the teeth, as this suggested that physical travel through interstellar space must be impossible, perhaps because of Man's frailty in the face of cosmic ray bombardment; and thus the whole development of intensive closed-cycle life-pods for single astronaut couriers must be deemed irrelevant. Yet a great boost too, since the possibility of a receiverless transmitter loomed. The now elderly Yang suggested that 1 December 1985 was actually a moment of lift-off to the stars. Where our passenger went then, in all his madness, was to a point in space thirty or forty light-years distant. The VSTM was thus the testing to destruction of a future man-beaming system and practical future models would only deal in distances (in times) of the order of seven to eight years. (Hence no other VSTMs had imploded into existence, hitherto.)

(2010)

I am tired with a lifetime's fruitless work; however, the human race at large is at once calmly loving and frenetic with hope. For we must be nearing our goal. Our passenger is in his thirties now (whether a live individual, or only an epiphenomenon of a system for transmitting the information present in a human being: literally a "ghost in the machine"). This sets a limit. It sets a limit. He couldn't have set off with such strength of mind much earlier than his twenties or (I sincerely hope not) his late teens. Although the teens *are* a prime time for taking vows of chastity, for entering monasteries, for pledging one's life to a cause....

(2015)

Boosted out of my weariness by the general euphoria, I have successfully put off my retirement for another four years. Our passenger is now in his middle twenties and a curious inversion in his "worship" is taking place, representing (I think) a subconscious groundswell of anxiety as well as joy. Joy, obviously, that the moment is coming when he makes his choice and steps into the VSTM, as Christ gave up carpentry and stepped out from Nazareth. Anxiety, though, at the possibility that he may pass beyond this critical point, towards infancy; ridiculous as this seems! He knows how to read books; he couldn't have taught himself to read. Nor could he have taught himself how to speak *in vitro*—and he has certainly delivered lucid, if mysterious, messages to us from time to time. The hit song of the whole world, nevertheless, this year is William Blake's *The Mental Traveller* set to sitar and gongs and glockenspiel....

> For as he eats and drinks he grows
> Younger and younger every day;
> And on the desert wild they both
> Wander in terror and dismay....

The unvoiced fear represented by this song's sweeping of the world being that he may yet evade us; that he may slide down towards infancy, and at the moment of his birth (whatever life-support mechanisms extrude to keep him alive till then!) the VSTM will implode back whence it came: sick joke of some alien superconsciousness, intervening in human affairs with a scientific "miracle" to make all human striving meaningless and pointless. Not many people feel this way openly. It isn't a popular view. A man could be torn limb from limb for espousing it in public. The human mind will never accept it; and purges this fear in a long song of joy which at once mocks and copies and adores the mystery of the VSTM.

Men put this supreme *man* into the machine. Even so, Madonna and Child does haunt the world's mind....and a soft femininity prevails—men's skirts are the new soft gracious mode of dress in the West. Yet he is now so noble, so handsome in his youth, so glowing and strong; such a Zarathustra, locked up in there.

(2018)

He can only be 21 or 22. The world adores him, mothers him, across the unbridgeable gulf of reversed time. No progress in the Solar System, let alone on the interstellar front. Why should we travel out and away, even as far as Mars, let alone Pluto, when a revelation is at hand; when all the secrets will be unlocked here on Earth? No progress on the tachyon or negative-time fronts, either. Nor any further messages from him. But he is his own message. His presence alone is sufficient to express Mankind: hopes, courage, holiness, determination.

(2019)

I am called back from retirement, for he is holding up signs again: the athlete holding up the Olympic Flame.

He holds them up for half an hour at a stretch—as though we are not all eyes agog, filming every moment in case we miss something, anything.

When I arrive, the signs that he has already held up have announced:

(*Sign One*) THIS IS A VERY SLOW TIME MACHINE. (And I amend accordingly, crossing out all the other titles we had bestowed on it successively, over the years. For a few seconds I wonder whether he was really naming the machine—defining it—or complaining about it! As though he'd been fooled into being its passenger on the assumption that a time machine should proceed to its destination *instanter* instead of at a snail's pace. But no. He was naming it.) TO TRAVEL INTO THE FUTURE, YOU MUST FIRST TRAVEL INTO THE PAST, ACCUMULATING HINDWARD POTENTIAL. (THIS IS CRAWLING DOWNHILL.)

(*Sign Two*) AS SOON AS YOU ACCUMULATE ONE LARGE QUANTUM OF TIME, YOU LEAP FORWARD BY THE SAME TIMESPAN AHEAD OF YOUR STARTING POINT. (THIS IS SLIDING UPHILL.)

(*Sign Three*) YOUR JOURNEY INTO THE FUTURE TAKES THE SAME TIME AS IT WOULD TAKE TO LIVE THROUGH THE YEARS IN REAL-TIME; YET YOU ALSO OMIT THE INTERVENING YEARS, ARRIVING AHEAD INSTANTLY. (PRINCIPLE OF CONSERVATION OF TIME.)

(*Sign Four*) SO, TO LEAP THE GAP, YOU MUST CRAWL THE OTHER WAY.

(*Sign Five*) TIME DIVIDES INTO ELEMENTARY QUANTA. NO MEASURING ROD CAN BE SMALLER THAN THE INDIVISIBLE ELEMENTARY ELECTRON; THIS IS ONE "ELEMENTARY LENGTH" (EL). THE TIME TAKEN FOR LIGHT TO TRAVEL ONE EL IS "ELEMENTARY TIME" (ET): I.E., 10^{23} SECONDS; THIS IS ONE ELEMENTARY QUANTUM OF TIME. TIME CONSTANTLY LEAPS AHEAD BY THESE TINY QUANTA FOR EVERY PARTICLE; BUT, NOT BEING SYNCHRONIZED, THESE FORM A CONTINUOUS TIME-OCEAN RATHER THAN SUCCESSIVE DISCRETE "MOMENTS" OR WE WOULD HAVE NO CONNECTED UNIVERSE.

(*Sign Six*) TIME REVERSAL OCCURS NORMALLY IN STRONG NUCLEAR INTERACTIONS: I.E. IN EVENTS OF ORDER 10^{23} SECS. THIS REPRESENTS THE "FROZEN GHOST"

OF THE FIRST MOMENT OF UNIVERSE WHEN AN "ARROW OF TIME" WAS FIRST STOCHASTICALLY DETERMINED.

(*Sign Seven*) (And this is when I arrived, to be shown Polaroid photographs of the first seven signs. Remarkably, he is holding up each sign in a linear sequence from *our* point of view; a considerable feat of forethought and memory, though no less than we expect of him.) NOW IT IS INVARIABLE & FROZEN IN; YET UNIVERSE AGES. STRETCHING OF SPACE-TIME BY EXPANSION PROPAGATES "WAVES" IN THE SEA OF TIME, CARRYING TIME-ENERGY WITH PERIOD (X) PROPORTIONAL TO THE RATE OF EXPANSION, AND TO RATIO OF TIME ELAPSED TO TOTAL TIME AVAILABLE FOR THIS COSMOS FROM INITIAL CONSTRAINTS. EQUATIONS FOR X YIELD A PERIOD OF 35 YEARS CURRENTLY AS ONE MOMENT OF MACRO-TIME WITHIN WHICH MACROSCOPIC TIME REVERSAL BECOMES POSSIBLE.

(*Sign Eight*) CONSTRUCT AN "ELECTRON SHELL" BY SYNCHRONIZING ELECTRON REVERSAL. THE LOCAL SYSTEM WILL THEN FORM A TIME-REVERSED MINI-COSMOS & PROCEED HINDWARDS TILL X ELAPSES WHEN TIME CONSERVATION OF THE TOTAL UNIVERSE WILL PULL THE MINI-COSMOS (OF THE VSTM) FORWARD INTO MESH WITH UNIVERSE AGAIN I.E. BY 35 PLUS 35 YEARS.

"But how?" we all cried. "How do you synchronize such an infinity of electrons? We haven't the slightest idea!"

Now at least we knew when he had set off: from 35 years after 1985. From *next year*. We are supposed to know all this by next year! Why has he waited so long to give us the proper clues?

And he is heading for the year 2055. What is there in the year 2055 that matters so much?

(*Sign Nine*) I DO NOT GIVE THIS INFORMATION TO YOU BECAUSE IT WILL LEAD TO YOUR INVENTING THE VSTM.

THE SITUATION IS QUITE OTHERWISE. TIME IS PROBABILISTIC, AS SOME OF YOU MAY SUSPECT. I REALIZE THAT I WILL PROBABLY PERVERT THE COURSE OF HISTORY & SCIENCE BY MY ARRIVAL IN YOUR PAST (MY MOMENT OF DEPARTURE FOR THE FUTURE); IT IS IMPORTANT THAT YOU DO NOT KNOW YOUR PREDICAMENT TOO EARLY OR YOUR FRANTIC EFFORTS TO AVOID IT WOULD GENERATE A TIME LINE WHICH WOULD UNPREPARE YOU FOR MY SETTING OFF. AND IT IS IMPORTANT THAT IT DOES ENDURE, FOR I AM THE MATRIX OF MAN. I AM LEGION. I SHALL CONTAIN MULTITUDES.

MY RETICENCE IS SOLELY TO KEEP THE WORLD ON TOLERABLY STABLE TRACKS SO THAT I CAN TRAVEL BACK ALONG THEM. I TELL YOU THIS OUT OF COMPASSION, AND TO PREPARE YOUR MINDS FOR THE ARRIVAL OF GOD ON EARTH.

"He's insane. He's been insane from the start."

"He's been isolated in there for some very good reason. Contagious insanity, yes."

"Suppose that a madman could project his madness—"

"He already has done that, for decades!"

"—no, I mean really project it, into the consciousness of the whole world; a madman with a mind so strong that he acted as a template, yes a matrix for everyone else, and made them all his dummies, his copies; and only a few people stayed immune who could build this VSTM to isolate him—"

"But there isn't time to research it now!"

"What good would it do shucking off the problem for another thirty-five years? He would only reappear—"

"Without his strength. Shorn. Senile. Broken. Starved of his connections with the human race. Dried up. A mental leech. Oh, he tried to conserve his strength. Sitting quietly. Reading, waiting. But he broke! Thank God for that. It was vital to the future that he went insane."

"Ridiculous! To enter the machine next year he must already be alive! He must already be out there in the world projecting this supposed madness of his. But he isn't. We're all separate sane individuals, all free to think what we want—"

"*Are we?* The whole world has been increasingly obsessed with him these last twenty years. Fashions, religions, life-styles: the whole world has been skewed by him ever since he was born! He must have been born about twenty years ago. Around 1995. Until then there was a lot of research into him. The tachyon hunt. All that. But he only began to obsess the world as a spiritual figure after that. From around 1995 or 6. When he was born as a baby. Only, we didn't focus our minds on his own infantile urges—because we had him here as an adult to obsess ourselves with—"

"Why should he have been born with infantile urges? If he's so unusual, why shouldn't he have been born already leeching on the world's mind; already knowing; already experiencing everything around him?"

"Yes, but the real charisma started then! All the emotional intoxication with him!"

"All the mothering. All the fear and adoration of his infancy. All the Bethlehem hysteria. Picking up as he grew and gained projective strength. We've been just as obsessed with Bethlehem as with Nazareth, haven't we? The two have gone hand in hand."

(*Sign Ten*) I AM GOD. AND I MUST SET YOU FREE. I MUST CUT MYSELF OFF FROM MY PEOPLE; CAST MYSELF INTO THIS HELL OF ISOLATION.

I CAME TOO SOON; YOU WERE NOT READY FOR ME.

We begin to feel very cold; yet we cannot feel cold. Something prevents us—a kind of malign contagious tranquillity.

It is all so *right*. It slots into our heads so exactly, like the missing jigsaw piece for which the hole lies cut and waiting, that we know what he said is true; that he is growing up out there in our obsessed, blessed world, only waiting to come to us.

(*Sign Eleven*) (Even though the order of the signs was time-reversed from his point of view, there was the sense of a real dialogue now between him and us, as though we were both synchronized. Yet this wasn't because the past was inflexible, and he was simply acting out a role he knew "from history." He was really as distant from us as ever. It was the looming presence of *himself* in the real world which cast its shadow on us, molded our thoughts and fitted our questions to his responses; and we all realized this now, as though scales fell from our eyes. We weren't guessing or fishing in the dark any longer; we were being dictated to by an overwhelming presence of which we were all conscious—and which wasn't locked up in the VSTM. The VSTM was Nazareth, the setting-off point; yet the whole world was also Bethlehem, womb of the embryonic God, his babyhood, childhood and youth combined into one synchronous sequence by his all-knowingness, with the accent on his wonderful birth that filtered through into human consciousness ever more saturatingly.)

MY OTHER SELF HAS ACCESS TO ALL THE SCIENTIFIC SPECULATIONS WHICH I HAVE GENERATED; AND ALREADY I HAVE THE SOLUTION OF THE TIME EQUATIONS. I SHALL ARRIVE SOON & YOU SHALL BUILD MY VSTM & I SHALL ENTER IT; YOU SHALL BUILD IT INSIDE AN EXACT REPLICA OF THIS LABORATORY, SOUTHWEST SIDE. THERE IS SPACE THERE. (Indeed it had been planned to extend the National Physical Laboratory that way, but the plans had never been taken up, because of the skewing of all our research which the VSTM had brought about.) WHEN I REACH MY TIME OF SETTING OUT, WHEN TIME REVERSES, THE PROBABILITY OF THIS LABORATORY WILL VANISH, & THE OTHER WILL ALWAYS HAVE BEEN THE TRUE LABORATORY THAT I AM IN, INSIDE THIS VSTM. THE WASTE LAND WHERE YOU BUILD, WILL NOW BE HERE. YOU CAN WITNESS THE INVERSION: IT WILL BE MY FIRST PROBABILISTIC MIRACLE. THERE ARE HYPERDIMENSIONAL REASONS FOR THE PROBABILISTIC INVERSION, AT THE INSTANT OF TIME REVERSAL. BE WARNED NOT TO BE INSIDE THIS LABORATORY WHEN I

SET OUT, WHEN I CHANGE TRACKS, FOR THIS SEGMENT OF REALITY HERE WILL ALSO CHANGE TRACKS, BECOMING IMPROBABLE, SQUEEZED OUT.

(*Sign Twelve*) I WAS BORN TO INCORPORATE YOU IN MY BOSOM; TO UNITE YOU IN A WORLD MIND, IN THE PHASE SPACE OF GOD. THOUGH YOUR INDIVIDUAL SOULS PERSIST, WITHIN THE FUSION. BUT YOU ARE NOT READY. YOU MUST BECOME READY IN 35 YEARS' TIME BY FOLLOWING THE MENTAL EXERCISES WHICH I SHALL DELIVER TO YOU, MY MEDITATIONS. IF I REMAINED WITH YOU NOW, AS I GAIN STRENGTH, YOU WOULD LOSE YOUR SOULS. THEY WOULD BE SUCKED INTO ME, INCOHERENTLY. BUT IF YOU GAIN STRENGTH, I CAN INCORPORATE YOU COHERENTLY WITHOUT LOSING YOU. I LOVE YOU ALL, YOU ARE PRECIOUS TO ME, SO I EXILE MYSELF.

THEN I WILL COME AGAIN IN 2055. I SHALL RISE FROM TIME, FROM THE USELESS HARROWING OF A LIMBO WHICH HOLDS NO SOULS PRISONER, FOR YOU ARE ALL HERE, ON EARTH.

That was the last sign. He sits reading again and listening to taped music. He is radiant; glorious. We yearn to fall upon him and be within him.

We hate and fear him too; but the Love washes over the Hate, losing it a mile deep.

He is gathering strength outside somewhere: in Wichita or Washington or Woodstock. He will come in a few weeks to reveal himself to us. We all know it now.

And then? Could we kill him? Our minds would halt our hands. As it is, we know that the sense of loss, the sheer bereavement of his departure hindwards into time will all but tear our souls apart.

And yet...I WILL COME AGAIN IN 2055, he has promised. And incorporate us, unite us, as separate thinking souls—if we follow all his meditations; or else he will suck us into him as dummies, as robots if we do not prepare ourselves. What then, when God rises from the grave of time, *insane*?

Surely he knows that he will end his journey in madness! That he will incorporate us all, as conscious living beings, into the matrix of his own insanity?

It is a fact of history that he arrived in 1985 ragged, jibbering and lunatic—tortured beyond endurance by being deprived of us.

Yet he demanded, jubilantly, in 1997, confirmation of his safe arrival; jubilantly, and we lied to him and said YES! YES! And he must have believed us. (Was he already going mad from deprivation?)

If a laboratory building can rotate into the probability of that same building adjacent to itself: if time is probabilistic (which we can never prove or disprove concretely with any measuring rod, for we can never see *what has not been*, all the alternative possibilities, though they might have been), we have to wish what we know to be the truth, not to have been the truth. We can only have faith that there will be another probabilistic miracle, beyond the promised inversion of laboratories that he speaks of, and that he will indeed arrive back in 1985 calm, well-kept, radiantly sane, his mind composed. And what is this but an entrée into madness for rational beings such as us? We must perpetrate an act of madness; we must believe the world to be other than what it was—so that we can receive among us a Sane, Blessed, Loving God in 2055. A fine preparation for the coming of a mad God! For if we drive ourselves mad, believing passionately what was not true, will we not infect him with our madness, so that he is/has to be/will be/and always was mad too?

Credo quia impossibilis; we have to believe because it is impossible. The alternative is hideous.

Soon. He will be coming. Soon. A few days, a few dozen hours. We all feel it. We are overwhelmed with bliss.

Then we must put him in a chamber, and lose Him, and drive Him mad with loss, in the sure and certain hope of a sane and loving resurrection thirty-five years hence—so that He does not harrow Hell, and carry it back to Earth with Him.

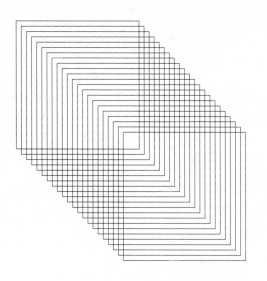

THE LOVE
LETTER

BY JACK FINNEY

've heard of secret drawers in old desks, of course; who hasn't? But the day I bought my desk I wasn't thinking of secret drawers and I know very well I didn't have any premonition or feeling of mystery about it. I spotted it in the window of a second-hand store near my apartment, went in to look it over, and the proprietor told me where he got it. It came from one of the last of the big old mid-Victorian houses in Brooklyn; they were tearing it down over on Brock Place a few blocks away, and he'd bought the desk along with some other furniture, dishes, glassware, light fixtures, and so on. But it didn't stir my imagination particularly; I never wondered or cared who might have used it long ago. I bought it and lugged it home because it was cheap and because it was small; a legless little wall desk that I fastened to my living-room wall with heavy screws directly into the studding.

I'm twenty-four years old, tall and thin, and I live in Brooklyn to save money and work in Manhattan to make it. When you're twenty-four and a bachelor, you usually figure you'll be married before much longer and since they tell me that takes money I'm reasonably ambitious and bring work home from the office every once in a while. And maybe every couple weeks or so I write a letter to my folks in Florida. So I'd been needing a desk; there's no table in my phone-booth kitchenette, and I'd been trying to work at a wobbly end table I couldn't get my knees under.

I bought the desk one Saturday afternoon and spent an hour or more fastening it to the wall. It was after six when I finished. I had a date that night, so I had time to stand and admire it for only a minute or so. It was made of heavy wood with a slant top like a kid's school desk and with the same sort of space underneath to put things into. But the back of it rose a good two feet above the desk top and was full of pigeonholes like an old-style roll-top desk. Underneath the pigeonholes was a row of three brass-knobbed little drawers. It was all pretty ornate; the drawer ends carved, some fancy scrollwork extending up over the back and out from the sides to help brace it against the wall. I dragged a chair up, sat down at the desk to try it for height, then got showered, shaved, and dressed, and went over to Manhattan to pick up my date.

THE LOVE LETTER

I'm trying to be honest about what happened and I'm convinced that includes the way I felt when I got home around two or two thirty that morning; I'm certain that what happened wouldn't have happened at all if I'd felt any other way. I'd had a good enough time that evening; we'd gone to an early movie that wasn't too bad, then had dinner, a drink or so and some dancing afterward. And the girl, Roberta Haig, is pretty nice—bright, pleasant, good-looking. But walking home from the subway, the Brooklyn streets quiet and deserted, it occurred to me that while I'd probably see her again I didn't really care whether I did or not. And I wondered as I often had lately, whether there was something wrong with me, whether I'd ever meet a girl I desperately wanted to be with—the only way a man can get married, it seems to me.

So when I stepped into my apartment I knew I wasn't going to feel like sleep for a while. I was restless, half-irritated for no good reason, and I took off my coat and yanked down my tie, wondering whether I wanted a drink or some coffee. Then—I'd half forgotten about it— I saw the desk I'd bought that afternoon and I walked over and sat down at it, thoroughly examining it for the first time.

I lifted the top and stared down into the empty space underneath it. Lowering the top, I reached into one of the pigeonholes and my hand and shirt cuff came out streaked with old dust; the holes were a good foot deep. I pulled open one of the little brass-knobbed drawers and there was a shred of paper in one of its corners, nothing else. I pulled the drawer all the way out and studied its construction, turning it in my hands: it was a solidly made, beautifully mortised little thing. Then I pushed my hand into the drawer opening; it went in to about the middle of my hand before my fingertips touched the back; there was nothing in there.

For a few moments I just sat at the desk, thinking vaguely that I could write a letter to my folks. Then it suddenly occurred to me that the little drawer in my hand was only half a foot long while the pigeonholes just above the drawer extended a good foot back.

Shoving my hand into the opening again, exploring with my finger tips, I found a tiny grooved indentation and pulled out the secret drawer which lay in back of the first. For an instant I was excited at the glimpse of papers inside it. Then I felt a stab of disappointment as I saw what they were. There was a little sheaf of folded writing paper, plain white but yellowed with age at the edges, and the sheets were all blank. There were three or four blank envelopes to match, and underneath them a small, round, glass bottle of ink; and because it had been upside down, the cork remaining moist and tight in the bottle mouth, a good third of the ink had remained unevaporated still. Beside the bottle lay a plain, black wooden pen holder, the pen point reddish-black with old ink. There was nothing else in the drawer.

And then, putting the things back into the drawer, I felt the slight extra thickness of one blank envelope, saw that it was sealed, and I ripped it open to find the letter inside. The folded paper opened stiffly, the crease permanent with age, and even before I saw the date I knew this letter was old. The handwriting was obviously feminine, and beautifully clear—it's called Spencerian, isn't it?—the letters perfectly formed and very ornate, the capitals especially being a whirl of dainty curlicues. The ink was rust-black, the date at the top of the page was May 14, 1882, and reading it I saw that it was a love letter. It began:

> *Dearest! Papa, Mamma, Willy and Cook are long retired and to sleep. Now, the night far advanced, the house silent, I alone remain awake, at last free to speak to you as I choose. Yes, I am willing to say it! Heart of mine, I crave your bold glance, I long for the tender warmth of your look; I welcome your ardency, and prize it; for what else should these be taken but sweet tribute to me?*

I smiled a little; it was hard to believe that people had once expressed themselves in elaborate phrasings of this kind, but they had. The letter continued, and I wondered why it had never been sent:

> *Dear one, do not change your ways. Never address me other than with what consideration my utterances should deserve. If I be foolish and whimsical, deride me sweetly if you will. But if I speak with*

seriousness, respond always with what care you deem my thoughts
worthy. For, oh my beloved, I am sick to death of the indulgent smile
and tolerant glance with which a woman's fancies are met. As I am
repelled by the false gentleness and nicety of manner which too often
ill conceal the wantonness they attempt to mask. I speak of the man
I am to marry; if you could but save me from that!

But you cannot. You are everything I prize; warmly and honestly
ardent, respectful in heart as well as in manner, true and loving. You
are as I wish you to be—for you exist only in my mind. But figment
though you are, and though I shall never see your like, you are more
dear to me than he to whom I am betrothed.

I think of you constantly. I dream of you. I speak with you in my
mind and heart; would you existed outside them! Sweetheart, good
night; dream of me, too.

> *With all my love, I am,*
> *your Helen*

At the bottom of the page, as I'm sure she'd been taught in school, was written, 'Miss Helen Elizabeth Worley, Brooklyn, New York', and as I stared down at it now I was no longer smiling at this cry from the heart in the middle of a long-ago night.

The night is a strange time when you're alone in it, the rest of your world asleep. If I'd found that letter in the daytime I'd have smiled and shown it to a few friends, then forgotten it. But alone here now, a window partly open, a cool late-at-night freshness stirring the quiet air, it was impossible to think of the girl who had written this letter as a very old lady or maybe long since dead. As I read her words, she seemed real and alive to me, sitting, or I so I pictured her, pen in hand at this desk in a long, white old-fashioned dress, her young hair piled on top of her head, in the dead of a night like this, here in Brooklyn almost in sight of where I now sat. And my heart went out to her as I stared down at her secret hopeless appeal against the world and time she lived in.

I am trying to explain why I answered that letter. There in the silence of a timeless spring night it seemed natural enough to uncork that old bottle, pick up the pen beside it, and then, spreading a sheet of yellowing old notepaper on the desk top, to begin to write. I felt that I was communicating with a still-living young woman when I wrote:

Helen: I have just read the letter in the secret drawer of your desk and I wish I knew how I could possibly help you. I can't tell what you might think of me if there were a way I could reach you. But you are someone I am certain I would like to know. I hope you are beautiful but you needn't be; you're a girl I could like, and maybe ardently, and if I did, I promise you I'd be true and loving. Do the best you can, Helen Elizabeth Worley, in the time and place you are; I can't reach you or help you. But I'll think of you. And maybe I'll dream of you, too.

> *Yours,*
> *Jake Belknap*

I was grinning a little sheepishly as I signed my name, knowing I'd read through what I'd written, then crumple the old sheet and throw it away. But I was glad I'd written it and I didn't throw it away. Still caught in the feeling of the warm, silent night, it suddenly seemed to me that throwing my letter away would turn the writing of it into a meaningless and foolish thing, though maybe what I did seems more foolish still. I folded the paper, put it into one of the envelopes and sealed it. Then I dipped the pen into the old ink, and wrote 'Miss Helen Worley' on the face of the envelope.

I suppose this can't be explained. You'd have to have been where I was and felt as I did to understand it, but I wanted to mail that letter. I simply quit examining my feelings and quit trying to be rational; I was suddenly determined to complete what I'd begun, just as far as I was able to go.

My parents sold their old home in New Jersey when my father retired two years ago, and now they live in Florida and enjoy it. And when my mother cleared out the old house I grew up in, she packed and mailed me a huge package of useless things I was glad to have.

There were class photographs dating from grammar school through college, old books I'd read as a kid, Boy Scout pins—a mass of junk of that sort, including a stamp collection I'd had in grade school. Now I found these things on my hall-closet shelf in the box they'd come in, and I found my old stamp album.

It's funny how things can stick in your mind over the years; standing at the open closet door I turned the pages of that beat-up old album directly to the stamps I remembered buying from another kid with seventy-five cents I'd earned cutting grass. There they lay, lightly fastened to the page with a little gummed-paper hinge—a pair of two, mint condition two-cent United States stamps, issued in 1869. Standing in the hallway looking down at them I once again got something of the thrill I'd had as a kid when I acquired them. It's a handsome stamp, square in shape, with an ornate border and a tiny engraving in the center, a rider on a galloping post horse. For all I knew they might have been worth a fair amount of money by now, especially an unseparated pair of two stamps. But back at the desk I pulled one of them loose, tearing carefully through the perforation, licked the back and fastened it to the faintly yellowing old envelope.

I'd thought no further than that; by now, I suppose, I was in a kind of trance. I shoved the old ink bottle and pen into a hip pocket, picked up my letter, and walked out of my apartment.

Brock Place, three blocks away, was deserted when I reached it; the parked cars motionless at the kerbs, the high, late moonlight softening the lines of the big concrete supermarket at the corner. Then, as I walked on, my letter in my hand, there stood the old house just past a little shoe-repair shop. It stood far back from the broken cast-iron fence in the center of its weed-grown lot, black-etched in the moonlight, and I stopped on the walk and stood staring up at it.

The high-windowed old roof was gone, the interior nearly gutted, the yard strewn with splintered boards and great chunks of torn plaster. The windows and doors were all removed, the openings hollow in the clear wash of light. But the high old walls, last of all to go, still stood tall and dignified in their old-fashioned strength and outmoded charm.

I walked through the opening where a gate had once hung, up the cracked and weed-grown brick pavement toward the wide old porch. And there on one of the ornate fluted posts I saw the house number deeply and elaborately carved into the old wood. At the wide, flat porch rail leading down to the walk I brought out my ink and pen and copied the number carefully on to my envelope; 972 I printed under the name of the girl who had once lived here, Brock Place, Brooklyn, New York. Then I turned towards the street again, my envelope in my hand.

There was a mailbox at the next corner and I stopped beside it. But to drop this letter into that box, knowing in advance that it could go only to the dead-letter office, would again, I couldn't help feeling, turn the writing of it into an empty meaningless act; and after a moment I walked on past the box, crossed the street and turned right, knowing exactly where I was going.

I walked four blocks through the night passing a hack stand with a single cab, its driver asleep with his arms and head cradled on the wheel; passing a night watchman sitting on a standpipe protruding from the building wall smoking a pipe—he nodded as I passed and I nodded in response. I turned left at the next corner, walked half a block more, then turned up on to the worn stone steps of the Wister postal substation.

It must easily be one of the oldest postal substations in the borough, built, I suppose, not much later than during the decade following the Civil War. And I can't imagine that the inside has changed much. The floor is marble, the ceiling high, the woodwork dark and carved. The outer lobby is open at all times as are post office lobbies everywhere, and as I pushed through the old swinging doors I saw that it was deserted. Somewhere behind the opaque windows a light burned dimly far in the rear of the post office and I had an impression of subdued activity back there. But the lobby was dim and silent and, as I walked across the worn stone of its floor, I knew I was seeing all around me precisely what Brooklynites had seen for no telling how many generations long dead.

The post office has always seemed an institution of mystery to me, an ancient, worn, but still functioning mechanism that is not operated but only tended by each succeeding generation of men to come along. It is a place where occasionally plainly addressed letters with clearly written return addresses go astray and are lost, to end up no one knows where and for reasons impossible to discover, as the postal employee from whom you inquire will tell you. Its air of mystery, for me, is made up of stories— well, you've read them, too, from time to time, the odd little stories in your newspaper. A letter bearing a postmark of 1906, written over half a century ago, is delivered today— simply because inexplicably it arrived at some post office along with the other mail with no explanation from anyone now alive. Sometimes it's a postcard of greeting—from the Chicago World's Fair of 1893, maybe. And once, tragically, as I remember reading, it was an acceptance of a proposal of marriage offered in 1901 and received today, a lifetime too late, by the man who made it and married someone else and is now a grandfather.

I pushed the worn brass plate open, dropped my letter into the silent blackness of the slot, and it disappeared forever with no sound. Then I turned and left to walk home with a feeling of fulfillment of having done, at least, everything I possibly could in response to the silent cry for help I'd found in the secrecy of the old desk.

Next morning I felt the way almost anyone might. Standing at the bathroom mirror shaving, I grinned, feeling foolish but at the same time secretly pleased with myself. I was glad I'd written and solemnly mailed that letter and now I realized why I'd put no return address on the envelope. I didn't want it to come forlornly back to me with no such person, or whatever the phrase is, stamped on the envelope. There'd once been such a girl and last night she still existed for me. And I didn't want to see my letter to her—rubber-stamped, scribbled on, and unopened—to prove that there no longer was.

I was busy all the next week. I work for a wholesale grocery company; we got a big new account, a chain of supermarkets, and that meant extra work for everyone. More often than not I had my lunch at my desk in the office and worked several evenings besides. I had dates the two evenings I was free. On Friday afternoon I was at the main public library in Manhattan at Fifth Avenue and Forty-second copying statistics from half a dozen trade publications for a memorandum I'd been assigned to write over the weekend on the new account.

Late in the afternoon the man sitting beside me at the big reading-room table closed his book, stowed away his glasses, picked up his hat from the table and left. I sat back in my chair glancing at my watch. Then I looked over at the book he'd left on the table. It was a big one-volume pictorial history of New York put out by Columbia University, and I dragged it over, and began leafing through it.

I skimmed over the first section on colonial and pre-colonial New York pretty quickly, but, when the old sketches and drawings began giving way to actual photographs, I turned the pages more slowly. I leafed past the first photos. taken around the mid-century, and then past those of the Civil War period. But when I reached the first photograph of the 1870s—it was a view of Fifth Avenue in 1871—I began reading the captions under each one.

I knew it would be too much to hope to find a photograph of Brock Place, in Helen Worley's time especially, and of course I didn't. But I knew there'd surely be photographs taken in Brooklyn during the 1880s, and a few pages farther on I found what I'd hoped I might. In clear, sharp detail and beautifully reproduced lay a big half-page photograph of a street less than a quarter mile from Brock Place; and staring down at it, there in the library, I knew that Helen Worley must often have walked along this very sidewalk. VARNEY STREET, 1881, the caption said. A TYPICAL BROOKLYN RESIDENTIAL STREET OF THE PERIOD.

Varney Street today—I walk two blocks of it every night coming home from work—is a wasteland. I pass four cinder-packed used-car lots; a shabby concrete garage, the dead earth in front of it littered with rusting car parts and old tires; and a half dozen or so nearly paintless boarding houses, one with a soiled card in its window reading MASSAGE. It's a nondescript joyless street and it's impossible to believe that there has ever been a tree on its entire length.

But there has been. There in sharp black-and-white in the book on the table before me lay Varney Street, 1881, and from the wide grass-covered parkways between the cut-stone kerb and sidewalks, the thick old long-gone trees rose high on both sides to meet, intertwine and roof the wide street with green. The photograph had been taken, apparently, from the street—it had been possible to do that in a day of occasional slow-trotting horses and buggies—and the camera was aimed at an angle to one side toward the sidewalk and the big houses beyond it, looking down the walk for several hundred feet.

The old walk, there in the foreground under the great trees, appeared to be at least six feet wide—spacious enough easily for a family to walk down it four or five abreast, as families did in those times walk together down the sidewalks under the trees. Beyond the walk, widely separated and set far back across the fine old lawns, rose the great houses, the ten-, twelve-, and fourteen-room family houses two or more storeys high and with attics above them for children to play in and discover the relics of childhoods before theirs. Their windows were tall and they were framed on the outside with ornamented wood. And in the solid construction of every one of those lost houses in that ancient photograph there had been left over the time, skill, money, and inclination to deco rate their eaves with scrollwork; to finish a job with craftsmanship and pride. And time, too, to build huge, wide porches on which families sat on summer evenings with palmleaf fans.

Far down that lovely tree-sheltered street—out of focus and indistinct—walked the retreating figure of a long-skirted puff-sleeved woman, her summer parasol open at her back. Of the thousands of long-dead girls it might have been I knew this could not be Helen Worley. Yet it wasn't completely impossible, I told myself; this was a street, precisely as I saw it now down which she must often have walked; and I let myself think that, yes, this was she. Maybe I live in what is for me the wrong time and I was filled now with the most desperate yearning to be there on that peaceful street—to walk off past the edges of the scene on the printed page before me into the old and beautiful Brooklyn of long ago. And to draw near and overtake that bobbing parasol in the distance, and then turn and look into the face of the girl who held it.

I worked that evening at home, sitting at my desk, with a can of beer on the floor beside me, but once more Helen Elizabeth Worley was in my mind. I worked steadily all evening and it was around twelve thirty when I finished—eleven hand-written pages which I'd get typed at the office on Monday. Then I opened the little center desk drawer into which I'd put a supply of rubber bands and paper clips, took out a clip and fastened the pages together, and sat back in my chair, taking a swallow of beer. The little center desk drawer stood half open as I'd left it and as my eye fell on it I realized that of course it, too, must have another secret drawer behind it.

I hadn't thought of that. It simply hadn't occurred to me the week before, in my interest and excitement over the letter I'd found behind the first drawer of the row; and I'd been too busy all week to think of it since. But now I set down my beer, pulled the center drawer all the way out, reached behind it, and found the little groove in the smooth wood I touched. Then I brought out the second secret little drawer.

I'll tell you what I think, what I'm certain of, though I don't claim to be speaking scientifically; I don't think science has a thing to do with it. The night is a strange time: things *are* different then, as every human being knows. And I think this: Brooklyn has changed over seven decades; it is no longer the same place at all. But here and there, still, are little islands—isolated remnants of the way things once were. And the Wister postal substation is one of them: it hasn't really changed at all. And I think that at night—late at night, the world asleep, when the sounds of things as they are now are nearly silent and the sight of things as they are now is vague in the darkness—the boundary between here and then wavers. At certain moments and places it fades. I think in the dimness of the old Wister post office in the dead of night lifting my letter to Helen Worley toward the old brass door of the letter drop—I think that I stood on one side of that slot in the year 1962 and that I dropped my letter, properly stamped, written and addressed in ink and on the very paper of Helen Worley's youth, into the Brooklyn of 1880s on the other side of that worn old slot.

I believe that—I'm not interested in proving it—but I believe it. Because now from that second secret little drawer I brought out the paper I found in it, opened it, and in rust-black ink on yellowing old paper I read:

Please, oh, please—who are you? Where can I reach you? Your letter arrived today in the second morning post, and I have wandered the house and garden ever since in an agony of excitement. I cannot conceive how you saw my letter in its secret place, but since you did, perhaps you will see this one too. Oh, tell me your letter is no hoax or cruel joke! Willy, if it is you; if you have discovered my letter and think to deceive your sister with a prank, I pray you to tell me! But if it is not—if I now address someone who has truly responded to my most secret hopes—do not longer keep me ignorant of who and where you are. For I, too—and I confess it willingly—long to see you! And I, too, feel and am most certain of it, that if I could know you I would love you. It is impossible for me to think otherwise.

I must hear from you again; I shall not rest until I do.

> *I remain, most sincerely,*
> *Helen Elizabeth Worley*

After a long time I opened the first drawer of the old desk and took out the pen and ink I'd found there, and a sheet of the note paper.

For minutes then, the pen in my hand, I sat there in the night staring down at the empty paper on the desk top; finally I dipped the pen into the old ink and wrote:

Helen my dear: I don't know how to say this so it will seem even comprehensible to you. But I do exist, here in Brooklyn, less than three blocks from where you now read this—in the year 1962. We are separated not by space but by the years which lie between us. Now I own the desk which you once had and at which you wrote the note I found in it. Helen, all I can tell you is that I answered that note, mailed it late at night at the old Wister station, and that somehow it reached you as I hope this will too. This is no hoax! Can you imagine anyone playing a joke that cruel? I live in a Brooklyn within sight of your house that you cannot imagine. It is a city whose streets are now crowded with wheeled vehicles propelled by engines. And it is a city extending far beyond the limits you know, with a population of millions, so crowded there is hardly room any longer for trees. From my window as I write I can see—across Brooklyn Bridge, which is hardly changed from the way you, too, can see it now—Manhattan Island, and rising from it are the lighted silhouettes of stone-and-steel buildings more than one thousand feet high.

You must believe me. I live, I exist eighty years after you read this, and with the feeling that I have fallen in love with you.

I sat for some moments staring at the wall, trying to figure out how to explain something I was certain was true. Then I wrote:

Helen, there are three secret drawers in our desk. Into the first you put only the letter I found. You cannot now add something to that drawer and hope that it will reach me. For I have already opened that drawer and found only the letter you put there. Nothing else can now come down through the years to me in that drawer for you cannot alter what you have already done.

Into the second drawer you put the note which lies before me, which I found when I opened that drawer a few minutes ago. You put nothing else into it, and now that, too, cannot be changed.

But I haven't opened the third drawer, Helen. Not yet! It is the last way you can still reach me and the last time. I will mail this as I did before, then wait. In a week I will open the last drawer.

Jake Belknap

It was a long week. I worked, I kept busy daytimes, but at night I thought of hardly anything but the third secret drawer in my desk. I was terribly tempted to open it earlier, telling myself whatever might lie in it had been put there decades before and must be there now, but I wasn't sure and I waited.

Then, late at night, a week to the hour I'd mailed my second letter at the old Wister post office, I pulled out the third drawer, reached in and brought out the last little secret drawer which lay behind it.

My hand was actually shaking and for a moment I couldn't bear to look directly—something lay in the drawer—and I turned my head away. Then I looked.

I'd expected a long letter, very long, of many pages, her last communication with me, and full of every thing she wanted to say. But there was no letter at all. It was a photograph, about three inches square, a faded sepia in color, mounted on heavy stiff cardboard, and with the photographer's name in tiny gold script down in the corner. *Brunner & Holland, Parisian Photography, Brooklyn, NY.*

The photograph showed the head and shoulders of a girl in a high-necked dark dress with a cameo brooch at the collar. Her dark hair was swept tightly back, covering the ears, in a style which no longer suits our ideas of beauty. But the stark severity of that dress and hair style couldn't spoil the beauty of the face that smiled out at me from the old photograph. It wasn't beautiful in any classic sense, I suppose. The brows were unplucked and somewhat heavier than we are used to. But it is the soft warm smile of her lips and her eyes—large and serene as she looks out at me over the years—that made Helen Elizabeth Worley a beautiful woman. Across the bottom of her photograph she has written, 'I will never forget.' And as I sat there at the old desk staring at what she had written, I understood that of course that was all there was to say—what else?—on this, the last time, as she knew, that she'd ever be able to reach me.

It wasn't the last time, though. There was one final way for Helen Worley to communicate with me over the years and it took me a long time, as it must have taken her, to realize it. Only a week ago, on my fourth day of searching, I finally found it. It was late in the evening and the sun was almost gone, when I found the old headstone among all the others stretching off in rows under the quiet trees. Then I read the inscription etched in the weathered old stone: HELEN ELIZABETH WORLEY—1861-1934. Under this were the words, I NEVER FORGOT.

And neither will I.

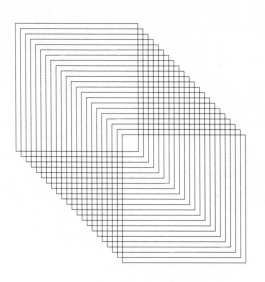

ON THE WATCHTOWER AT PLATAEA

BY GARRY KILWORTH

There was the chilling possibility, despite Miriam's assurance that she would dissuade the government from physical confrontation, that I might receive the order to go out and kill my adversary in the temple. They might use the argument that our future existence depended on answers to be dredged from further back in the past. I wondered if I could do such a thing: and if so, how? Would I sneak from the watchtower in the night, like an assassin, and murder him in his bed? Or challenge him to single combat, like a true noble warrior is supposed to? The whole idea of such a confrontation made me feel ill and I prayed that if it should come to such a pass, they would send someone else to do the bloody job. I have no stomach for such things.

It was a shock to find that the expedition could go no further back than BC 429: though for some of us, it was not an unwelcome one. Miriam was perhaps the only one amongst us who was annoyed that we couldn't get to Pericles. He had died earlier, in the part of the year we couldn't reach. So near—but we had hit a barrier, as solid as a rockface on the path of linear time, in the year that the Peloponnesian War was gaining momentum. It was the night that Sparta and its allies were to take positive action against the Athenians by attacking a little walled city-state called Plataea. Plataea, with its present garrison of 400—local hoplites and some 80 seconded Athenians, was virtually the only mainland supporter of Athens in the war amongst the Greeks. It was a tiny city-state, even by ancient world standards—perhaps a mile in circumference, and it was heavily outnumbered by the besieging troops led by the Spartan king, Archidamus. It didn't stand a chance, but by God it put up resistance which rivaled The Alamo for stubbornness, and surpassed it for inventiveness.

Miriam suggested we set up the recording equipment in an old abandoned watchtower on a hill outside the city. From there we could see the main gates, and could record both the Spartan attempts at breaching the walls, and the defenders as they battled to keep the invaders at bay. The stonework of the watchtower was unstable, the timber rotting, and it was probably only used to shelter goats. We did not, therefore, expect to be interrupted while we settled in. In any case, while we were 'travelling', we appeared as insubstantial beings and were seldom confronted. The tower was ideal. It gave us the height we needed to command a good view, and had aged enough to be a respectable establishment for spectral forms.

There were three of us in the team. Miriam was the expedition's leader; John was responsible for the recording equipment; and I was the official communicator, in contact with base camp, 2017 AD. By 429, we were not at our harmonious best, having been away from home for a very long time, long enough for all our habits and individual ways to get on each other's nerves to the point of screaming. I suppose we were all missing home to a certain extent, though why we should want to go back to a world where four-fifths of the population was on the streets, starving, and kept precariously at bay by the private military armies of privileged groups, was never raised. We ourselves, of course, belonged to one of those groups, but we were aware of the instability of the situation and the depressingly obvious fact that we could do nothing to influence it. The *haves* were no longer in a position to help the *have nots*, even given the desire to do such. One of the reasons for coming on the expedition was to escape my guilt—and the constant wars between the groups. It was, as always, a mess.

"What does base say?" asked Miriam.

I could see the watch fires on the nearby city walls through her ghostly form, as she moved restlessly around the walkway of the tower. John was doing something below.

"They believe the vortex must have an outer limit," I said. "It would appear that we've reached it."

This didn't satisfy her, and I didn't expect it to. Miriam did not operate on beliefs. She liked people to *know*.

"But why here? Why now? What's so special about the year 429? It doesn't make any sense."

"You expect it to make sense?"

"I had hoped…oh, I don't know. An answer which wasn't still a question I suppose. Doesn't it worry you? That suddenly we come up against a wall, without any apparent reason?"

I shrugged. "Surely natural limitations are a good enough reason.

Human endeavor has often come up against such things—the sound barrier for example. They believed that was impassable at the time, but they got through it in the end. Maybe this is a comparable problem?"

"It's a bitch, I know that much," she replied in a bitter tone. "I really wanted Pericles—and the earlier battles. Marathon. Thermopylae. Damn it, there's so much we'll have to leave. Mycenae and Agamemnon. We could have confirmed all that. If we can't go back any further, Troy will remain covered in mist...."

Which was not altogether a bad thing as far as I was concerned. Already too many illusions had been wiped away. Why destroy all myth and legend, simply for the sake of facts? It's a pretty boring world, once the magic has been stripped off.

"Well, perhaps we shouldn't do it all at once," I suggested. "I feel as if I'm drowning as it is...let someone else destroy Homer."

She said, "We're not *destroying* anything. We're merely recording..."

"The *truth*" I said, unable to keep the sarcasm out of my tone. She glared at me, a silvery frown marring her handsome features. We had clashed in the same way several times recently and I think she was getting tired of my outbursts.

"You have an attitude problem, Stan—don't make it my problem too."

"I won't," I said, turning away.

In the distance, I could hear the jingle of brass: the Spartan army tromping through the night, their torches clearly visible. These sounds and sights were the cause of some consternation and excitement amongst the Plataeans on the walls of the city. The enemy had arrived. Little figures ran to and fro, between the watch fires. They had known for a few hours that Archidamus was coming: Theban traitors, spies and double agents had been busy during the day, earning a crust. The warnings had come too late for flight however and it was now a case of defying the vastly superior force, or surrendering the city. Some of the defenders were relying on the fact that Plataea was sacred ground—it had been consecrated after a successful battle with the Persians earlier in the century—but

Archidamus was not a man to take much notice of that. There were ways of appealing to the gods for a suspension of holy rights, if the need was there.

I wondered how the Spartans would react if they knew they were being recorded, visually. They were already pretty good at strutting around in grand macho style, cuffing slaves and flaunting their long hair. We had been told that historical recordings such as this would be studied for possible answers to the problems of our own time. I couldn't help but feel cynical about this idea, though I did not have the whole picture. The future, beyond my own time, had been investigated by another team and the result was a secret known only to that expedition and our illustrious government, but I couldn't help feeling it was a very bleak picture.

Besides Spartans, the invading army consisted of slave-auxiliaries, a few mercenaries, and volunteer forces from the cities allied with Sparta: Corinth, Megara, Elis, Thebes, many others. These cities looked to their big cousin to lead them against the upstart Athens, a city-state of little significance until the early part of the century, when it had thrashed a hugely superior force of Persians at the Battle of Marathon, and had since become too big for its sandals. If there was one thing the Ancient Greeks could not stand, it was someone thinking they were better than everyone else.

Except for Plataea, Athens stood virtually alone in mainland Greece, though its maritime empire encompassed almost all the Aegean islands and the coast of Asia Minor. One of the reasons why the war would last so long was because a stalemate was inevitable. Athens was a strongly   walled city, which included its harbor, and could not be penetrated by a land force. Its formidable bronze-toothed fleet of ramming triremes discouraged any idea of a naval blockade. On the other hand, Sparta had no ships to speak of, was an inland unwalled city, but positively encouraged an invasion of their territory since they relished battles and their hoplites were considered almost invincible in battle. Certainly no Spartan would leave a field alive unless victory had been assured. Direct confrontations with such warriors, cool and unafraid of death, were not courted at all keenly, even by brave Athenians.

So, a military might and a naval power, and rarely the twain met. Stalemate. Little Plataea was in fact nothing more than a whipping boy on which Sparta could vent some of its frustration and spleen.

Miriam was looking through night viewers at the advancing hordes. She said, "This may be the last historical battle we're able to record."

I was glad of that. Expeditions like ours tend to start out fortified by enthusiasms and good nature, only to end in disillusionment and bitter emotions, as any geographical explorer will tell you. Discoveries exact a high price from the finders, who have to pay for them with pieces of their souls.

There was a terrible scream from down below, sending lizards racing up my back. I stared at Miriam. A few moments later, John came up the makeshift ladder, looking disgusted.

"Goatboy," he explained. "Wandered in looking for a place to hide from the troops I suppose, now that they've closed the city gates. He saw me and ran. That earth floor already stinks to high heaven with goat droppings. They must have been using it for decades."

Miriam said, "Pull up the ladder, John. We may as well settle for the night. Nothing's going to happen until morning."

Below us, the weary Allies began to arrive and put up tents, out of range of any archers who might be on the walls of the city. Trumpets were sounded, informing the Plataeans that a bloody business was about to begin, as if they didn't know that already. They were pretty noisy in unloading their gear, clattering pots and clanking bits of armor; bawling to one another as new groups arrived, in the hearty fashion of the soldier before the killing starts. We required rest, though we did not sleep while we were travelling, any more than we needed to eat or drink.

"Noisy bastards," I grumbled. "I wish they'd shut up."

John, saying his prayers as he always did at that time of night, looked up sharply from his kneeling position and frowned. He did not like interruptions during such a time, and I found myself apologizing.

Here we were, making sure these squabbles amongst humankind reached a pitch of historical accuracy nobody needed. What the hell was it all about? And were our recordings doing even that useless job? I doubted it. Going back into history, you tend to get caught in the confusion of one small corner of an issue, just as if you lived in the times. One needs God's eyes to see the whole, and weigh the reasons.

It might be that God dwells beyond some far ripple of the time vortex. If you think of the vortex as an old-fashioned long playing record and the groove as linear time, you will have some idea how travellers are able to skip through the ages, as a too-light arm of a record deck skates over a disc. It is a mental process, requiring no vehicle. Somewhere beyond those grooves, dwells the Almighty. Who wants to meet God and see *absolute truth* in all its blinding whiteness? Not me. Not me, my friend. *Eyes I dare not meet in dreams*, as the poet Eliot said.

By the next morning the Spartans had surrounded Plataea and were intent on encircling it with a palisade of sharpened stakes, leaning inwards. Archidamus wanted to be sure that no one could escape from the city. He wanted to teach the inhabitants a lesson: that siding with those nasty imperialists and free-thinkers, the Athenians, was a dangerous thing to do.

It was true that Athens had created a confederacy, mostly consisting of island states, which she subsequently milked of funds, using the money to build the Parthenon, generally beautify the city, and increase the number of ships in her fleet. It was true that anyone who requested to leave the confederacy found the equivalent of several British gunboats in their harbor within a few days. But it was equally true that the Spartans, with their two kings (one to stay at home, while the other was at war) really could not give a damn about anyone but themselves. Athens was full of woolly-minded intellectuals who not only indulged in progressive thinking and innovations, but were carefree and undisciplined with it. Sparta had long since fossilized. They had put a stop to progress some time ago. In Sparta it was forbidden to write new songs, poetry or plays, or introduce anything into society with a flavor of change about it, let alone the *avant-garde* stuff allowed in Athens. Why, the northern city was positively licentious in its attitudes towards art and science. Nothing which would disturb the perfection of the lifestyle Spartans had achieved at an earlier time, was permitted in Lacedaemonia. Asceticism, the mobility of war, plain food and state-raised children destined for the army: these were the ideals to be upheld. Give a Spartan a coarse-hair shirt, a plate of salty porridge, a lusty three-hundred-year-old song to sing, and send him out onto the battlefield, and he'll die thanking you. To the Athenians, who loved good food, new mathematics, eccentric old men asking interminable questions, incomprehensible philosophies, weird inventions, plays making fun of the gods, love, life and the pursuit of happiness—to these people the Spartans were homicidal lunatics.

I suppose it was little wonder that these two Hellenic city-states disliked each other so much.

While the thousands of figures, the keen ones still sweating in their armor, scurried about below us, busy with siege engines, we got on with our regular tasks. John had set up a hologram at the entrance to the tower. It was supposed to represent Apollo and appeared instantly on any human approach, to warn away hoplites who would have otherwise used the tower as a toilet. The hologram uttered its threats in what was probably an appalling accent, but it was the best we could do with the devices to hand. It seemed to do its job, because by noon on the first day gifts had been placed at a respectable distance from the entrance to the watchtower. They could see us, of course, drifting around the top of the tower, but I suppose we were gods too, witnessing the heroic struggles of mortals. I did my best to assume a Zeus-like posture. We had some 'thunder and lightning' for emergencies, but hadn't needed them up to that point.

The heat of the day made us generally testy and irritable, for although many of our bodily functions were suspended, we still had our senses. I found some shade under the parapet and proceeded to contact base. This time they had a little news for us, which was still very vague. Something—they were not sure quite what, but told us to watch for the unusual—something was preventing a further spread of the vortex.

Watch for something unusual? Only those bloody deskriders back at base would say something like that to travellers in an antique world, where the unusual was all around, in almost every facet of daily life. Personally, I hoped they didn't solve the problem. I was weary and homesick and a solution would mean continuing the journey. I didn't say that, of course.

I told Miriam what base had said, and she nodded.

"Thanks. We'll have to wait and see." Boredom, that's what time travel is mostly about. Like war, it's five percent feverish action, and ninety-five percent sitting around with nothing to do. I settled down wearily for a game of chess with John.

"You're the Athenians and I'm the Spartans, so I get to have two kings," he joked.

I thought John uncomplicated and open, and we seemed to get on well together, though he was a good deal younger than me. I was reticent, but he didn't seem to mind that. He had not lost the bubbling enthusiasm of youth, took religion seriously (both of which got on my nerves sometimes, when I was feeling bloody), and had a love for his fellows which was difficult to resist.

Miriam was of a similar disposition to myself. Sometimes to while away the hours, I imagined a romantic connection between us, which was actually as farfetched as any fairytale romance. Although she is a fine-looking woman, with a strong will and good mind, I was not in the least attracted to her. Interested in her, but not attracted. One of those chemical negatives I suppose. I'm sure the feeling was mutual, if she thought about it at all. She had a husband back home, and two kids, not that she ever talked about them. I expect they were none of our damn business.

"Your move."

John shifted his head, to interfere with my line of vision.

"Oh, yes—sorry. Daydreaming."

"Occupational hazard," he said, with more seriousness than was warranted, but I didn't have time to question his tone. At that moment a bird, a bee-eater I think, flew into the parapet with a *smack*. I picked the beautiful creature up, whereupon it pecked me, struggled from my grasp and took groggily to the air. It seemed to be all right.

John gave me a significant stare. It is one of his theories that the vortex interferes with the orientation of natural creatures (time travellers being *unnatural* I expect) and he intended to write something of the sort when we returned to civilization. He could be right, but if he believed that anyone would care about such things, he was in for a disappointment. It is one of *my* theories that, back at base camp, they don't even care about the orientation of humans, let alone bee-eaters.

Over the next few weeks we watched the activity below with a little more interest. It became a battle of wits, not swords, the main combatants being the engineering corps of both sides. The Spartan army labored long and hard to build an earth ramp against the city wall, up which they intended to march and take the city, at the same time catapulting fireballs through the air and making futile attempts at scaling the walls with ladders. Before the ramp was completed the wily Plataeans had raised the height of the wall at that point, cannibalizing their houses for stone blocks. It became a race. The taller grew the ramp, the higher went the wall. In the end, Archidamus put every available man on earth-carrying duty and by this means he managed to gain on the Plataeans, threatening to reach the top of the wall.

Undaunted, the defenders then tunneled underneath their own wall and through the earth ramp, removing the loose soil until the ramp collapsed. On seeing his beautiful mound fall in on itself, Archidamus stamped around threatening death and destruction. He sacrificed a dozen goats to us, and to another shrine—a small temple about half a mile from our position—hoping we would intervene divinely on his behalf in subduing these irksome Plataeans. He came to us in full armor, wearing the classic Corinthian helmet, with its decorated, elongated cheek-pieces and transverse crest of horsehair, his brass-faced shield and muscled greaves, and a heavy bell cuirass. For a Spartan he was pretty flashy, but then he was a king. It was obvious that he was hot and testy, and I think it took all his reserve to remain polite to the gods who were giving his troops such a hard time. The goats' entrails stank like hell when thrown into the copper bowl of flames and we retreated below for a while, leaving a hologram of Athena to receive promises of temples to be erected, and pilgrimages to be undertaken, once victory was within Spartan grasp.

On reflection it was not the most tactful thing to have done, since Athena was the goddess protector of Athens, but we didn't think about that at the time. In any case, what was irritating Archidamus was the fact that the enemy would not come out and fight like men. Spartans do not make the best besieging troops in the world. They hate messing around with mud, sticks and stones, when they could be looking their best, charging across a windy plain with their long black hair streaming and their mouths uttering terrible war cries, ready to stick or be stuck by some sharp instrument. There were lots of jokes about the Spartans, even amongst their own allies. The one about the shrew's brain in a lion's skin was a particular favorite.

After delivering his dubious gifts, Archidamus then went to the small temple, inside the palisade, and repeated the exercise. Miriam became very curious about this rival for our affections and managed to find a spot around the tower wall where she could see the building through her viewers. Finally she asked John to take some footage, though it was not possible to see directly into the obliquely positioned temple and our line of sight was hampered by the points of some tall stakes on the palisade. We ran this through, afterwards, and managed to catch a glimpse of a figure between the marble columns. He had some kind of legged device with him, the head of which seemed to incorporate revolving flaps of stiff material, that flashed like mirrors when it was operated. More significant than this, however, was the fact that the white-robed figure working this machine seemed to have semitransparent flesh. Certainly he was treated with distant, wary reverence by the Greeks, in the same way that we were ourselves. There was very good reason to suppose that we and this elusive person, and possibly any companions hidden by the temple walls, had a great deal in common.

"Look at those beggars—you've got to hand it to them," said John, with admiration in his voice. He was of course talking about the Plataeans. Archidamus's engineers had stopped the Plataeans' little game of removing earth from under the ramp by packing baskets with clay and placing them as foundation blocks for the ramp. These could not be drawn away like loose earth. The defenders met this device by digging a subterranean mine to beyond the ramp and allowing the whole effort to collapse again. By this time the earth was having to be carried from some considerable distance by the besiegers and they were becoming dispirited and thoroughly disgruntled by the whole affair. Deserters began to drift by our watchtower at night, and one or two minor kings packed their tents and took their citizen-soldiers home. Archidamus executed some malefactors, possibly to create an interesting diversion to the grueling manual labour, but was unable to stem the increasing tide of dissatisfaction amongst his troops. He had sent for some Scythian archers of his own, but the Plataeans erected animal-hide screens on top of the walls to protect themselves and the bowmen were less than effective. Added to this there was the smell of sickness in the air, which was part of the sordid business of a war in stalemate.

Some time after calling base regarding the possible presence of another group of travellers, we were asked to obtain further information. Miriam had already spent a great deal of time studying the mysterious occupants of the small temple through the viewer, but there were too many obstacles in the way to get anything concrete.

"We'll have to go over there," she said, "and get a closer look."

John and I glanced at one another. Although the watchtower was far from secure against aggressive action, it provided protection for us in that it had become a sacred building to the Greeks and was unlikely to be violated. It ensured that we remained distant, aloof figures which could be avoided simply by giving the crumbling structure a wide berth. Once we started wandering amongst them, like ordinary mortals, we were in danger of becoming too familiar. It was not beyond the realms of possibility that some brave hoplite might decide to challenge the 'gods;' after all, Odysseus had got away with it. It was a risky business. Of course, we could protect ourselves with our own weapons, but never having had to resort to such drastic action, we were unsure of the consequences.

"What do you suggest?" asked John.

Miriam said, "I'll take the portable and go over there for some close-ups—Stan, you come with me."

Not *too* close, I thought, but nodded in assent. I must admit, the anticipation of some excitement gave me a charge, despite my apprehension.

We set off just as the Hellenic dawn was coming up. Miriam carried the hand recorder, while I self-consciously cradled a weapon in my arms. I knew how to use it, but it was more a question of whether it knew how to use me. I have never had to hurt anyone in my life—physically, that is. We walked between tents and lean-to shacks that had been raised by the invaders, without hindrance, though one or two wide-eyed early risers moved quickly out of our way. When we got to the gate in the palisade of stakes we had a problem. It was closed.

"What do we do?" I said. "We can't walk through the damn thing. And gods don't fiddle with gates, wondering how they open." Before Miriam could answer, one of the sentries rushed forward and pulled at a leather thong. The gate swung open. He had not, of course, understood the language of the gods, but our intentions were obvious and the mere fact that I had voiced some strange words must have spurred him to action.

We made our way toward the temple. I prayed that the archers on the walls of Plataea would be too overawed by the sight of a pair of semi-transparent beings to fire any arrows.

We stood off about a hundred yards from the temple, where we had a clear view into the interior, and Miriam began recording. Half-hidden in the heavy shadows thrown by the columns we could see a translucent form operating the instrument with the metallic flaps, which was possibly some sort of heliogravic recording device, though it looked like something knocked-up in a Swiss toymaker's workshop for an Arabian prince. The stand was fashioned of polished wood covered in hieroglyphics and there were lead weights on plumblines which balanced wooden arms connected to cogged wheels. Behind the operator, hanging from the walls, were two elongated scrolls of painted parchment, one with a picture of a dog's body with a monkey's head, the other depicting some sort of wading bird.

As we stood, both he and us, recording each other—a situation that struck me as rather ironical—another wraith-like figure appeared, wearing a long, flowing robe and decorated headcloth. He whispered to his companion, then went back into a side-room. I was sure that the directional mike would capture that whisper, which when amplified, would reveal their language.

Miriam gestured to me without speaking and we stopped recording, making our way back.

The gate had been left open for us and we passed through without any problem, but on the other side of the palisade it was a different matter. Word had got around that the gods were abroad and a huge crowd had gathered, though there was a wide path through the middle of it leading to the tower. I could see John on the ramparts of the watchtower with a weapon in his hands.

"Okay," said Miriam, "let's go, Stan. Don't look back...."

I had no intention of doing anything of the sort. All I wanted to do was reach the tower, safely.

As we walked down the avenue a murmuring broke out amongst the troops, which grew in volume to uncoordinated chants. I hadn't any doubt we were being petitioned for various miracles, both collective and individual. Two thirds of the way along there was a horrible incident. A young man broke from the crowd and threw himself at my feet, attempting to clutch my ankle. Before he could lay a hand on me, he was pinned to the mud by several spears, thrown by his comrades. I wanted to be sick on the spot as I watched him squirming in the dust like some wounded porcupine. We made the tower without any further problems and shortly afterward the crowd broke up as Spartan officers moved amongst them with whips. The young man's body was removed, and as he was carried away I wondered what had made him so desperate as to brave touching a god. Maybe his mother or father was terminally ill? Or a close friend had been killed whom he wished us to raise from the dead? Or perhaps he was just a helot, a slave, who thought we could free him from the oppression of his Spartan masters with a wave of our hands? Poor bastard.

Later, I went to Miriam and asked her about our friends in the temple. We had already mentioned the word *Egyptian* to each other, though all we had as evidence for that were the hieroglyphics and the pictures. A group of future Ancient Egyptian revivalists? Just because they wore the costume and carried the artifacts didn't make them residents from the banks of the Nile. Though there didn't seem any logical reason for a masquerade, cults are seldom founded on reason, or by rational thinkers.

"The bird picture was an ibis," said Miriam, "and the dog-monkey, well, the Ancient Egyptian god Zehuti was represented by both those symbolic characters."

"Zehuti?" I knew a little of the culture in question, but this was a new one to me.

"Sorry, you probably know him as Thoth—Zehuti is his older name. The Greeks identified him with Hermes, which makes sense. Hermes the messenger—a *traveller?*"

"Anything else?"

"Yes—Thoth was also the patron of science and inventions, the spokesman of the gods and their keeper of the records. Thoth invented all the arts and sciences, including surveying, geometry, astronomy, soothsaying, magic…do I need to go on?"

"No. I get the picture. If you wanted a god of time-travel, Thoth fits the bill quite nicely. So what do we do now?"

She gave me a grim smile.

"Wait. What else? Once you've transmitted the recording back to base, we wait until they come up with definites."

So we did what we were best, and worst, at: waiting. One evening the three of us were sitting, more or less in a rough circle, engaged in frivolous tasks. I was actually doing nothing. The stars were out, above us, and I could hear the snuffling of livestock and the clank of pots from down below. The area around Plataea was becoming as unsavory as the no-man's-land of World War Two, with cess pits filling the air with an appalling stink and churned mud giving the landscape an ugly, open-wound appearance. We had been discussing our situation. Something was preventing the outer ring of our vortex from going any further, and base believed that what was stopping it was another vortex, coming from the other direction, the distant past. The two whirlpools were touching each other, and neither could proceed before the other retreated. Our friends were indeed, early

Egyptians. It had taken a while for this idea to sink in, but when I thought deeply about it, it was not at all farfetched.

On a simple level, time travel involved a psychological state induced by the use of darkness and light, resulting in the fusion of infinites, of space and time. The dark and light became unified into a substance which formed a shape. That shape was common enough in the night sky: a spiral on a flat plane, moving outwards from the center of the group, some of whom remained behind to form an anchor point for the vortex. The base camp group. The room in which we had begun the vigil was no longer a room, but something else: a super-physical universe that possibly exists in all minds at some level of perception. There was no technological reason why an earlier civilization could not have made the same mental discovery. On the other hand, people of our rank were still not privy to the source of the discovery, and it could well be that the knowledge had come from the past. Egyptian documents perhaps, only recently decoded? I remembered something about mirrors being used to flood the dark interior passages of the pyramids with light from the sun.

I wanted to rush up the ladder and look at the temple that housed this other group, though what good that would do me, I don't know. In any case, there was nothing to be done.

A horrible thought occurred to me.

"We're not going stay here, until they go back?"

Miriam shrugged.

"I don't know. I'm awaiting instructions from base."

"Now look, we're the ones that are here. Not them."

"You know how it is, as well as I do, Stan."

I stared at her.

"I know how it is," I said, bitterly.

Her phantom features produced a faint smile.

I lay awake that night, thinking about the stalemate I had got myself into. Egyptians? If they had had time travel for so long, why hadn't they visited future centuries? But then of course, they probably had, and we had run screaming from them, just as the goatboy had fled from us. They probably had a similar policy to ourselves: no interference, just record and return. So, on their umpteenth journey into the future, they had come to a halt, suddenly, and had no doubt come to the same conclusion as we had: someone was blocking the path.

It wasn't difficult, either, to see how such a discovery might be lost to future civilizations. Hadn't certain surgical techniques been lost too? Time travel would undoubtedly have been in the hands of an elite: probably a priesthood. Some pharaoh, his brain addled as the result of a long lineage of incestuous relationships, had destroyed the brotherhood in a fit of pique; or the priests had been put to death by invading barbarians, their secret locked in stone vaults.

On the current front, the Plataeans were still one jump ahead of the Spartans. They had abandoned their mining operations and instead had built another crescent-shaped wall inside their own, so that when the ramp was finally completed, the Spartans were faced with a second, higher obstacle. Peltasts tried lobbing spears over the higher wall, only to find the distance was too great. Archidamus had his men fill the gap between the two walls with faggots and set light to it, but a chance storm doused this attempt to burn down the city. We got a few indignant looks from the Spartans after that. As gods, we were responsible for the weather. The war trumpets of the invaders filled the air with bleating notes which we felt sure were a criticism of us and our seeming partiality towards the defenders.

Finally, battering rams were employed, over the gap between the walls, but the Plataeans had a device—a huge beam on chains— which they dropped onto the ram-headed war machines and snapped off the ends.

Archidamus gave up. He ordered yet another wall to be built, outside the palisade of stakes, and left part of his army to guard it. Winter was beginning to set in and the king had had enough of the inglorious mudbath in which he had been wallowing. He went home, to his family in the south.

The majority of the Egyptians too, withdrew at this point. One of them remained behind.

We received our orders from base.

"One of us must stay," said Miriam, "until a relief can be sent. If we all go back, the vortex will recede with us and the Egyptians will move forward, gain on us."

"A Mexican stand-off," I said, disgustedly.

"Right. We can't allow them the opportunity to invade the territory we already hold…."

"Shit," I said, ignoring a black look from John, "now we've got a cold war on our hands. Even *time* isn't safe from ownership. First it was things, then it was countries…now it's time itself. Why don't we build a bloody great wall across this year, like Archidamus, and send an army of guards to defend it?"

Miriam said, "Sarcasm won't help at this stage, Stan."

"No, I don't suppose it will, but it makes me feel good. So what happens now? We draw straws?"

"I suggest we do it democratically." She produced three shards of pottery that she had gathered from the ground below, and distributed one to each of us.

"We each write the name of the person we think most competent to remain behind," she explained, "and then toss them in the middle."

"Most competent—I like the diplomatic language," I muttered. John, I knew, would put down his own name. He was one of those selfless types, who volunteered for everything. His minor household gods were Duty and Honor. He would actually *want* to stay.

I picked up my piece of pot. It was an unglazed shard depicting two wrestlers locked in an eternal, motionless struggle, each seemingly of equal strength and skill, and each determined not to give ground. I turned it over and wrote JOHN in clear letters, before placing it, picture-side up, in the middle of the ring.

Two other pieces clattered against mine. Miriam sorted through them, turning them over.

My name was on two of them.

I turned to John.

"Thanks," I said.

"It had to be somebody. You're the best man for the job."

"Bullshit," I said. I turned to Miriam. "What if I refuse to stay? I'll resign, terminate my contract."

Miriam shook her head. "You won't do that. You'd never get another trip and while you get restless in the field, you get even worse at home. I know your type, Stan. Once you've been back a couple of weeks you'll be yelling to go again."

She was right, damn her. While I got bored in the field, I was twice as bad back home.

"I'm not a type," I said, and got up to go below. Shortly afterwards, Miriam followed me.

"I'm sorry, Stan." She touched my arm. "You see it for what it is—another political attempt at putting up fences by possessive, parochial old farts. Unless I go back and convince them otherwise, they'll be sending death squads down the line to wipe out the Egyptians. You do understand?"

"So it had to be me."

"John's too young to leave here alone. I'll get them to replace you as soon as I can—until then…"

She held out her slim hand and I placed my own slowly and gently into her grip. The touch of her skin was like warm silk.

"Goodbye," I said.

She went up the ladder and John came down next.

I said coldly, "What is this? Visiting day?"

"I came to say goodbye," he said, stiffly.

I stared hard at him, hoping I was making it difficult, hoping the bastard was uncomfortable and squirming.

"Why me, John? You had a reason."

He suddenly looked very prim, his spectral features assuming a sharp quality. "I thought about volunteering myself, but that would have meant you two going back alone—together, that is…." He became flustered. "She's a married woman, Stan. She'll go back to her husband and forget you."

I rocked on my heels.

"*What?* What the hell are you talking about?"

"Miriam. I've seen the way you two look at each other."

I stared at him, finding it difficult to believe he could be so stupid.

"You're a fool, John. The worst kind of fool. It's people like you, with twisted minds, that start things like that war out there. Go on, get out of my sight."

He started to climb the ladder, then he looked down and gave me a Parthian shot. "You put *my* name on your shard. Why should I feel guilty about putting yours?"

And he was right, but that didn't stop me from wanting to jerk the ladder from under him and break his bloody neck.

They were both gone, within the hour, leaving me to haunt the Greeks all on my own, a solitary ghost moving restlessly around the parapet of the tower. I saw my Egyptian counterpart once, in the small hours, as a shimmering figure came out into the open to stare at my prison. I thought for a moment he or she was going to wave again, but nothing so interesting happened, and I was left to think about my predicament once more. I knew how slowly things moved back home. They had all the time in the world. I wondered whether Egyptians could learn to play chess. It was a pity Diogenes wasn't yet alive, or I might have been tempted to wander down to Corinth. He would certainly have enjoyed a game, providing I stayed out of his sun. Me and Diogenes, sitting on top of his barrel playing chess a thousand years before the game was invented—that would have been something. Plato was a new-born babe in arms. Socrates was around, in his early forties, but who would want to play with that cunning man. Once he got the hang of it, you'd never win a game.

Flurries of snow began to drift in, over the mountains. The little Plataeans were in for a hard winter. I knew the result of the siege of course. Three hundred Plataeans and seconded Athenians would make a break for it in a year's time, killing the sentries left by Archidamus on the outer wall and getting away in the dark. All of them would make it, to Athens, fooling their pursuers into following a false trail, their inventive minds never flagging when it came to survival. Those Plataeans whose hearts failed them when it came to risking the escape, almost two hundred, would be put to death by the irate Spartans. The city itself would be rased. Perhaps the Spartans would learn something from the incident, but I doubted it. There was certainly a lot of patience around, in the ancient world.

Patience. I wondered how much patience those people from the land of the pharaohs had, because it occurred to me that the natural movement of time was on their side. Provided we did nothing but maintain the *status quo*, standing nose to nose on the edges of our own vortices, they would gain, ever so gradually. Hour by hour, day by day, we were moving back to that place I call home.

We might replace our frontier guards, by one or by thousands, but the plain fact of the matter is we will eventually be pushed back to where we belong. Why, they've already gained several months as it is…only another 25 centuries and I'll be back in my own back yard.

Then again, I might receive that terrible message I have been dreading, which would turn me from being the Athenian I believe I am, into a Spartan. Which would have me laying down my scroll and taking up the spear and shield. A ghost-warrior from the future, running forth to meet a god-soldier from the past. I can only hope that the possible historical havoc such action might cause will govern any decision made back home. I can't help thinking, however, that the wish for sense to prevail must have been on the lips of a million-million such as I, who killed or died on fields, in trenches, in deserts and jungles, on seas and in the air.

The odds are stacked against me.

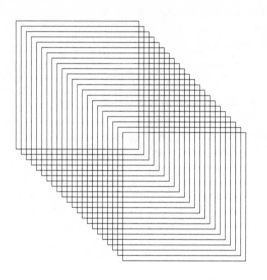

THE TWONKY

BY LEWIS PADGETT

The turnover at Mideastern Radio was so great that Mickey Lloyd couldn't keep track of his men. Employees kept quitting and going elsewhere, at a higher salary. So when the big-headed little man in overalls wandered vaguely out of a storeroom, Lloyd took one look at the brown dungaree suit—company provided—and said mildly, "The whistle blew half an hour ago. Hop to work."

"Work-k-k?" The man seemed to have trouble with the word.

Drunk? Lloyd, in his capacity as foreman, couldn't permit that. He flipped away his cigarette, walked forward and sniffed. No, it wasn't liquor. He peered at the badge on the man's overalls.

"Two-o-four, m-mm. Are you new here?"

"New. Huh?" The man rubbed a rising bump on his forehead. He was an odd-looking little chap, bald as a vacuum tube, with a pinched, pallid face and tiny eyes that held dazed wonder.

"Come on, Joe. Wake up!" Lloyd was beginning to sound impatient. "You work here, don't you?"

"Joe," said the man thoughtfully. "Work. Yes, I work. I make them." His words ran together oddly, as though he had a cleft palate.

With another glance at the badge, Lloyd gripped Joe's arm and ran him through the assembly room. "Here's your place. Hop to it. Know what to do?"

The other drew his scrawny body erect. "I am—expert," he remarked. "Make them better than Ponthwank."

"O.K.," Lloyd said. "Make 'em, then." And he went away.

The man called Joe hesitated, nursing the bruise on his head. The overalls caught his attention, and he examined them wonderingly. Where—oh, yes. They had been hanging in the room from which he had first emerged. His own garments had, naturally, dissipated during the trip—what trip?

Amnesia, he thought. He had fallen from the...the something...when it slowed down and stopped. How odd this huge, machine-filled barn looked! It struck no chord of remembrance.

Amnesia, that was it. He was a worker. He made things. As for the unfamiliarity of his surroundings, that meant nothing. He was still dazed. The clouds would lift from his mind presently. They were beginning to do that already.

Work. Joe scuttled around the room, trying to goad his faulty memory. Men in overalls were doing things. Simple, obvious things. But how childish—how elemental! Perhaps this was a kindergarten.

After a while Joe went out into a stock room and examined some finished models of combination radio-phonographs. So that was it. Awkward and clumsy, but it wasn't his place to say so. No. His job was to make Twonkies.

Twonkies? The name jolted his memory again. Of course he knew how to make Twonkies. He'd made them; all his life—had been specially trained for the job. Now they were using a different model of Twonky, but what the hell! Child's play for a clever workman.

Joe went back into the shop and found a vacant bench. He began to build a Twonky. Occasionally he slipped off and stole the material he needed. Once, when he couldn't locate any tungsten, he hastily built a small gadget and made it.

His bench was in a distant corner, badly lighted, though it seemed quite bright to Joe's eyes. Nobody noticed the console that was swiftly growing to completion there. Joe worked very, very fast. He ignored the noon whistle, and, at quitting time, his task was finished. It could, perhaps, stand another coat of paint; it lacked the Shimmertone of a standard Twonky. But none of the others had Shimmertone. Joe sighed, crawled under the bench, looked in vain for a relaxopad, and went to sleep on the floor.

A few hours later he woke up. The factory was empty. Odd! Maybe the working hours had changed. Maybe Joe's mind felt funny. Sleep had cleared away the mists of amnesia, if such it had been, but he still felt dazed.

Muttering under his breath, he sent the Twonky into the stock room and compared it with the others. Superficially it was identical with a console radio-phonograph combination of the latest model. Following the pattern of the others, Joe had camouflaged and disguised the various organs and reactors.

He went back into the shop. Then the last of the mists cleared from his mind. Joe's shoulders jerked convulsively.

"Great Snell!" he gasped. "So that was it! I ran into a temporal snag!"

With a startled glance around, he fled to the storeroom from which he had first emerged. The overalls he took off and returned to their hook. After that, Joe went over to a corner, felt around in the air, nodded with satisfaction and seated himself on nothing, three feet above the floor. Then Joe vanished.

"Time," said Kerry Westerfield, "is curved. Eventually it gets back to the same place where it started. That's duplication." He put his feet up on a conveniently outjutting rock of the chimney and stretched luxuriously. From the kitchen Martha made clinking noises with bottles and glasses.

"Yesterday at this time I had a Martini," Kerry said. "The time curve indicates that I should have another one now. Are you listening, angel?"

"I'm pouring," said the angel distantly.

"You get my point, then. Here's another. Time describes a spiral instead of a circle. If you call the first cycle 'a,' the second one's 'a plus 1'—see? Which means a double Martini tonight."

"I knew where that would end," Martha remarked, coming into the spacious, oak-raftered living room. She was a small, dark-haired woman, with a singularly pretty face and a figure to match. Her tiny gingham apron looked slightly absurd in combination with slacks and silk blouse, "And they don't make infinity-proof gin. Here's your Martini." She did things with the shaker and manipulated glasses.

"Stir slowly," Kerry cautioned. "Never shake. Ah—that's it." He accepted the drink and eyed it appreciatively. Black hair, sprinkled with gray, gleamed in the lamplight as he sipped the Martini. "Good. Very good."

Martha drank slowly and eyed her husband. A nice guy, Kerry Westerfield. He was forty-odd, pleasantly ugly, with a wide mouth and with an occasional sardonic gleam in his gray eyes as he contemplated life. They had been married for twelve years, and liked it.

From outside, the late, faint glow of sunset came through the windows, picking out the console cabinet that stood against the wall by the door. Kerry peered at it with appreciation.

"A pretty penny," he remarked. "Still—"

"What? Oh. The men had a tough time getting it up the stairs. Why don't you try it, Kerry?"

"Didn't you?"

"The old one was complicated enough," Martha said in a baffled manner. "Gadgets. They confuse me. I was brought up on an Edison. You wound it up with a crank, and strange noises came out of a horn. That I could understand. But now—you push a button, and extraordinary things happen. Electric eyes, tone selections, records that get played on both sides, to the accompaniment of weird groanings and clickings from inside the console—probably you understand those things. I don't even want to. Whenever I play a Crosby record in a superduper like that, Bing seems embarrassed."

Kerry ate his olive. "I'm going to play some Debussy." He nodded towards a table. "There's a new Crosby record for you. The latest."

Martha wriggled happily. "Can I, maybe, huh?"

"Uh-huh."

"But you'll have to show me how."

"Simple enough," said Kerry, beaming at the console, "Those babies are pretty good, you know. They do everything but think."

"I wish they'd wash the dishes," Martha remarked. She set down her glass, got up and vanished into the kitchen.

Kerry snapped on a lamp nearby and went over to examine the new radio, Mideastern's latest model, with all the new improvements. It had been expensive—but what the hell? He could afford it. And the old one had been pretty well shot.

It was not, he saw, plugged in. Nor were there any wires in evidence of even a ground. Something new, perhaps. Built-in antenna and ground. Kerry crouched down, looked for a socket, and plugged the cord into it.

That done, he opened the doors and eyed the dials with every appearance of satisfaction. A beam of bluish light shot out and hit him in the eyes. From the depths of the console a faint, thoughtful clicking proceeded. Abruptly it stopped. Kerry blinked, fiddled with dials and switches, and bit at a fingernail.

The radio said, in a distant voice, "Psychology pattern checked and recorded."

"Eh?" Kerry twirled a dial. "Wonder what that was? Amateur station—no, they're off the air. Hm-m-m." He shrugged and went over to a chair beside the shelves of albums. His gaze ran swiftly over the titles and composers' names. Where was the *Swan of Tuonela?* There it was, next to *Finlandia.* Kerry took down the album and opened it in his lap. With his free hand he extracted a cigarette from his pocket, put it between his lips and fumbled for the matches on the table beside him. The first match he lit went out.

He tossed it into the fireplace and was about to reach for another when a faint noise caught his attention. The radio was walking across the room towards him. A whiplike tendril flicked out from somewhere, picked up a match, scratched it beneath the table top— as Kerry had done—and held the flame to the man's cigarette.

Automatic reflexes took over. Kerry sucked in his breath, and exploded in smoky, racking coughs. He bent double, gasping and momentarily blind.

When he could see again, the radio was back in its accustomed place.

Kerry caught his lower lip between his teeth. "Martha," he called.

"Soup's on," her voice said.

Kerry didn't answer. He stood up, went over to the radio and looked at it hesitantly. The electric cord had been pulled out of its socket. Kerry gingerly replaced it.

He crouched to examine the console's legs. They looked like finely finished wood. His exploratory hand told him nothing. Wood—hard and brittle.

How in hell—

"Dinner!" Martha called.

Kerry threw his cigarette into the fireplace and slowly walked out of the room. His wife, setting a gravy boat in place stared at him.

"How many Martinis did you have?"

"Just one," Kerry said in a vague way. "I must have dozed off for a minute. Yeah. I must have."

THE TWONKY

"Well, fall to," Martha commanded. "This is the last chance you'll have to make a pig of yourself on my dumplings, for a week, anyway."

Kerry absently felt for his wallet, took out an envelope and tossed it at his wife. "Here's your ticket, angel. Don't lose it."

"Oh? I rate a compartment!" Martha thrust the paste board back into its envelope and gurgled happily. "You're a pal. Sure you can get along without me?"

"Huh? Hm-m-m—I think so." Kerry salted his avocado. He shook himself and seemed to come out of a slight daze. "Sure, I'll be all right. You trot off to Denver and help Carol have her baby. It's all in the family."

"We-ell, my only sister—" Martha grinned. "You know how she and Bill are. Quite nuts. They'll need a steadying hand just now."

There was no reply. Kerry was brooding over a forkful of avocado. He muttered something about the Venerable Bede.

"What about him?"

"Lecture tomorrow. Every term we bog down on the Bede, for some strange reason. Ah, well."

"Got your lecture ready?"

Kerry nodded. "Sure." For eight years he had taught at the University, and he certainly should know the schedule by this time!

Later, over coffee and cigarettes, Martha glanced at her wristwatch. "Nearly train time. I'd better finish packing. The dishes—"

"I'll do 'em." Kerry wandered after his wife into the bedroom and made motions of futile helpfulness. After a while, he carried the bags down to the car. Martha joined him, and they headed for the depot.

The train was on time. Half an hour after it had pulled out, Kerry drove the car back into the garage, let himself into the house and yawned mightily. He was tired. Well, the dishes, and then beer and a book in bed.

With a puzzled look at the radio, he entered the kitchen and started on the dishes. The hall phone rang. Kerry wiped his hands on a dish towel and answered it.

It was Mike Fitzgerald, who taught psychology at the University.

"Hiya, Fitz."

"Hiya. Martha gone?"

"Yeah. I just drove her to the train."

"Feel like talking, then? I've got some pretty good Scotch. Why not run over and gab a while?"

"Like to," Kerry said, yawning again, "but I'm dead. Tomorrow's a big day. Rain check?"

"Sure. I just finished correcting papers, and felt the need of sharpening my mind. What's the matter?"

"Nothing. Wait a minute." Kerry put down the phone and looked over his shoulder, scowling. Noises were coming from the kitchen. What the hell!

He went along the hall and stopped in the doorway, motionless and staring. The radio was washing the dishes.

After a while he returned to the phone. Fitzgerald said, "Something?"

"My new radio," Kerry told him carefully. "It's washing the dishes."

Fitz didn't answer for a moment. His laugh was a bit hesitant. "Oh?"

"I'll call you back," Kerry said, and hung up. He stood motionless for a while, chewing his lip. Then he walked back to the kitchen and paused to watch.

The radio's back was towards him. Several limber tentacles were manipulating the dishes, expertly sousing them in hot, soapy water, scrubbing them with the little mop, dipping them into the rinse water and then stacking them neatly in the metal rack. Those whip-lashes were the only sign of unusual activity. The legs were apparently solid.

"Hey!" Kerry said.

There was no response.

He sidled around till he could examine the radio more closely. The tentacles emerged from a slot under one of the dials. The electric cord was dangling. No juice, then. But what—

Kerry stepped back and fumbled out a cigarette. Instantly the radio turned, took a match from its container on the stove and walked forward. Kerry blinked, studying the legs. They couldn't be wood. They were bending as the—the thing moved, elastic as rubber. The radio had a peculiar sidling motion unlike anything else on earth.

It lit Kerry's cigarette and went back to the sink, where it resumed the dishwashing.

Kerry phoned Fitzgerald again. "I wasn't kidding. I'm having hallucinations or something. That damned radio just lit a cigarette for me."

"Wait a minute." Fitzgerald's voice sounded undecided. "This is a gag, eh?"

"No. And I don't think it's a hallucination, either. It's up your alley. Can you run over and test my knee-jerks?"

"All right," Fitz said. "Give me ten minutes. Have a drink ready."

He hung up, and Kerry, laying the phone back into its cradle, turned to see the radio walking out of the kitchen toward the living room. Its square, boxlike contour was subtly horrifying, like some bizarre sort of hobgoblin. Kerry shivered.

He followed the radio, to find it in its former place, motionless and impassive. He opened the doors, examining the turntable, the phonograph arm and the other buttons and gadgets. There was nothing apparently unusual. Again he touched the legs. They were not wood, after all. Some plastic, which seemed quite hard. Or— maybe they were wood, after all. It was difficult to make certain, without damaging the finish. Kerry felt a natural reluctance to use a knife on his new console.

He tried the radio, getting local stations without trouble. The tone was good—unusually good, he thought. The phonograph—

He picked up Halvorsen's *Entrance of the Boyars* at random and slipped it into place, closing the lid. No sound emerged. Investigation proved that the needle was moving rhythmically along the groove, but without audible result. Well?

Kerry removed the record as the doorbell rang. It was Fitzgerald, a gangling, saturnine man with a leathery, wrinkled face and a tousled mop of dull gray hair. He extended a large, bony hand.

"Where's my drink?"

"'Lo, Fitz. Come in the kitchen. I'll mix. Highball?"

"Highball."

"O.K." Kerry led the way. "Don't drink it just yet, though. I want to show you my new combination."

"The one that washes dishes?" Fitzgerald asked. "What else does it do?"

Kerry gave the other a glass. "It won't play records."

"Oh, well. A minor matter, if it'll do the housework. Let's take a look at it." Fitzgerald went into the living room, selected *Afternoon of a Faun* and approached the radio. "It isn't plugged in."

"That doesn't matter a bit," Kerry said wildly,

"Batteries?" Fitzgerald slipped the record in place and adjusted the switches. "Ten inch—there. Now we'll see." He beamed triumphantly at Kerry. "Well? It's playing now."

It was.

Kerry said, "Try that Halvorsen piece. Here." He handed the disk to Fitzgerald, who pushed the reject switch and watched the lever arm lift.

But this time the phonograph refused to play. It didn't like *Entrance of the Boyars*.

"That's funny," Fitzgerald grunted. "Probably the trouble's with the record. Let's try another."

There was no trouble with *Daphnis* and *Chloë*. But the radio silently rejected the composer's *Bolero*.

Kerry sat down and pointed to a nearby chair. "That doesn't prove anything. Come over here and watch. Don't drink anything yet. You, uh, you feel perfectly normal?"

"Sure. Well?"

Kerry took out a cigarette. The console walked across the room, picking up a matchbook on the way and politely held the flame. Then it went back to its place against the wall.

Fitzgerald didn't say anything. After a while he took a cigarette from his pocket and waited. Nothing happened.

"So?" Kerry asked.

"A robot. That's the only possible answer. Where in the name of Petrarch did you get it?"

"You don't seem much surprised."

"I am, though. But I've seen robots before; Westinghouse tried it, you know. Only this—" Fitzgerald tapped his teeth with a nail. "Who made it?"

"How the devil should I know?" Kerry demanded. "The radio people, I suppose."

Fitzgerald narrowed his eyes. "Wait a minute. I don't quite understand—"

"There's nothing to understand. I bought this combination a few days ago. Turned in the old one. It was delivered this afternoon, and..." Kerry explained what had happened.

"You mean you didn't know if was a robot?"

"Exactly. I bought it as a radio. And—and—the damn thing seems almost alive to me."

"Nope." Fitzgerald shook his head, rose and inspected the console carefully. "It's a new kind of robot. At least—" He hesitated. "What else is there to think? I suggest you get in touch with the Mideastern people tomorrow and check up."

"Let's open the cabinet and look inside," Kerry suggested.

Fitzgerald was willing, but the experiment proved impossible. The presumably wooden panels weren't screwed into place, and there was no apparent way of opening the console. Kerry found a screwdriver and applied it, gingerly at first, then with a sort of repressed fury. He could neither pry free a panel nor even scratch the dark, smooth finish of the cabinet.

"Damn!" he said finally. "Well, your guess is as good as mine. It's a robot. Only I didn't know they could make 'em like this. And why in a radio?"

"Don't ask me." Fitzgerald shrugged. "Check up tomorrow. That's the first step. Naturally, I'm pretty baffled. If a new sort of specialized robot has been invented, why put it in a console? And what makes those legs move? There aren't any casters."

"I've been wondering about that, too."

"When it moves, the legs look—rubbery. But they're not. They're hard as—as hardwood. Or plastic."

"I'm afraid of the thing," Kerry said.

"Want to stay at my place tonight?"

"No-no. No. I guess not. The—robot can't hurt me."

"I don't think it wants to. It's been helping you, hasn't it?"

"Yeah," Kerry said, and went off to mix another drink.

The rest of the conversation was inconclusive. Fitzgerald, several hours later, went home rather worried. He wasn't as casual as he had pretended, for the sake of Kerry's nerves. The impingement of something so entirely unexpected on normal life was subtly frightening. And yet, as he had said, the robot didn't seem menacing.

Kerry went to bed, with a new detective mystery. The radio followed him into the bedroom and gently took the book out of his hand. Kerry instinctively snatched for it.

"Hey!" he said. "What the devil—"

The radio went back into the living room. Kerry followed, in time to see the book replaced on the shelf. After a bit Kerry retreated, locking his door, and slept uneasily till dawn.

In dressing gown and slippers, he stumbled out to stare at the console. It was back in its former place, looking as though it had never moved. Kerry, rather white around the gills, made breakfast.

He was allowed only one cup of coffee. The radio appeared, reprovingly took the second cup from his hand and emptied it into the sink.

That was quite enough for Kerry Westerfield. He found his hat and topcoat and almost ran out of the house. He had a horrid feeling that the radio might follow him, but it didn't, luckily for his sanity. He was beginning to be worried.

During the morning he found time to telephone Mideastern. The salesman knew nothing. It was a standard model combination, the latest. If it wasn't giving satisfaction, of course, he'd be glad to—

"It's O.K.," Kerry said. "But who made the thing? That's what I want to find out."

"One moment, sir." There was a delay. "It came from Mr. Lloyd's department. One of our foremen."

"Let me speak to him, please."

But Lloyd wasn't very helpful. After much thought, he remembered that the combination had been placed in the stock room without a serial number. It had been added later.

"But who made it?"

"I just don't know. I can find out for you, I guess. Suppose I ring you back."

"Don't forget," Kerry said, and went back to his class. The lecture on the Venerable Bede wasn't too successful.

At lunch he saw Fitzgerald, who seemed relieved when Kerry came over to his table. "Find out any more about your pet robot?" the psychology professor demanded.

No one else was within hearing. With a sigh Kerry sat down and lit a cigarette. "Not a thing. It's a pleasure to be able to do this myself." He drew smoke into his lungs. "I phoned the company."

"And?"

"They don't know anything. Except that it didn't have a serial number."

"That may be significant," Fitzgerald said.

Kerry told the other about the incidents of the book and the coffee, and Fitzgerald squinted thoughtfully at his milk. "I've given you some psyche tests. Too much stimulation isn't good for you."

"A detective yarn!"

"Carrying it a bit to extremes, I'll admit. But I can understand why the robot acted that way, though I dunno how it managed it" He hesitated. "Without intelligence, that is."

"Intelligence?" Kerry licked his lips. "I'm not so sure that it's just a machine. And I'm not crazy."

"No, you're not. But you say the robot was in the front room. How could it tell what you were reading?"

"Short of X-ray vision and superfast scanning and assimilative powers, I can't imagine. Perhaps it doesn't want me to read anything."

"You've said something," Fitzgerald grunted. "Know much about theoretical machines of that type?"

"Robots?"

"Purely theoretical. Your brain's a colloid, you know. Compact, complicated—but slow. Suppose you work out a gadget with a multi-million radioatom unit embedded in an insulating material. The result is a brain, Kerry. A brain with a tremendous number of units interacting at light-velocity speeds. A radio tube adjusts current flow when it's operating at forty million separate signals a second. And, theoretically, a radioatomic brain of the type I've mentioned could include perception, recognition, consideration, reaction and adjustment in a hundred-thousandth of a second."

"Theory."

"I've thought so. But I'd like to find out where your radio came from."

A page came over. "Telephone call for Mr. Westerfield."

Kerry excused himself and left. When he returned, there was a puzzled frown knitting his dark brows. Fitzgerald looked at him inquiringly.

"Guy named Lloyd, at the Mideastern plant. I was talking to him about the radio."

"Any luck?"

Kerry shook his head. "No. Well, not much. He didn't know who had built the thing."

"But it was built in the plant?"

"Yes. About two weeks ago—but there's no record of who worked on it. Lloyd seemed to think that was very, very funny. If a radio's built in the plant, they know who put it together."

"So?"

"So nothing. I asked him how to open the cabinet, and he said it was easy. Just unscrew the panel in back."

"There aren't any screws," Fitzgerald said.

"I know."

They looked at one another.

Fitzgerald said, "I'd give fifty bucks to find out whether that robot was really built only two weeks ago."

"Why?"

"Because a radioatomic brain would need training. Even in such matters as the lighting of a cigarette."

"It saw me light one."

"And followed the example. The dishwashing—hm-mm. Induction, I suppose. If that gadget has been trained, it's a robot. If it hasn't—" Fitzgerald stopped.

Kerry blinked. "Yes?"

"I don't know what the devil it is. It bears the same relation to a robot that we bear to Eohippus. One thing I do know, Kerry; it's very probable that no scientist today has the knowledge it would take to make a—a thing like that."

"You're arguing in circles," Kerry said. "It was made."

"Uh-huh. But how—when—and by whom? That's what's got me worried."

"Well, I've a class in five minutes. Why not come over tonight?"

"Can't. I'm lecturing at the Hall. I'll phone you after, though."

With a nod Kerry went out, trying to dismiss the matter from his mind. He succeeded pretty well. But dining alone in a restaurant that night, he began to feel a general unwillingness to go home. A hobgoblin was waiting for him.

"Brandy," he told the waiter. "Make it double."

Two hours later a taxi let Kerry out at his door. He was remarkably drunk. Things swam before his eyes. He walked unsteadily toward the porch, mounted the steps with exaggerated care and let himself into the house.

He switched on a lamp.

The radio came forward to meet him. Tentacles, thin but strong as metal, coiled gently around his body, holding him motionless. A pang of violent fear struck through Kerry. He struggled desperately and tried to yell, but his throat was dry.

From the radio panel a beam of yellow light shot out, blinding the man. It swung down, aimed at his chest. Abruptly a queer taste was perceptible under Kerry's tongue.

After a minute or so, the ray clicked out, the tentacles flashed back out of sight and the console returned to its corner. Kerry staggered weakly to a chair and relaxed, gulping.

He was sober. Which was quite impossible. Fourteen brandies infiltrate a definite amount of alcohol into the system. One can't wave a magic wand and instantly reach a state of sobriety. Yet that was exactly what had happened.

The robot was trying to be helpful. Only Kerry would have preferred to remain drunk.

He got up gingerly and sidled past the radio to the bookshelf. One eye on the combination, he took down the detective novel he had tried to read on the preceding night. As he had expected, the radio took it from his hand and replaced it on the shelf. Kerry, remembering Fitzgerald's words, glanced at his watch. Reaction time, four seconds.

He took down a Chaucer and waited, but the radio didn't stir. However, when Kerry found a history volume, it was gently removed from his fingers. Reaction time, six seconds.

Kerry located a history twice as thick.

Reaction time, ten seconds.

Uh-huh So the robot did read the books. That meant X-ray vision and superswift reactions. Jumping Jehoshaphat!

Kerry tested more books, wondering what the criterion was. *Alice in Wonderland* was snatched from his hands; Millay's poems were not. He made a list, with two columns, for future reference.

The robot, then, was not merely a servant. It was a censor. But what was the standard of comparison?

After a while he remembered his lecture tomorrow, and thumbed through his notes. Several points needed verification. Rather hesitantly he located the necessary reference book—and the robot took it away from him.

"Wait a minute," Kerry said. "I need that." He tried to pull the volume out of the tentacle's grasp, without success.

The console paid no attention. It calmly replaced the book on the shelf.

Kerry stood biting his lip. This was a bit too much. The damned robot was a monitor. He sidled towards the book, and was out in the hall before the radio could move.

The thing was coming after him. He could hear the soft padding of it—its feet. Kerry scurried into the bedroom and locked the door. He waited, heart thumping, as the knob was tried gently.

A wire-thin cilium crept through the crack of the door and fumbled with the key. Kerry suddenly jumped forward and shoved the auxiliary bolt into position. But that didn't help, either. The robot's precision tools—the specialized antennae—slid it back; and then the console opened the door, walked into the room and came toward Kerry.

He felt a touch of panic. With a little gasp he threw the book at the thing, and it caught it deftly. Apparently that was all that was wanted, for the radio turned and went out, rocking awkwardly on its rubbery legs, carrying the forbidden volume. Kerry cursed quietly.

The phone rang. It was Fitzgerald.

"Well? How'd you make out?"

"Have you got a copy of Cassen's *Social Literature of the Ages?*"

"I don't think so, no. Why?"

"I'll get it in the University library tomorrow, then." Kerry explained what had happened. Fitzgerald whistled softly.

"Interfering, is it? Hm-m-m. I wonder…"

"I'm afraid of the thing."

"I don't think it means you any harm. You say it sobered you up?"

"Yeah. With a light ray. That isn't very logical."

"It might be. The vibrationary equivalent of thiamine chloride."

"Light?"

"There's vitamin content in sunlight, you know. That isn't the important point. It's censoring your reading—and apparently it reads the books, with superfast reactions. That gadget, whatever it is, isn't merely a robot."

"You're telling me," Kerry said grimly. "It's a Hitler." Fitzgerald didn't laugh. Rather soberly, he suggested, "Suppose you spend the night at my place?"

"No," Kerry said, his voice stubborn. "No so-and-so radio's going to chase me out of my house. I'll take an ax to the thing first."

"We-ell, you know what you're doing, I suppose. Phone me if—if anything happens."

"O.K.," Kerry said, and hung up. He went into the living room and eyed the radio coldly. What the devil was it—and what was it trying to do? Certainly it wasn't merely a robot. Equally certainly, it wasn't alive, in the sense that a colloid brain is alive.

Lips thinned, he went over and fiddled with the dials and switches. A swing band's throbbing, erratic tempo came from the console. He tried the short-wave band—nothing unusual there. So?

So nothing. There was no answer.

After a while he went to bed.

At luncheon the next day he brought Cassen's *Social Literature* to show Fitzgerald.

"What about it?"

"Look here." Kerry flipped the pages and indicated a passage. "Does this mean anything to you?"

Fitzgerald read it. "Yeah. The point seems to be that individualism is necessary for the production of literature. Right?"

Kerry looked at him. "I don't know."

"Eh?"

"My mind goes funny."

Fitzgerald rumpled his gray hair, narrowing his eyes and watching the other man intently. "Come again. I don't quite—"

With angry patience, Kerry said. "This morning I went into the library and looked up this reference. I read it all right. But it didn't mean anything to me. Just words. Know how it is when you're fagged out and have been reading a lot? You'll run into a sentence with a lot of subjunctive clauses, and it doesn't percolate. Well, it was like that."

"Read it now," Fitzgerald said quietly, thrusting the book across the table.

Kerry obeyed, looking up with a wry smile. "No good."

"Read it aloud. I'll go over it with you, step by step."

But that didn't help. Kerry seemed utterly unable to assimilate the sense of the passage.

"Semantic block, maybe," Fitzgerald said, scratching his ear. "Is this the first time it's happened?"

"Yes—no. I don't know."

"Got any classes this afternoon? Good. Let's run over to your place."

"All right. I'm not hungry, "Kerry thrust away his plate." Whenever you're ready—"

Half an hour later they were looking at the radio. It seemed quite harmless. Fitzgerald wasted some time trying to pry a panel off, but finally gave it up as a bad job. He found pencil and paper, seated himself opposite Kerry and began to ask questions.

At one point he paused. "You didn't mention that before."

"Forgot it, I guess."

"Hm-m-m." Fitzgerald tapped his teeth with the pencil. "The first time the radio acted up—"

"It hit me in the eye with a blue light."

"Not that. I mean—what it said."

Kerry blinked. "What it said?" He hesitated. "'Psychology pattern checked and noted, or something like that. I thought I'd tuned in on some station and got part of a quiz program or something. You mean—"

"Were the words easy to understand? Good English?"

"No, now that I remember it," Kerry scowled. "They were slurred quite a lot. Vowels stressed."

"Uh-huh. Well, let's get on." They tried a word-association test.

Finally Fitzgerald leaned back, frowning. "I want to check this stuff with the last tests I gave you a few months ago. It looks funny to me—damned funny. I'd feel a lot better if I knew exactly what memory was. We've done considerable work on mnemonics—artificial memory. Still it may not be that at all."

"Eh?"

"That—machine. Either it's got an artificial memory, has been highly trained, or else it's adjusted to a different milieu and culture. It has affected you—quite a lot."

Kerry licked dry lips. "How?"

"Implanted blocks in your mind. I haven't correlated them yet. When I do, we may be able to figure out some sort of answer. No, that thing isn't a robot. It's a lot more than that."

Kerry took out a cigarette; the console walked across the room and lit it for him. The two men watched with a faint shrinking horror.

"You'd better stay with me tonight," Fitzgerald suggested.

"No," Kerry said. He shivered.

The next day Fitzgerald looked for Kerry at lunch, but the younger man did not appear. He telephoned the house, and Martha answered the call.

"Hello! When did you get back?"

"Hello, Fitz. About an hour ago. My sister went ahead and had her baby without me—so I came back." She stopped, and Fitzgerald was alarmed at her tone.

"Where's Kerry?"

"He's here. Can you come over, Fitz? I'm worried."

"What's the matter with him?"

"I—I don't know. Come right away."

"O.K.," Fitzgerald said, and hung up, biting his lips. He was worried. When, a short while later, he rang the Westerfield bell, he discovered that his nerves were badly out of control. But sight of Martha reassured him.

He followed her into the living room. Fitzgerald's glance went at once to the console, which was unchanged, and then to Kerry, seated motionless by a window. Kerry's face had a blank, dazed look. His pupils were dilated, and he seemed to recognize Fitzgerald only slowly.

"Hello, Fitz," he said.

"How do you feel?"

Martha broke in. "Fitz, what's wrong? Is he sick? Shall I call the doctor?"

Fitzgerald sat down. "Have you noticed anything funny about the radio?"

"No. Why?"

"Then listen." He told the whole story, watching incredulity struggle with reluctant belief on Martha's face. Presently she said, "I can't quite—"

"If Kerry takes out a cigarette, the thing will light it for him. Want to see how it works?"

"No—no. Yes. I suppose so." Martha's eyes were wide.

Fitzgerald gave Kerry a cigarette. The expected happened. When the console had returned to its place, she shivered and went over to Kerry. He looked at her vaguely.

"He needs a doctor, Fitz."

"Yes." Fitzgerald didn't mention that a doctor might be quite useless.

"What is that thing?"

"It's more than a robot. And it's been readjusting Kerry. I told you what's happened. When I checked Kerry's psychology patterns, I found that they'd altered. He's lost most of his initiative."

"Nobody on earth could have made that—"

Fitzgerald scowled. "I thought of that. It seems to be the product of a well-developed culture, quite different from ours. Martian, perhaps. It's such a specialized thing that it naturally fits into a complicated culture. But I do not understand why it looks exactly like a Mideastern console radio."

Martha touched Kerry's hand. "Camouflage?"

"But why? You were one of my best pupils in psyche, Martha. Look at this logically. Imagine a civilization where a gadget like that has its place. Use inductive reasoning."

"I'm trying to. I can't think very well. Fitz, I'm worried about Kerry."

Fitzgerald put his finger tips together. "It isn't a radio so much as a monitor. In this other civilization, perhaps every man has one, or maybe only a few—the ones who need it. It keeps them in line."

"By destroying initiative?"

Fitzgerald made a helpless gesture. "I don't know! It worked that way in Kerry's case. In others—I don't know."

Martha stood up. "I don't think we should talk any more. Kerry needs a doctor. After that we can decide upon that." She pointed to the console.

Fitzgerald said, "It'd be rather a shame to wreck it, but—" His look was significant.

The console moved. It came out from its corner with a sidling, rocking gait and walked toward Fitzgerald. As he sprang up, the whiplike tentacles flashed out and seized him. A pale ray shone into the man's eyes.

Almost instantly it vanished; the tentacles withdrew, and the radio returned to its place. Fitzgerald stood motionless. Martha was on her feet, one hand at her mouth.

"Fitz!" Her voice shook.

He hesitated. "Yes? What's the matter?"

"Are you hurt? What did it do to you?"

Fitzgerald frowned a little. "Eh? Hurt? I don't—"

"The radio. What did it do?"

He looked toward the console "Something wrong with it? Afraid I'm not much of a repairman, Martha"

"Fitz." She came forward and gripped his arm. "Listen to me." Quick words spilled from her mouth. The radio. Kerry. Their discussion.

Fitzgerald looked at her blankly, as though he didn't quite understand. "I guess I'm stupid today. I can't quite understand what you're talking about."

"The radio—you know! You said it changed Kerry—" Martha paused, staring at the man.

Fitzgerald was definitely puzzled. Martha was acting strangely. Queer! He'd always considered her a pretty level-headed girl. But now she was talking nonsense. At least, he couldn't figure out the meaning of her words; there was no sense to them.

And why was she talking about the radio? Wasn't it satisfactory? Kerry had said it was a good buy, with a fine tone and the latest gadgets in it. Fitzgerald wondered, for a fleeting second, if Martha had gone crazy.

In any case, he was late for his class. He said so. Martha didn't try to stop him when he went out. She was pale as chalk.

Kerry took out a cigarette. The radio walked over and held a match. "Kerry!"

"Yes, Martha?" His voice was dead.

She stared at the—the radio. Mars? Another world—another civilization? What was it? What did it want? What was it trying to do?

Martha let herself out of the house and went to the garage. When she returned, a small hatchet was gripped tightly in her hand.

Kerry watched. He saw Martha walk over to the radio and lift the hatchet. Then a beam of light shot out, and Martha vanished. A little dust floated up in the afternoon sunlight.

"Destruction of life-form threatening attack," the radio said, slurring the words together.

Kerry's brain turned over. He felt sick—dazed and horribly empty. Martha—

His mind churned. Instinct and emotion fought with something that smothered them. Abruptly the dams crumbled, and the blocks were gone, the barriers down. Kerry cried out hoarsely, inarticulately, and sprang to his feet.

"Martha!" he yelled.

She was gone. Kerry looked around. Where—

What had happened? He couldn't remember.

He sat down in the chair again, rubbing his forehead. His free hand brought up a cigarette, an automatic reaction that brought instant response. The radio walked forward and held a lighted match ready.

Kerry made a choking, sick sound and flung himself out of the chair. He remembered now. He picked up the hatchet and sprang towards the console, teeth bared in a mirthless rictus.

Again the light beam flashed out.

Kerry vanished. The hatchet thudded onto the carpet The radio walked back to its place and stood motionless once more. A faint clicking proceeded from its radioatomic brain.

"Subject basically unsuitable," it said, after a moment. "Elimination has been necessary." Click! "Preparation for next subject completed." Click.

"We'll take it," the boy said.

"You won't be making a mistake," smiled the rental agent. "It's quiet, isolated and the price is quite reasonable."

"Not so very," the girl put in. "But it is just what we've been looking for."

The agent shrugged. "Of course, an unfurnished place would run less. But—"

"We haven't been married long enough to have furniture," the boy grinned. He put an arm around his wife. "Like it, Hon?"

"Hm-m-m. Who lived here before?"

The agent scratched his cheek. "Let's see. Some people named Westerfield, I think. It was given to me for listing just about a week ago. Nice place. If I didn't own my own house, I'd jump at it myself."

"Nice radio," the boy said. "Late model, isn't it?" He went over to examine the console.

"Come along," the girl urged. "Let's look at the kitchen again."

"O.K., Hon."

They went out of the room. From the hall came the sound of the agent's smooth voice, growing fainter. Warm afternoon sunlight slanted through the windows.

For a moment there was silence. Then—

Click!

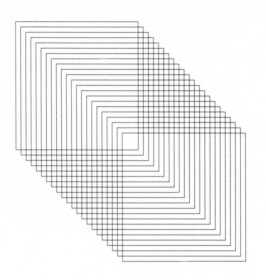

THE NEW ACCELERATOR

BY H. G. WELLS

Certainly, if ever a man found a guinea when he was looking for a pin it is my good friend Professor Gibberne. I have heard before of investigators overshooting the mark, but never quite to the extent that he has done. He has really, this time at any rate, without any touch of exaggeration in the phrase, found something to revolutionize human life. And that when he was simply seeking an all-round nervous stimulant to bring languid people up to the stresses of these pushful days. I have tasted the stuff now several times, and I cannot do better than describe the effect the thing had on me. That there are astonishing experiences in store for all in search of new sensations will become apparent enough.

Professor Gibberne, as many people know, is my neighbor in Folkestone. Unless my memory plays me a trick, his portrait at various ages has already appeared in *The Strand Magazine*—I think late in 1889; but I am unable to look it up because I have lent that volume to someone who has never sent it back. The reader may, perhaps, recall the high forehead and the singularly long black eye-brows that give such a Mephistophelian touch to his face. He occupies one of those pleasant detached houses in the mixed style, that make the western end of the Upper Sandgate Road so interesting. His is the one with the Flemish gables and the Moorish portico, and it is in the room with the mullioned bay window that he works when he is down here, and in which of an evening we have so often smoked and talked together. He is a mighty jester, but, besides, he likes to talk to me about his work; he is one of those men who find a help and stimulus in talking, and so I have been able to follow the conception of the New Accelerator right up from a very early stage. Of course, the greater portion of his experimental work is not done in Folkestone, but in Gower Street, in the fine new laboratory next to the hospital that he has been the first to use.

As everyone knows, or at least as all intelligent people know, the special department in which Gibberne has gained so great and deserved a reputation among physiologists is the action of drugs upon the nervous system. Upon soporifics, sedatives, and anesthetics he is, I am told, unequaled. He is also a chemist of considerable eminence, and I suppose in the subtle and complex jungle of riddles that centers about the ganglion cell and the axis fiber there are little cleared places of his making, glades of illumination, that, until he sees fit to publish his results, are inaccessible to every other living man. And in the last few years he has been particularly assiduous upon this question of nervous stimulants, and already, before the discovery of the New Accelerator, very successful with them. Medical science has to thank him for at least three distinct and absolutely safe invigorators of unrivaled value to practicing men. In cases of exhaustion the preparation known as Gibberne's B Syrup has, I suppose, saved more lives already than any lifeboat round the coast.

"But none of these things begin to satisfy me yet," he told me nearly a year ago. "Either they increase the central energy without affecting the nerves or they simply increase the available energy by lowering the nervous conductivity; and all of them are unequal and local in their operation. One wakes up the heart and viscera and leaves the brain stupefied, one gets at the brain champagne fashion and does nothing good for the solar plexus, and what I want—and what, if it's an earthly possibility, I mean to have—is a stimulant that stimulates all round, that wakes you up for a time from the crown of your head to the tip of your great toe, and makes you go two—or even three to everybody else's one. Eh? That's the thing I'm after."

"It would tire a man," I said.

"Not a doubt of it. And you'd eat double or treble—and all that. But just think what the thing would mean. Imagine yourself with a little phial like this"—he held up a bottle of green glass and marked his points with it—"and in this precious phial is the power to think twice as fast, move twice as quickly, do twice as much work in a given time as you could otherwise do."

"But is such a thing possible?"

"I believe so. If it isn't, I've wasted my time for a year. These various preparations of the hypophosphites, for example, seem to show that something of the sort...Even if it was only one and a half times as fast it would do."

"It *would* do," I said.

"If you were a statesman in a corner, for example, time rushing up against you, something urgent to be done, eh?"

"He could dose his private secretary," I said.

"And gain—double time. And think if *you*, for example, wanted to finish a book."

"Usually," I said, "I wish I'd never begun 'em."

"Or a doctor, driven to death, wants to sit down and think out a case. Or a barrister—or a man cramming for an examination."

"Worth a guinea a drop," said I, "and more—to men like that."

"And in a duel again," said Gibberne, "where it all depends on your quickness in pulling the trigger."

"Or in fencing," I echoed.

"You see," said Gibberne, "if I get it as an all-round thing it will really do you no harm at all—except perhaps to an infinitesimal degree it brings you nearer old age. You will just have lived twice to other people's once—"

"I suppose," I meditated, "in a duel—it would be fair?"

"That's a question for the seconds," said Gibberne.

I harked back farther. "And you really think such a thing *is* possible?" I said.

"As possible," said Gibberne, and glanced at something that went throbbing by the window, "as a motor-bus. As a matter of fact—

He paused and smiled at me deeply, and tapped slowly on the edge of his desk with the green phial. "I think I know the stuff....Already I've got something coming." The nervous smile upon his face betrayed the gravity of his revelation. He rarely talked of his actual experimental work unless things were very near the end. "And it may be, it may be—I shouldn't be surprised—it may even do the thing at a greater rate than twice."

"It will be rather a big thing," I hazarded.

"It will be, I think, rather a big thing."

But I don't think he quite knew what a big thing it was to be, for all that.

I remember we had several subsequent talks about the stuff, "The New Accelerator" he called it, and his tone about it grew more confident on each occasion. Sometimes he talked nervously of unexpected physiological results its use might have, and when he would get a bit unhappy; at others he was frankly mercenary, and we debated long and anxiously how the preparation might be turned to commercial account. "It's a good thing," said Gibberne, "a tremendous thing. I know I'm giving the world something and I think it only reasonable we should expect the world to pay. The dignity of science is all very well, but I think somehow I must have the monopoly of the stuff for, say, ten years. I don't see why all the fun in life should go to the dealers in ham."

My own interest in the coming drug certainly did not wane in the time. I have always had a queer twist towards metaphysics in my mind. I have always been given to paradoxes about space and time, and it seemed to me that Gibberne was really preparing no less than the absolute acceleration of life. Suppose a man repeatedly dosed with such a preparation: he would live an active and record life indeed, but he would be an adult at eleven, middle-aged at twenty-five, and by thirty well on the road to senile decay. It seemed to me that so far Gibberne was only going to do for anyone who took this drug exactly what Nature has done for the Jews and Orientals, who are men in their teens and aged by fifty, and quicker in thought and act than we are all the time. The marvel of drugs has always been great to my mind; you can madden a man, calm a man, make him incredibly strong and alert or a helpless log, quicken his passion and allay that, all by means of drugs, and here was a new miracle to be added to this strange armory of phials the doctors use! But Gibberne was far too eager upon his technical points to enter very keenly into my aspect of the question.

It was the 7th or 8th of August when he told me the distillation that would decide his failure or success for a time was going forward as we talked, and it was on the 10th that he told me the thing was done and the New Accelerator a tangible reality in the world. I met him as I was going up the Sandgate Hill towards Folkestone—I think I was going to get my hair cut; and he came hurrying down to meet me—I suppose he was coming to my house to tell me at once of his success. I remember that his eyes were unusually bright and his face flushed, and I noted even then the swift alacrity of his step.

"It's done," he cried, and gripped my hand, speaking very fast; "it's more than done. Come up to my house and see."

"Really?"

"Really!" he shouted. "Incredibly! Come up and see."

"And it goes—twice?"

"It does more, much more. It scares me. Come up and see the stuff. Taste it! Try it! It's the most amazing stuff on earth." He gripped my arm and, walking at such a pace that he forced me into a trot, went shouting with me up the hill. A whole charabancful of people turned and stared at us in unison after the manner of people in charabancs. It was one of those hot, clear days that Folkestone sees so much of, every colour incredibly bright and every outline hard. There was a breeze, of course, but not so much breeze as sufficed under these conditions to keep me cool and dry. I panted for mercy.

"I'm not walking fast, am I?" cried Gibberne, and slackened his pace to a quick march.

"You've been taking some of this stuff," I puffed.

"No," he said. "At the utmost a drop of water that stood in a beaker from which I had washed out the last traces of the stuff. I took some last night, you know. But that is ancient history, now."

"And it goes twice?" I said, nearing his doorway in a grateful perspiration.

"It goes a thousand times, many thousand times!" cried Gibberne, with a dramatic gesture, flinging open his Early English carved oak gate.

"Phew!" said I, and followed him to the door.

"I don't know how many times it goes," he said, with his latch-key in his hand.

"And you—"

"It throws all sorts of light on nervous physiology, it kicks the theory of vision into a perfectly new shape!…Heaven knows how many thousand times. We'll try all that after—The thing is to try the stuff now."

"Try the stuff?" I said, as we went along the passage.

"Rather," said Gibberne, turning on me in his study. "There it is in that little green phial there! Unless you happen to be afraid?"

I am a careful man by nature, and only theoretically adventurous. I *was* afraid. But on the other hand there is pride.

"Well," I haggled. "You say you've tried it?"

"I've tried it," he said, "and I don't look hurt by it, do I? I don't even look livery and I *feel*—"

I sat down. "Give me the potion," I said. "If the worst comes to the worst it will save having my hair cut, and that I think is one of the most hateful duties of a civilized man. How do you take the mixture?"

"With water," said Gibberne, whacking down a carafe.

He stood up in front of his desk and regarded me in his easy chair; his manner was suddenly reflected by a touch of the Harley Street specialist. "It's rum stuff, you know," he said.

I made a gesture with my hand.

"I must warn you in the first place as soon as you've got it down to shut your eyes, and open them very cautiously in a minute or so's time. One still sees. The sense of vision is a question of length of vibration, and not of multitude of impacts; but there's a kind of shock to the retina, a nasty giddy confusion just at the time if the eyes are open. Keep 'em shut."

"Shut," I said. "Good!"

"And the next thing is, keep still. Don't begin to whack about. You may fetch something a nasty rap if you do. Remember you will be going several thousand times faster than you ever did before, heart, lungs, muscles, brain—everything—and you will hit hard without knowing it. You won't know it, you know. You'll feel just as you do now. Only everything in the world will seem to be going ever so many thousand times slower than it ever went before. That's what makes it so deuced queer."

"Lor'," I said. "And you mean—"

"You'll see," said he, and took up a measure. He glanced at the material on his desk. "Glasses," he said, "water. All here. Mustn't take too much for the first attempt."

The little phial glucked out its precious contents. "Don't forget what I told you," he said, turning the contents of the measure into a glass in the manner of an Italian waiter measuring whisky. "Sit with your eyes tightly shut and in absolute stillness for two minutes," he said. "Then you will hear me speak."

He added an inch or so of water to the dose in each glass.

"By-the-by," he said, "don't put your glass down. Keep it in your hand and rest your hand on your knee. Yes—so. And now—"

He raised his glass.

"The New Accelerator," I said

"The New Accelerator," he answered, and we touched glasses and drank, and instantly I closed my eyes.

You know that blank nonexistence into which one drops when one has taken "gas." For an indefinite interval it was like that. Then I heard Gibberne telling me to wake up, and I stirred and opened my eyes. There he stood as he had been standing, glass still in hand. It was empty, that was all the difference.

"Well?" said I.

"Nothing out of the way?"

"Nothing. A slight feeling of exhilaration, perhaps. Nothing more."

"Sounds?"

"Things are still," I said. "By Jove! yes! They *are* still. Except the sort of faint pat, patter, like rain falling on different things. What is it?"

"Analyzed sounds," I think he said, but I am not sure. He glanced at the window. "Have you ever seen a curtain before a window fixed in that way before?"

I followed his eyes, and there was the end of the curtain, frozen, as it were, corner high, in the act of flapping briskly in the breeze.

"No," said I; "that's odd:"

"And here," he said, and opened the hand that held the glass. Naturally I winced, expected the glass to smash. But so far from smashing it did not even seem to stir; it hung in mid-air motionless. "Roughly speaking," said Gibberne, "an object in these latitudes falls sixteen feet in the first second. This glass is falling sixteen feet in a second now. Only, you see, it hasn't been falling yet for the hundredth part of a second. That gives you some idea of the pace of my Accelerator." And he waved his hand round and round, over and over the slowly sinking glass. Finally he took it by the bottom, pulled it down and placed it very carefully on the table. "Eh?" he said to me, and laughed.

"That seems all right," I said, and began very gingerly to raise myself from my chair. I felt perfectly well, very light and comfortable, and quite confident in my mind. I was going fast all over. My heart, for example, was beating a thousand times a second, but it caused me no discomfort at all. I looked out of the window. An immovable cyclist, head down and with a frozen puff of dust behind his driving-wheel, scorched to overtake a galloping charabanc that did not stir. I gaped in amazement at this incredible spectacle. "Gibberne," I cried, "how long will this confounded stuff last?"

"Heaven knows!" he answered. "Last time I took it I went to bed and slept it off. I tell you, I was frightened. It must have lasted some minutes, I think—it seemed like hours. But after a bit it slows down rather suddenly, I believe."

I was proud to observe that I did not feel frightened—I suppose because there were two of us. "Why shouldn't we go out?" I asked.

"Why not?"

"They'll see us."

"Not they. Goodness, no! Why, we shall be going a thousand times faster than the quickest, conjuring trick that was ever done. Come along! Which way shall we go? Window, or door?"

And out by the window we went.

Assuredly of all the strange experiences that I have ever had, or imagined, or read of other people having or imagining, that little raid I made with Gibberne on the Folkestone Leas, under the influence of the New Accelerator, was the strangest and maddest of all. We went out by his gate into the road, and there we made a minute examination of the statuesque passing traffic. The tops of the wheels and some of the legs of the horses of this charabanc, the end of the whip-lash and the lower jaw of the conductor—who was just beginning to yawn—were perceptibly in motion, but all the rest of the lumbering conveyance seemed still. And quite noiseless except for a faint rattling that came from one man's throat! And as parts of this frozen edifice there were a driver, you know, and a conductor, and eleven people! The effect as we walked about the thing began by being madly queer and ended by being—disagreeable. There they were, people like ourselves and yet not like ourselves, frozen in careless attitudes, caught in mid-gesture. A girl and a man smiled at one another, a leering smile that threatened to last for evermore; a woman in a floppy capelline rested her arm on the rail and stared at Gibberne's house with the unwinking stare of eternity; a man stroked his mustache like a figure of wax, and another stretched a tiresome stiff hand with extended fingers towards his loosened hat. We stared at them, we laughed at them, we made faces at them, and then a sort of disgust of them came upon us, and we turned away and walked round in front of the cyclist towards the Leas.

"Goodness!" cried Gibberne, suddenly; "look there!"

He pointed, and there at the tip of his finger and sliding down the air with wings flapping slowly and at the speed of an exceptionally languid snail—was a bee.

And so we came out upon the Leas. There the thing seemed madder than ever. The band was playing in the upper stand, though all the sound it made for us was a low-pitched, wheezy rattle, a sort of prolonged last sigh that passed at times into a sound like the slow muffled ticking of some monstrous clock. Frozen people stood erect; strange, silent, self-conscious-looking dummies hung unstably in mid-stride, promenading upon the grass. I passed close to a poodle dog suspended in the act of leaping, and watched the slow movement of his legs as he sank to earth. "Lord, look *here!*" cried Gibberne, and we halted for a moment before a magnificent person in white faint-striped flannels, white shoes, and a Panama hat, who turned back to wink at two gaily dressed ladies he had passed. A wink, studied with such leisurely deliberation as we could afford, is an unattractive thing. It loses any quality of alert gaiety, and one remarks that the winking eye does not completely close, that under its drooping lid appears the lower edge of an eyeball and a line of white. "Heaven give me memory," said I, "and I will never wink again."

"Or smile," said Gibberne, with his eye on the ladies' answering teeth.

"It's infernally hot, somehow," said I. "Let's go slower."

"Oh, come along!" said Gibberne.

We picked our way among the bath-chairs in the path. Many of the people sitting in the chairs seemed almost natural in their passive poses, but the contorted scarlet of the bandsmen was not a restful thing to see. A purple-faced gentleman was frozen in the midst of a violent struggle to refold his newspaper against the wind; there were many evidences that all these people in their sluggish way were exposed to a considerable breeze, a breeze that had no existence so far as our sensations went. We came out and walked a little way from the crowd, and turned and regarded it. To see all that multitude changed to a picture, smitten rigid, as it were, into the semblance of realistic wax, was impossibly wonderful. It was absurd, of course; but it filled me with an irrational, an exultant sense of superior advantage. Consider the wonder of it! All that I had said and thought and done since the stuff had begun to work in my veins had happened, so far as those people, so far as the world in general went, in the twinkling of an eye. "The New Accelerator—" I began, but Gibberne interrupted me.

"There's that infernal old woman," he said.

"What old woman?"

"Lives next door to me," said Gibberne. "Has a lapdog that yaps. Gods! The temptation is strong!"

There is something very boyish and impulsive about Gibberne at times. Before I could expostulate with him he had dashed forward, snatched the unfortunate animal out of visible existence, and was running violently with it towards the cliff of the Leas. It was most extraordinary. The little brute, you know, didn't bark or wriggle or make the slightest sign of vitality. It kept quite stiffly in an attitude of somnolent repose, and Gibberne held it by the neck. It was like running about with a dog of wood. "Gibberne," I cried, "put it down!" Then I said something else. "If you run like that, Gibberne," I cried, "you'll set your clothes on fire. Your linen trousers are going brown as it is!"

He clapped his hand on his thigh and stood hesitating on the verge. "Gibberne," I cried, coming up, "put it down. This heat is too much! It's our running so! Two or three miles a second! Friction of the air!"

"What?" he said, glancing at the dog.

"Friction of the air," I shouted. "Friction of the air. Going too fast. Like meteorites and things. Too hot. And, Gibberne! Gibberne I'm all over pricking and a sort of perspiration. You can see people stirring slightly. I believe the stuff's working off! Put that dog down."

"Eh?" he said.

"It's working off," I repeated. "We're too hot and the stuff's working off! I'm wet though."

He stared at me. Then at the band, the wheezy rattle of whose performance was certainly going faster. Then with a tremendous sweep of the arm he hurled the dog away from him and it went spinning upward, still inanimate and hung at last over the grouped parasols of a knot of chattering people. Gibberne was gripping my elbow. "By Jove!" he cried. "I believe it is! A sort of hot pricking and—yes. That man's moving his pocket-handkerchief! Perceptibly. We must get out of this sharp."

But we could not get out of it sharply enough. Luckily perhaps! For we might have run, and if we had run we should, I believe, have burst into flames. Almost certainly we should have burst into flames! You know we had neither of us thought of that....But before we could even begin to run the action of the drug had ceased. It was the business of a minute fraction of a second. The effect of the New Accelerator passed like the drawing of a curtain, vanished in the movement of a hand. I heard Gibberne's voice in infinite alarm. "Sit down," he said, and flop, down upon the turf at the edge of the Leas I sat—scorching as I sat. There is a patch of grass burnt there still where I sat down. The whole stagnation seemed to wake up as I did so, the disarticulated vibration of the band rushed together into a blast of music, the promenaders put their feet down and walked their ways, the papers and flags began flapping, smiles passed into words, the winker finished his wink and went on his way complacently, and all the seated people moved and spoke.

The whole world had come alive again, was going as fast as we were, or rather we were going no faster than the rest of the world. It was like slowing down as one comes into a railway station. Everything seemed to spin round for a second or two, I had the most transient feeling of nausea, and that was all. And the little dog which had seemed to hang for a moment when the force of Gibberne's arm was expended fell with a swift acceleration clean through a lady's parasol.

That was the saving of us. Unless it was for one corpulent old gentleman in a bath-chair, who certainly did start at the sight of us and afterwards regarded us at intervals with a darkly suspicious eye, and finally, I believe, said something to his nurse about us, I doubt if a solitary person remarked our sudden appearance among them. Plop! We must have appeared abruptly. We ceased to smolder almost at once, though the turf beneath me was uncomfortably hot. The attention of everyone—including even the Amusements Association band, which on this occasion, for the only time in its history, got out of tune—was arrested by the amazing fact, and the still more amazing yapping and uproar caused by the fact, that a respectable, over-fed lapdog sleeping quietly to the east of the bandstand should suddenly fall through the parasol of a lady on the west—in a slightly singed condition due to the extreme velocity of its movements through the air. In these absurd days, too, when we are all trying to be as psychic and silly and superstitious as possible! People got up and trod on other people, chairs were overturned, the Leas policeman ran. How the matter settled itself I do not know—we were much too anxious to disentangle ourselves from the affair and get out of range of the eye of the old gentleman in the bath-chair to make minute inquiries. As soon as we were sufficiently cool and sufficiently recovered from our giddiness and nausea and confusion of mind to do so we stood up and, skirting the crowd, directed our steps back along the road below the Metropole towards Gibberne's house. But amidst the din I heard very distinctly the gentleman who had been sitting beside the lady of the ruptured sunshade using quite unjustifiable threats and language to one of those chair-attendants who have "Inspector" written on their caps. "If you didn't throw the dog," he said, "who *did?*"

The sudden return of movement and familiar noises, and our natural anxiety about ourselves (our clothes were still dreadfully hot, and the fronts of the thighs of Gibberne's white trousers were scorched a drabbish brown), prevented the minute observations I should have liked to make on all these things. Indeed, I really made no observations of any scientific value on that return. The bee, of course, had gone. I looked for that cyclist, but he was already out of sight as we came into the Upper Sandgate Road or hidden from us by traffic; the charabanc, however, with its people now all alive and stirring, was clattering along at a spanking pace almost abreast of the nearer church.

We noted, however, that the window-sill on which we had stepped in getting out of the house was slightly singed, and that the impressions of our feet on the gravel of the path were unusually deep.

So it was I had my first experience of the New Accelerator. Practically we had been running about and saying and doing all sorts of things in the space of a second or so of time. We had lived half an hour while the band had played, perhaps, two bars. But the effect it had upon us was that the whole world had stopped for our convenient inspection. Considering all things, and particularly considering our rashness in venturing out of the house, the experience might certainly have been much more disagreeable than it was. It showed, no doubt, that Gibberne has still much to learn before his preparation is a manageable convenience, but its practicability is certainly demonstrated beyond all cavil.

Since that adventure he has been steadily bringing its use under control, and I have several times, and without the slightest bad result, taken measured doses under his direction: though I must confess I have not yet ventured abroad again while under its influence. I may mention, for example, that this story has been written at one sitting and without interruption, except for the nibbling of some chocolate, by its means. I began at 6.25, and my watch is now very nearly at the minute past the half-hour. The convenience of securing a long, uninterrupted spell of work in the midst of a day full of engagements cannot be exaggerated. Gibberne is now working at the quantitative handling of his preparation, with especial reference to its distinctive effects upon different types of constitution. He then hopes to find a Retarder with which to dilute its present rather excessive potency. The Retarder will, of course, have the reverse effect to the Accelerator; used alone it should enable the patient to spread a few seconds over many hours of ordinary time, and so to maintain an apathetic inaction, a glacier-like absence of alacrity, amidst the most animated or irritating surroundings. The two things together must necessarily work an entire revolution in civilized existence. It is the beginning of our escape from that Time Garment of which Carlyle speaks. While this Accelerator will enable us to concentrate ourselves with tremendous impact upon any moment or occasion that demands our utmost sense and vigor, the Retarder will enable us to pass in passive tranquillity through infinite hardship and tedium. Perhaps I am a little optimistic about the Retarder, which has indeed still to be discovered, but about the Accelerator there is no possible sort of doubt whatever. Its appearance upon the market in a convenient, controllable, and assimilable form is a matter of the next few months. It will be obtainable of all chemists and druggists, in small green bottles, at a high but, considering its extraordinary qualities, by no means excessive price. Gibberne's Nervous Accelerator it will be called, and he hopes to be able to supply it in three strengths: one in 200, one in 900, and one in 2000, distinguished by yellow, pink, and white labels respectively.

No doubt its use renders a great number of very extraordinary things possible; for, of course, the most remarkable and, possibly, even criminal proceedings may be effected with impunity by thus dodging, as it were, into the interstices of time. Like all potent preparations it will be liable to abuse. We have, however, discussed this aspect of the question very thoroughly, and we have decided that this is purely a matter of medical jurisprudence and altogether outside our province. We shall manufacture and sell the Accelerator, and, as for the consequences we shall see.

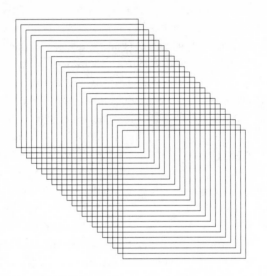

MAN IN HIS TIME

BY BRIAN W. ALDISS

His absence

Janet Westermark sat watching the three men in the office: the administrator who was about to go out of her life, the behaviourist who was about to come into it, and the husband whose life ran parallel to but insulated from her own.

She was not the only one playing a watching game. The behaviourist, whose name was Clement Stackpole, sat hunched in his chair with his ugly strong hands clasped round his knee, thrusting his intelligent and simian face forward, the better to regard his new subject, Jack Westermark.

The administrator of the Mental Research Hospital spoke in a lively and engaged way. Typically, it was only Jack Westermark who seemed absent from the scene.

Your particular problem, restless

His hands upon his lap lay still, but he himself was restless, though the restlessness seemed directed. It was as if he were in another room with other people, Janet thought. She saw that he caught her eye when in fact she was not entirely looking at him, and by the time she returned the glance, he was gone, withdrawn.

"Although Mr. Stackpole has not dealt before with your particular problem," the administrator was saying, "he has had plenty of field experience. I know—"

"I'm sure we won't," Westermark said, folding his hands and nodding his head slightly.

Smoothly, the administrator made a penciled note of the remark, scribbled the precise time beside it, and continued, "I know Mr. Stackpole is too modest to say this, but he is a great man for working in with people—"

"If you feel it's necessary," Westermark said. "Though I've seen enough of your equipment for a while."

The pencil moved, the smooth voice proceeded. "Good. A great man for working in with people, and I'm sure you and Mr. Westermark will soon find you are glad to have him around. Remember, he's there to help both of you."

Janet smiled, and said from the island of her chair, trying to smile at him and Stackpole, "I'm sure that everything will work—" She was interrupted by her husband, who rose to his feet, letting his hands drop to his sides and saying, turning slightly to address thin air, "Do you mind if I say good-bye to Nurse Simmons?"

Her voice no longer wavered

"Everything will be all right, I'm sure," she said hastily. And Stackpole nodded at her, conspiratorially agreeing to see her point of view.

"We'll all get on fine, Janet," he said. She was in the swift process of digesting that unexpected use of her Christian name, and the administrator was also giving her the sort of encouraging smile so many people had fed her since Westermark was pulled out of the ocean off Casablanca, when her husband, still having his lonely conversation with the air, said, "Of course, I should have remembered."

His right hand went halfway to his forehead—or his heart? Janet wondered—and then dropped, as he added, "Perhaps she'll come round and see us some time." Now he turned and was smiling faintly at another vacant space with just the faintest nod of his head, as if slightly cajoling. "You'd like that, wouldn't you, Janet?"

She moved her head, instinctively trying to bring her eyes into his gaze as she replied vaguely, "Of course, darling." Her voice no longer wavered when she addressed his absent attention.

There was sunlight through which they could see each other

There was sunlight in one corner of the room, coming through the windows of a bay angled towards the sun. For a moment she caught, as she rose to her feet, her husband's profile with the sunlight behind it. It was thin and withdrawn. Intelligent: she had always thought him over-burdened with his intelligence, but now there was a lost look there, and she thought of the words of a psychiatrist who had been called in on the case earlier: "You must understand that the waking brain is perpetually lapped by the unconscious."

Lapped by the unconscious

Fighting the words away, she said, addressing the smile of the administrator—that smile which must have advanced his career so much—"You've helped me a lot. I couldn't have got through these months without you. Now we'd better go."

She heard herself chopping her words, fearing Westermark would talk across them, as he did: "Thank you for your help. If you find anything…"

Stackpole walked modestly over to Janet as the administrator rose and said, "Well, don't either of you forget us if you're in any kind of trouble."

"I'm sure we won't."

"And, Jack, we'd like you to come back here to visit us once a month for a personal check-up. Don't want to waste all our expensive equipment, you know, and you are our star—er, patient." He smiled rather tightly as he said it, glancing at the paper on his desk to check Westermark's answer. Westermark's back was already turned on him, Westermark was already walking slowly to the door, Westermark had said his goodbyes, perched out on the lonely eminence of his existence.

Janet looked helplessly, before she could guard against it, at the administrator and Stackpole. She hated it that they were too professional to take note of what seemed her husband's breach of conduct. Stackpole looked kindly in a monkey way and took her arm with one of his thick hands.

"Shall we be off then? My car's waiting outside."

Not saying anything, nodding, thinking, and consulting watches

She nodded, not saying anything, thinking only, without the need of the administrator's notes to think it, "Oh yes, this was when he said, 'Do you mind if I say good-bye to Nurse'—who's it?—Simpson?" She was learning to follow her husband's footprints across the broken path of conversation. He was now out in the corridor, the door swinging to behind him and to empty air the administrator was saying, "It's her day off today."

"You're good on your cues," she said, feeling the hand tighten on her arm. She politely brushed his fingers away, horrid Stackpole, trying to recall what had gone only four minutes before. Jack had said something to her; she couldn't remember, didn't speak, avoided eyes, put out her hand and shook the administrator's firmly.

"Thanks," she said.

"Au revoir to both of you," he replied firmly, glancing swiftly: watch, notes, her, the door. "Of course," he said. "If we find anything at all. We are very hopeful...."

He adjusted his tie, looking at the watch again.

"Your husband has gone now, Mrs. Westermark," he said, his manner softening. He walked towards the door with her and added, "You have been wonderfully brave, and I do realize—we all realize—that you will have to go on being wonderful. With time, it should be easier for you; doesn't Shakespeare say in Hamlet that 'Use almost can change the stamp of nature'? May I suggest that you follow Stackpole's and my example and keep a little notebook and a strict check on the time?"

They saw her tiny hesitation, stood about her, two men round a personable women, not entirely innocent of relish. Stackpole cleared his throat, smiled, said, "He can so easily feel cut off, you know. It's essential that you of all people answer his questions, or he will feel cut off."

Always a pace ahead

"The children?" she asked.

"Let's see you and Jack well settled in at home again, say for a fortnight or so," the administrator said, "before we think about having the children back to see him."

"That way's better for them and Jack *and* you, Janet," Stackpole said. "Don't be glib," she thought; "consolation I need, God knows, but that's too facile." She turned her face away, fearing it looked too vulnerable these days.

In the corridor, the administrator said, as valediction, "I'm sure Grandma's spoiling them terribly, Mrs. Westermark, but worrying won't mend it, as the old saw says."

She smiled at him and walked quickly away, a pace ahead of Stackpole.

Westermark sat in the back of the car outside the administrative block. She climbed in beside him. As she did so, he jerked violently back in his seat.

"Darling, what is it?" she asked. He said nothing.

Stackpole had not emerged from the building, evidently having a last word with the administrator. Janet took the moment to lean over and kiss her husband's cheek, aware as she did so that a phantom wife had already, from his viewpoint, done so. His response was a phantom to her.

"The countryside looks green," he said. His eyes were flickering over the grey concrete block opposite.

"Yes," she said.

Stackpole came bustling down the steps, apologizing as he opened the car door, settled in. He let the clutch back too fast and they shot forward. Janet saw then the reason for Westermark's jerking backwards a short while before. Now the acceleration caught him again; his body was rolled helplessly back. As they drove along, he set one hand fiercely on the side grip, for his sway was not properly counterbalancing the movement of the car.

Once outside the grounds of the institute, they were in the country, still under a mid-August day.

His theories

Westermark, by concentrating, could bring himself to conform to some of the laws of the time continuum he had left. When the car he was in climbed up his drive (familiar, yet strange with the rhododendrons unclipped and no signs of children) and stopped by the front door, he sat in his seat for three and a half minutes before venturing to open his door. Then he climbed out and stood on the gravel, frowning down at it. Was it as real as ever, as material? Was there a slight glaze on it?—as if something shone through from the interior of the earth, shone through all things? Or was it that there was a screen between him and everything else? It was important to decide between the two theories, for he had to live under the discipline of one. What he hoped to prove was that the permeation theory was correct; that way he was merely one of the factors comprising the functioning universe, together with the rest of humanity. By the glaze theory, he was isolated not only from the rest of humanity but from the entire cosmos (except Mars?). It was early days yet; he had a deal of thinking to do, and new ideas would undoubtedly emerge after observation and cogitation. Emotion must not decide the issue; he must be detached. Revolutionary theories could well emerge from this—suffering.

He could see his wife by him, standing off in case they happened embarrassingly or painfully to collide. He smiled thinly at her through her glaze. He said, "I am, but I'd prefer not to talk." He stepped towards the house, noting the slippery feel of gravel that would not move under his tread until the world caught up. He said, "I've every respect for the *Guardian*, but I'd prefer not to talk at present."

Famous Astronaut Returns Home

As the party arrived, a man waited in the porch for them, ambushing Westermark's return home with a deprecatory smile. Hesitant but businesslike, he came forward and looked interrogatively at the three people who had emerged from the car.

"Excuse me, you are Captain Jack Westermark, aren't you?"

He stood aside as Westermark seemed to make straight for him.

"I'm the psychology correspondent for the *Guardian*, if I might intrude for a moment."

Westermark's mother had opened the front door and stood there smiling welcome at him, one hand nervously up to her grey hair. Her son walked past her. The newspaper man stared after him.

Janet told him apologetically, "You'll have to excuse us. My husband did reply to you, but he's really not prepared to meet people yet."

"*When* did he reply, Mrs. Westermark? Before he heard what I had to say?"

"Well, naturally not—but his life stream...I'm sorry, I can't explain."

"He really is living ahead of time, isn't he? Will you spare me a minute to tell me how you feel now the first shock is over?"

"You really must excuse me," Janet said, brushing past him. As she followed her husband into the house, she heard Stackpole say, "Actually, I read the *Guardian*, and perhaps I could help you. The Institute has given me the job of remaining with Captain Westermark. My name's Clement Stackpole—you may know my book. *Persistent Human Relations*, Methuen. But you must not say that Westermark is living ahead of time. That's quite incorrect. What you can say is that some of his psychological and physiological processes have somehow been transposed forward—"

"Ass!" she exclaimed to herself. She had paused by the threshold to catch some of his words. Now she whisked in.

Talk hanging in the air among the long watches of supper

Supper that evening had its discomforts, although Janet Westermark and her mother-in-law achieved an air of melancholy gaiety by bringing two Scandinavian candelabra, relics of a Copenhagen holiday, to the table and surprising the two men with a gay-looking hors d'oeuvre. But the conversation was mainly like the hors d'oeuvre, Janet thought: little tempting isolated bits of talk, not nourishing.

Mrs. Westermark senior had not yet got the hang of talking to her son, and confined her remarks to Janet, though she looked towards Jack often enough. "How are the children!" he asked her. Flustered by the knowledge that he was waiting a long while for her answer, she replied rather incoherently and dropped her knife.

To relieve the tension, Janet was cooking up a remark on the character of the administrator at the Mental Research Hospital, when Westermark said, "Then he is at once thoughtful and literate. Commendable and rare in men of this type. I got the impression, as you evidently did, that he was as interested in his job as in advancement. I suppose one might say one even *liked* him. But you know him better, Stackpole; what do you think of him?"

Crumbling bread to cover his ignorance of whom they were supposed to be conversing about, Stackpole said, "Oh, I don't know;

it's hard to say really," spinning out time, pretending not to squint at his watch.

"The administrator was quite a charmer, didn't you think Jack?" Janet remarked—perhaps helping Stackpole as much as Jack.

"He looks as if he might make a slow bowler," Westermark said, with an intonation that suggested he was agreeing with something as yet unsaid.

"Oh, him!" Stackpole said. "Yes, he seems a satisfactory sort of chap on the whole."

"He quoted Shakespeare to me and thoughtfully told me where the quotation came from," Janet said.

"No thank you, Mother," Westermark said.

"I don't have much to do with him," Stackpole continued. "Though I have played cricket with him a time or two. He makes quite a good slow bowler."

"Are you really?" Westermark exclaimed.

That stopped them. Jack's mother looked helplessly about, caught her son's glazed eye, said, covering up, "Do have some more sauce, Jack, dear," recalled she had already had her answer, almost let her knife slide again, gave up trying to eat.

"I'm a batsman, myself," Stackpole said, as if bringing an old pneumatic drill to the new silence. When no answer came, he doggedly went on, expounding on the game, the pleasure of it. Janet sat and watched, a shade perplexed that she was admiring Stackpole's performance and wondering at her slight perplexity; then she decided that she had made up her mind to dislike Stackpole, and immediately dissolved the resolution. Was he not on their side? And even the strong hairy hands became a little more acceptable when you thought of them gripping the rubber bat-handle; and the broad shoulders swinging… She closed her eyes momentarily, and tried to concentrate on what he was saying.

A batsman himself

Later, she met Stackpole on the upper landing. He had a small cigar in his mouth, she had two pillows in her arms. He stood in her way.

"Can I help at all, Janet?"

"I'm only making up a bed, Mr. Stackpole."

"Are you not sleeping in with your husband?"

"He would like to be on his own for a night or two, Mr. Stackpole. I shall sleep in the children's room for the time being."

"Then please permit me to carry the pillows for you. And do please call me Clem. All my friends do."

Trying to be pleasanter, to unfreeze, to recall that Jack was not moving her out of the bedroom permanently, she said, "I'm sorry. It's just that we once had a terrier called Clem." But it did not sound as she had wished it to do.

He put the pillows on Peter's blue bed, switched on the bedside lamp, and sat on the edge of the bed, clutching his cigar and puffing at it.

"This may be a bit embarrassing, but there's something I feel I should say to you, Janet." He did not look at her. She brought him an ashtray and stood by him.

"We feel your husband's mental health may be endangered, although I hasten to assure you that he shows no signs of losing his mental equilibrium beyond what we may call an inordinate absorption in phenomena—and even there, we cannot say, of course we can't, that his absorption is any greater than one might expect. Except in the totally unprecedented circumstances, I mean. We must talk about this in the next few days."

She waited for him to go on, not unamused by the play with the cigar. Then he looked straight up at her and said, "Frankly, Mrs. Westermark, we think it would help your husband if you could have sexual relations with him."

A little taken aback, she said, "Can you imagine—" Correcting herself, she said, "That is for my husband to say. I am not unapproachable."

She saw he had caught her slip. Playing a very straight bat, he said, "I'm sure you're not, Mrs. Westermark."

With the light out, living, she lay in Peter's bed

She lay in Peter's bed with the light out. Certainly she wanted him: pretty badly, now she allowed herself to dwell on it. During the long months of the Mars expedition, while she had stayed at home and he had got farther from home, while he actually had existence on that other planet, she had been chaste. She had looked after the children and driven round the countryside and enjoyed writing those articles for women's magazines and being interviewed on TV when the ship was reported to have left Mars on its homeward journey. She had been, in part, dormant.

Then came the news, kept from her at first, that there was confusion in communicating with the returning ship. A sensational tabloid broke the secrecy by declaring that the nine-man crew had all gone mad. And the ship had overshot its landing area, crashing into the Atlantic. Her first reaction had been purely a selfish one—no, not selfish, but from the self: He'll never lie with me again. And infinite love and sorrow.

After his rescue, the only survivor, miraculously unmaimed, her hope had revived. Since then, it had remained embalmed, as he was now embalmed in time. She tried to visualize love as it would be now, with everything happening first to him, before she had begun to—With his movement of pleasure even before she—No, it wasn't possible! But of course it was, if they worked it out first intellectually; then if she just lay flat...But what she was trying to visualize, all she could visualize, was not love-making, merely a formal prostration to the exigencies of glands and time flow.

She sat up in bed, longing for movement, freedom. She jumped out and opened the lower window; there was still a tang of cigar smoke in the dark room.

If they worked it out intellectually

Within a couple of days, they had fallen into routine. It was as if the calm weather, perpetuating mildness, aided them. They had to be careful to move slowly through doors, keeping to the left, so as not to bump into each other—a tray of drinks was dropped before they agreed on that. They devised simple knocking systems before using the bathroom. They conversed in bulletins that did not ask questions unless questions were necessary. They walked slightly apart. In short, they made detours round each other's lives.

"It's really quite easy as long as one is careful," Mrs. Westermark senior said to Janet. "And dear Jack is *so* patient!"

"I even get the feeling he likes the situation."

"Oh, my dear, how could he like such an unfortunate predicament?"

"Mother, you realize how we all exist together, don't you? No, it sounds too terrible—I daren't say it."

"Now don't you start getting silly ideas. You've been very brave, and this is not the time for us to be getting upset, just as things are going well. If you have any worries, you must tell Clem. That's what he's here for."

"I know."

"Well then."

She saw Jack walk in the garden. As she looked, he glanced up, smiled, said something to himself, stretched out a hand, withdrew it, and went, still smiling, to sit on one end of the seat on the lawn. Touched, Janet hurried over to the French windows, to go and join him.

She paused. Already, she saw ahead, saw her sequence of actions, for Jack had already sketched them into the future. She would go on to the lawn, call his name, smile, and walk over to him when he smiled back. Then they would stroll together to the seat and sit down, one at each end.

The knowledge drained all spontaneity from her. She might have been working a treadmill, for what she was about to do had already been done as far as Jack was concerned, with his head's start in time. Then if she did not go, if she mutinied, turned back to the discussion of the day's chores with her mother-in-law… That left Jack mouthing like a fool on the lawn, indulging in a fantasy there was no penetrating. Let him do that, let Stackpole see; then they could drop this theory about Jack's being ahead of time and would have to treat him for a more normal sort of hallucinatory insanity. He would be safe in Clem's hands.

But Jack's actions proved that she would go out there. It was insane for her not to go out there. Insane? To disobey a law of the universe was impossible, not insane. Jack was not disobeying—he had simply tumbled over a law that nobody knew was there before the first expedition to Mars; certainly they had discovered something more momentous than anyone had expected, and more unforeseen. And she had lost—No, she hadn't lost yet! She ran out on to the lawn, calling to him, letting the action quell the confusion in her mind.

And in the repeated event there was concealed a little freshness for she remembered how his smile, glimpsed through the window, had held a special warmth, as if he sought to reassure her. What had he said? That was lost. She walked over to the seat and sat beside him.

He had been saving a remark for the statutory and unvarying time lapse.

"Don't worry, Janet," he said. "It could be worse."

"How?" she asked, but he was already answering: "We could be a day apart. 3.3077 minutes at least allows us a measure of communication."

"It's wonderful how philosophical you are about it," she said. She was alarmed at the sarcasm in her tone.

"Shall we have a talk together now?"

"Jack, I've been wanting to have a private talk with you for some time."

"*I?*"

The tall beeches that sheltered the garden on the north side were so still that she thought, "They will look exactly the same for him as for me."

He delivered a bulletin, looking at his watch. His wrists were thin. He appeared frailer than he had done when they left hospital. "I am aware, my darling, how painful this must be for you. We are both isolated from the other by this amazing shift of temporal function, but at least I have the consolation of experiencing the new phenomenon, whereas you—"

"*I?*"

Talking of interstellar distances

"I was going to say that you are stuck with the same old world all of mankind has always known, but I suppose you don't see it that way." Evidently a remark of hers had caught up with him, for he added inconsequentially, "I've wanted a private talk with you."

Janet bit off something she was going to say, for he raised a finger irritably and said, "Please time your statements, so that we do not talk at cross purposes. Confine what you have to say to essentials. Really, darling, I'm surprised you don't do as Clem suggests, and make notes of what is said at what time."

"That—I just wanted—we can't act as if we were a board meeting. I want to know your feelings, how you are, what you are thinking, so that I can help you, so that eventually you will be able to live a normal life again."

He was timing it so that he answered almost at once, "I am not suffering from any mental illness, and I have completely recovered my physical health after the crash. There is no reason to foresee that my perceptions will ever lapse back into phase with yours. They have remained an unfluctuating 3.3077 minutes ahead of terrestrial time ever since our ship left the surface of Mars."

He paused. She thought, "It is now about 11.03 by my watch, and there is so much I long to say. But it's 11.06 and a bit by his time, and he already knows I can't say anything. It's such an effort of endurance, talking across this three and a bit minutes; we might just as well be talking across an interstellar distance."

Evidently he too had lost the thread of the exercise, for he smiled and stretched out a hand, holding it in the air; Janet looked round. Clem Stackpole was coming out towards them with a tray full of drinks. He set it carefully down on the lawn, and picked up a martini, the stem of which he slipped between Jack's fingers.

"Cheers!" he said smiling, and "Here's your tipple," giving Janet her gin and tonic. He had brought himself a bottle of pale ale.

"Can you make my position clearer to Janet, Clem? She does not seem to understand it yet."

Angrily, she turned to the behaviourist "This was meant to be a private talk, Mr. Stackpole, between my husband and myself."

"Sorry you're not getting on too well, then. Perhaps I can help you sort out a bit. It is difficult, I know."

3.3077

Powerfully, he wrenched the top off the beer bottle and poured the liquid into the glass. Sipping, he said, "We have always been used to the idea that everything moves forward in time at the same rate. We speak of the course of time, presuming it only has one rate of flow. We've assumed, too, that anything living on another planet in any other part of our universe might have the same rate of flow. In other words, although we've long been accustomed to some oddities of time, thanks to relativity theories, we have accustomed ourselves, perhaps, to certain errors of thinking. Now we're going to have to think differently. You follow me."

"Perfectly."

"The universe is by no means the simple box our predecessors imagined. It may be that each planet is encased in its own time field, just as it is in its own gravitational field. From the evidence, it seems that Mars's time field is 3.3077 minutes ahead of ours on Earth. We deduce this from the fact that your husband and the eight other men with him on Mars experienced no sensation of temporal difference among themselves, and were unaware that anything was untoward until they were away from Mars and attempted to get into communication again with Earth, when the temporal discrepancy at once showed up. Your husband is still living in Mars time. Unfortunately, the other members of the crew did not survive the crash; but we can be sure that if they did, they too would suffer from the same effect. That's clear, isn't it?"

"Entirely. But I still cannot see why this effect, if it is as you say—"

"It's not what *I* say, Janet, but the conclusion arrived at by much cleverer men than I." He smiled as he said that, adding parenthetically, "Not that we don't develop and even alter our conclusions every day."

"Then why was a similar effect not noticed when the Russians and Americans returned from the moon?"

"We don't know. There's so much we don't know. We surmise that because the moon is a satellite of Earth's, and thus within its gravitational field, there is no temporal discrepancy. But until we have more data, until we can explore further, we know so little, and can only speculate so much. It's like trying to estimate the runs of an entire innings when only one over has been bowled. After the expedition gets back from Venus, we shall be in a much better position to start theorizing."

"*What* expedition to Venus?" she asked, shocked.

"It may not leave for a year yet, but they're speeding up the program. That will bring us really invaluable data."

Future time with its uses and abuses

She started to say, "But after this surely they won't be fool enough—" Then she stopped. She knew they would be fool enough. She thought of Peter saying, "I'm going to be a spaceman too. I want to be the first man on Saturn!"

The men were looking at their watches. Westermark transferred his gaze to the gravel to say, "This figure of 3.3077 is surely not a universal constant. It may vary—I think it will vary—from planetary body to planetary body. My private opinion is that it is bound to be connected with solar activity in some way. If that is so, then we may find that the men returning from Venus will be perceiving on a continuum slightly in arrears of Earth time."

He stood up suddenly, looking dismayed, the absorption gone from his face.

"That's a point that hadn't occurred to me" Stackpole said, making a note. "If the expedition to Venus is primed with these points beforehand, we should have no trouble about organizing their return. Ultimately, this confusion will be sorted out, and I've no doubt that it will eventually vastly enrich the culture of mankind. The possibilities are of such enormity that…"

"It's awful! You're all crazy!" Janet exclaimed. She jumped up and hurried off towards the house.

Or then again

Jack began to move after her towards the house. By his watch, which showed Earth time, it was 11.18 and twelve seconds; he thought, not for the first time, that he would invest in another watch, which would be strapped to his right wrist and show Martian time. No, the one on his left wrist should show Martian time, for that was the wrist he principally consulted and the time by which he lived, even when going through the business of communicating with the earth-bound human race.

He realized he was now moving ahead of Janet, by her reckoning. It would be interesting to have someone ahead of *him* in perception; then he would wish to converse, would want to go to the labor of it. Although it would rob him of the sensation that he was perpetually first in the universe, first everywhere, with everything dewy in that strange light—Mars-light! He'd call it that, till he had it classified, the romantic vision preceding the scientific, with a touch of the grand permissible before the steadying discipline closed in. Or then again, suppose they were wrong in their theories, and the perceptual effect was some freak of the long space journey itself; supposing time were quantal…Supposing *all* time were quantal. After all, aging was a matter of steps, not a smooth progress for much of the inorganic world as for the organic.

Now he was standing quite still on the lawn. The glaze was coming through the grass, making it look brittle, almost tingeing each blade with a tiny spectrum of light. If his perceptual time were further ahead than it was now, would the Mars-light be stronger, the Earth more translucent? How beautiful it would look! After a longer star journey one would return to a cobweb of a world, centuries behind one in perceptual time, a mere embodiment of light, a prism. Hungrily, he visualized it. But they needed more knowledge.

Suddenly he thought, "If I could get on the Venus expedition! If the Institute's right, I'd be perhaps six, say five and a half—no, one can't say—but I'd be ahead of Venerean time. I *must* go. I'd be valuable to them. I only have to volunteer, surely."

He did not notice Stackpole touch his arm in cordial fashion and go past him into the house. He stood looking at the ground and through it, to the stony vales of Mars and the unguessable landscapes of Venus.

The figures move

Janet had consented to ride into town with Stackpole. He was collecting his cricket books, which had been restudded; she thought she might buy a roll of film for her camera. The children would like photos of her and Daddy together. Standing together.

As the car ran beside trees, their shadow flickered red and green before her vision. Stackpole held the wheel very capably, whistling under his breath. Strangely, she did not resent a habit she would normally have found irksome, taking it as a sign that he was not entirely at his ease.

"I have an awful feeling you now understand my husband better than I do," she said.

He did not deny it. "Why do you feel that?"

"I believe he does not mind the terrible isolation he must be experiencing."

"He is a brave man."

Westermark had been home a week now. Janet saw that each day they were more removed from each other, as he spoke less and stood frequently as still as a statue, gazing at the ground raptly. She thought of something she had once been afraid to utter aloud to her mother-in-law; but with Clem Stackpole she was safer.

"You know why we manage to exist in comparative harmony," she said. He was slowing the car, half-looking at her. "We only manage to exist by banishing all events from our lives, all children, all seasons. Otherwise we'd be faced at every moment with the knowledge of how much at odds we really are."

Catching the note in her voice, Stackpole said soothingly, "You are every bit as brave as he is, Janet."

"Damn being brave. What I can't bear is—nothing!"

Seeing the sign by the side of the road, Stackpole glanced in his driving mirror and changed gear. The road was deserted in front as well as behind. He whistled through his teeth again, and Janet felt compelled to go on talking.

"We've already interfered with time too much—all of us, I mean. Time is a European invention. Goodness knows how mixed up in it we are going to get if—well, if this goes on." She was irritated by the lack of her usual coherence.

As Stackpole spoke next, he was pulling the car into a lay-by, stopping it by overhanging bushes. He turned to her, smiling tolerantly. "Time was God's invention, if you believe in God, as I prefer to do. We observe it, tame it, exploit it where possible."

"Exploit it!"

"You mustn't think of the future as if we were all wading knee deep in treacle or something." He laughed briefly, resting his hands on the steering wheel. "What lovely weather it is! I was wondering— on Sunday I'm playing cricket over in the village. Would you like to come and watch the match? And perhaps we could have tea somewhere afterwards."

All events, all children, all seasons

She had a letter next morning from Jane, her five-year-old daughter, and it made her think. All the letter said was: "Dear Mummy, Thank you for the dollies. With love from Jane," but Janet knew the labor that had gone into the inch-high letters. How long could she bear to leave the children away from their home and her care?

As soon as the thought emerged, she recalled that during the previous evening she had told herself nebulously that if there was going to be "anything" with Stackpole, it was as well the children would be out of the way—purely, she now realized, for her convenience and for Stackpole's. She had not thought then about the children; she had thought about Stackpole who, despite the unexpected delicacy he had shown, was not a man she cared for.

"And another intolerably immoral thought," she muttered unhappily to the empty room, "what alternative have I to Stackpole?"

She knew Westermark was in his study. It was a cold day, too cold and damp for him to make his daily parade round the garden. She knew he was sinking deeper into isolation, she longed to help, she feared to sacrifice herself to that isolation, longed to stay outside it, in life. Dropping the letter, she held her head in her hands, closing her eyes as in the curved bone of her skull she heard all her possible courses of action jar together, future lifelines that annihilated each other.

As Janet stood transfixed, Westermark's mother came into the room.

"I was looking for you," she said. "You're so unhappy, my dear, aren't you?"

"Mother, people always try and hide from others how they suffer. Does everyone do it?"

"You don't have to hide it from me—chiefly, I suppose, because you can't."

"But I don't know how much you suffer, and it ought to work both ways. Why do we do this awful covering up? What are we afraid of—pity or derision?"

"Help, perhaps."

"Help! Perhaps you're right…. That's a disconcerting thought." They stood there staring at each other, until the older woman said, awkwardly, "We don't often talk like this, Janet."

"No." She wanted to say more. To a stranger in a train, perhaps she would have done; here, she could not deliver.

Seeing nothing more was said on that subject, Mrs. Westermark said, "I was going to tell you, Janet, that I thought perhaps it would be better if the children didn't come back here while things are as they are. If you want to go and see them and stay with them at your parents' house, I can look after Jack and Mr. Stackpole for a week. I don't think Jack wants to see them."

"That's very kind, Mother. I'll see. I promised Clem—well, I told Mr. Stackpole that perhaps I'd go and watch him play cricket tomorrow afternoon. It's not important, of course, but I did say—anyhow, I might drive over to see the children on Monday, if you could hold the fort."

"You've still plenty of time if you feel like going today. I'm sure Mr. Stackpole will understand your maternal feelings."

"I'd prefer to leave it till Monday," Janet said—a little distantly, for she suspected now the motive behind her mother-in-law's suggestion.

Where the Scientific American did not reach

Jack Westermark put down the *Scientific American* and stared at the table top. With his right hand, he felt the beat of his heart. In the magazine was an article about him, illustrated with photographs of him taken at the Research Hospital. This thoughtful article was far removed from the sensational pieces that had appeared elsewhere, the shallow things that referred to him as The Man Who Has Done More Than Einstein To Wreck Our Cosmic Culture; and for that very reason it was the more startling, and presented some aspects of the matter that Westermark himself had not considered.

As he thought over its conclusions, he rested from the effort of reading terrestrial books, and Stackpole sat by the fire, smoking a cigar and waiting to take Westermark's dictation. Even reading a magazine represented a feat in space-time, a collaboration, a conspiracy. Stackpole turned the pages at timed intervals, Westermark read when they lay flat. He was unable to turn them when, in their own narrow continuum, they were not being turned; to his fingers, they lay under the jellylike glaze, that visual hallucination that represented an unconquerable cosmic inertia.

The inertia gave a special shine to the surface of the table as he stared into it and probed into his own mind to determine the truths of the *Scientific American* article.

The writer of the article began by considering the facts and observing that they tended to point towards the existence of "local times" throughout the universe; and that if this were so, a new explanation might be forthcoming for the recession of the galaxies and different estimates arrived at for the age of the universe (and of course for its complexity). He then proceeded to deal with the problem that vexed other writers on the subject; namely, why, if Westermark lost Earth time on Mars, he had not reciprocally lost Mars time back on Earth. This, more than anything, pointed to the fact that "local times" were not purely mechanistic but to some extent at least a psycho-biological function.

In the table top, Westermark saw himself being asked to travel again to Mars, to take part in a second expedition to those continents of russet sand where the fabric of space-time was in some mysterious and insuperable fashion 3.3077 minutes ahead of Earth norm. Would his interior clock leap forward again? What then of the sheen on things earthly? And what would be the effect of gradually drawing away from the iron laws under which, since its scampering Pleistocene infancy, humankind had lived?

Impatiently he thrust his mind forward to imagine the day when Earth harbored many local times, gleaned from voyages across the vacancies of space; those vacancies lay across time, too, and that little-understood concept (McTaggart had denied its external reality, hadn't he?) would come to lie within the grasp of man's understanding. Wasn't that the ultimate secret, to be able to understand the flux in which existence is staged as a dream is staged in the primitive reaches of the mind?

And—But—Would not that day bring the annihilation of Earth's local time? That was what he had started. It could only mean that "local time" was not a product of planetary elements; there the writer of the Scientific American article had not dared to go far enough; local time was entirely a product of the psyche. That dark innermost thing that could keep accurate time even while a man lay unconscious was a mere provincial; but it could be educated to be a citizen of the universe. He saw that he was the first of a new race, unimaginable in the wildest mind a few months previously. He was independent of the enemy that, more than Death, menaced contemporary man: Time. Locked within him was a entirely new potential. Superman had arrived.

Painfully, Superman stirred in his seat. He sat so rapt that his limbs grew stiff and dead without his noticing it.

Universal thoughts may occur if one times carefully enough one's circumbendibus about a given table

"Dictation," he said, and waited impatiently until the command had penetrated backwards to the limbo by the fire where Stackpole sat. What he had to say was so terribly important—yet it had to wait on these people.

As was his custom, he rose and began to walk round the table, speaking in phrases quickly delivered. This was to be the testament to the new way of life....

"Consciousness is not expendable but concurrent.... There may have been many time nodes at the beginning of the human race.... The mentally deranged often revert to different time rates. For some, a day seems to stretch on for ever.... We know by experience that for children time is seen in the convex mirror of consciousness, enlarged and distorted beyond its focal point...." He was momentarily irritated by the scared face of his wife appearing outside the study window, but he brushed it away and continued.

"....its focal point... Yet man in his ignorance has persisted in pretending time was some of uni-directional flow, and homogenous at that...despite the evidence to the contrary... Our conception of ourselves—no, this erroneous conception has become a basic life assumption...."

Daughters of daughters

Westermark's mother was not given to metaphysical speculation, but as she was leaving the room, she turned and said to her daughter-in-law, "You know what I sometimes think? Jack is so strange, I wonder at nights if men and women aren't getting more and more apart in thought and in their ways with every generation—you know, almost like separate species. My generation made a great attempt to bring the two sexes together in equality and all the rest, but it seems to have come to nothing."

"Jack will get better." Janet could hear the lack of confidence in her voice.

"I thought the same thing—about men and women getting wider apart I mean—when my husband was killed."

Suddenly all Janet's sympathy was gone. She had recognized a familiar topic drifting on to the scene, knew well the careful tone that ironed away all self-pity as her mother-in-law said, "Bob was dedicated to speed, you know. That was what killed him really, not the fool backing into the road in front of him."

"No blame was attached to your husband," Janet said. "You should try not to let it worry you still."

"You see the connection though….This progress thing. Bob so crazy to get round the next bend first, and now Jack… Oh well, there's nothing a woman can do."

She closed the door behind her. Absently, Janet picked up the message from the next generation of women: "Thank you for the dollies."

The resolves and the sudden risks involved

He was their father. Perhaps Jane and Peter should come back, despite the risks involved. Anxiously, Janet stood there, moving herself with a sudden resolve to tackle Jack straight away. He was so irritable, so unapproachable, but at least she could observe how busy he was before interrupting him.

As she slipped into the side hall and made for the back door, she heard her mother-in-law call her. "Just a minute!" she answered.

The sun had broken through, sucking moisture from the damp garden. It was now unmistakably autumn. She rounded the corner of the house, stepped round the rose bed, and looked into her husband's study.

Shaken, she saw he leaned half over the table. His hands were over his face, blood ran between his fingers and dripped on to an open magazine on the table top. She was aware of Stackpole sitting indifferently beside the electric fire.

She gave a small cry and ran round the house again, to be met at the back door by Mrs. Westermark.

"Oh, I was just—Janet, what is it?"

"Jack, Mother! He's had a stroke or something terrible!"

"But how do you know?"

"Quick, we must phone the hospital—I must go to him."

Mrs. Westermark took Janet's arm. "Perhaps we'd better leave it to Mr. Stackpole, hadn't we? I'm afraid—"

"Mother, we must do what we can. I know we're amateurs. Please let me go."

"No, Janet, we're—it's *their* world. I'm frightened. They'll come if they want us." She was gripping Janet in her fright. Their wild eyes stared momentarily at each other as if seeing something else, and then Janet snatched herself away. "I must go to him," she said.

She hurried down the hall and pushed open the study door. Her husband stood now at the far end of the room by the window, while blood streamed from his nose.

"Jack!" she exclaimed. As she ran towards him, a blow from the empty air struck her on the forehead, so that she staggered aside, falling against a bookcase. A shower of smaller volumes from the upper shelf fell on her and round her. Exclaiming, Stackpole dropped his notebook and ran round the table to her. Even as he went to her aid, he noted the time from his watch: 10.24.

Aid after 10.24 and the tidiness of bed
Westermark's mother appeared in the doorway.

"Stay where you are," Stackpole shouted, "or there will be more trouble! Jack, I'm right with you—God knows what you've felt, isolated without aid for three and a third minutes!" Angrily, he went across and stood within arm's length of his patient. He threw his handkerchief down on to the table.

"Mr. Stackpole—" Westermark's mother said tentatively from the door, an arm round Janet's waist.

He looked back over his shoulder only long enough to say, "Get towels! Phone the Research Hospital for an ambulance and tell them to be here right away."

By midday, Westermark was tidily in bed upstairs and the ambulance staff, who had treated him for what after all was only nosebleed, had left. Stackpole, as he turned from closing the front door, eyed the two women.

"I feel it is my duty to warn you," he said heavily, "that another incident such as this might well prove fatal. This time we escaped very lightly. If anything else of this sort happens, I shall feel obliged to recommend to the board that Mr. Westermark is moved back to the hospital."

Current way to define accidents

"He wouldn't want to go," Janet said. "Besides, you are being absurd; it was entirely an accident. Now I wish to go upstairs and see how he is."

"Just before you go, may I point out that what happened was *not* an accident—or not as we generally define accidents, since you saw the results of your interference through the study window before you entered. Where you were to blame—"

"But that's absurd—" both women began at once. Janet went on to say, "I never would have rushed into the room as I did had I not seen through the window that he was in trouble."

"What you saw was the result on your husband of your later interference."

In something like a wail, Westermark's mother said, "I don't understand any of this. What did Janet bump into when she ran in?"

"She ran, Mrs. Westermark, into the spot where her husband had been standing 3.3077 minutes earlier. Surely by now you have grasped this elementary business of time inertia?"

When they both started speaking at once, he stared at them until they stopped and looked at him. Then he said, "We had better go into the living room. Speaking for myself, I would like a drink."

He helped himself, and not until his hand was round a glass of whisky did he say, "Now, without wishing to lecture to you ladies, I think it is high time you both realized that you are not living in the old safe world of classical mechanics ruled over by a god invented by eighteenth-century enlightenment. All that has happened here is perfectly rational, but if you are going to pretend it is beyond your female understandings—"

"Mr. Stackpole," Janet said sharply. "Can you please keep to the point without being insulting? Will you tell me why what happened was not an accident? I understand now that when I looked through the study window I saw my husband suffering from a collision that to him had happened three and something minutes before and to me would not happen for another three and something minutes, but at that moment I was so startled that I forgot—"

"No, no, your figures are wrong. The *total* time lapse is only 3.3077 minutes. When you saw your husband, he had been hit half that time—1.65385 minutes—ago, and there was another 1.65385 minutes to go before you completed the action by bursting into the room and striking him."

"But she *didn't* strike him!" the older woman cried.

Firmly, Stackpole diverted his attention long enough to reply. "She struck him at 10.24 Earthtime, which equals 10.20 plus about 36 seconds Mars or his time, which equals 9.59 or whatever Neptune time, which equals 156 and a half Sirius time. It's a big universe, Mrs. Westermark! You will remain confused as long as you continue to confuse event with time. May I suggest you sit down and have a drink?"

"Leaving aside the figures," Janet said, returning to the attack—loathsome opportunist the man was—"how can you say that what happened was no accident? You are not claiming I injured my husband deliberately, I hope? What you say suggests that I was powerless from the moment I saw him through the window."

" 'Leaving aside the figures...'" he quoted. "That's where your responsibility lies. What you saw through the window was the result of your act; it was by then inevitable that you should complete it, for it had already been completed."

Through the window, draughts of time blow

"I can't understand!" she clutched her forehead, gratefully accepting a cigarette from her mother-in-law, while shrugging off her consolatory "Don't try to understand, dear!" "Supposing when I had seen Jack's nose bleeding, I had looked at my watch and thought, 'It's 10.20 or whenever it was, and he may be suffering from my interference, so I'd better not go in,' and I *hadn't* gone in? Would his nose then miraculously have healed?"

"Of course not. You take such a mechanistic view of the universe. Cultivate a mental approach, try and live in your own century! You could not think what you suggest because that is not in your nature:

just as it is not in your nature to consult your watch intelligently, just as you always 'leave aside the figures', as you say. No, I'm not being personal: it's all very feminine and appealing in a way. What I'm saying is that if *before* you looked into the window you had been able to think, 'However I see my husband now, I must recall he has the additional experience of the next 3-3077 minutes', then you could have looked in and seen him unharmed, and you would not have come bursting in as you did."

She drew on her cigarette, baffled and hurt. "You're saying I'm a danger to my own husband."

"You're saying that."

"God, how I hate men!" she exclaimed. "You're so bloody logical, so bloody smug!"

He finished his whisky and set the glass down on a table beside her so that he leant close. "You're upset just now," he said.

"Of course I'm upset! What do you think?" She fought a desire to cry or slap his face. She turned to Jack's mother, who gently took her wrist.

"Why don't you go off straight away and stay with the children for the weekend, darling! Come back when you feel like it. Jack will be all right and I can look after him—as much as he wants looking after."

She glanced about the room.

"I will. I'll pack right away. They'll be glad to see me." As she passed Stackpole on the way out, she said bitterly, "At least *they* won't be worrying about the local time on Sirius!"

"They may," said Stackpole, imperturbably from the middle of the room, "have to one day."

All events, all children, all seasons

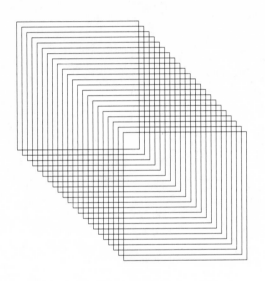

"—AND SUBSEQUENT CONSTRUCTION"

BY SPIDER ROBINSON

G od gets away with things no one else could.
Want proof?

The greatest comedians of the last century, the ones who lasted longest commercially and physically, were named *hope* (who always looked young), *burns* (who always looked old), and *miltin' b[oy/g]irl* (remembered for his drag routines). Then there were *skel[e]ton*, who slumped when he got tired; *'kay*, who was absurdly agreeable; and *Cid Caesar*, who returned from the dead when he slowed down, slimmed down, and got control of his ego. The only woman one can call to mind from that generation was named *ball*, whom they loved loose, see?; enough said there. Not many would accept irony that heavy-handed from an author...yet the twentieth century swallowed it from God without comment, laughing their heads off. Today, in 2010, I'm the only one who seems to have noticed.

Remember that: it may help you with what follows.

I'm a mathematician by training, and I've been a relativist. I've logged trips to six different star systems. I pray not to a god, but to the Nameless; and I don't try to send my prayers anywhere—I just try to *be* them. I remember well the prayer I was being that night as I drove from home to my lab....

Thank you, Nameless!

For all my life, the statement [(good luck) > (bad luck)] has tended to obtain—consistently enough to compensate for my basic tragedy: having been born a supergenius. Want proof? The foster parents who have always sworn they picked their little Iris on the basis of my toothless smile happened to be a NASA image specialist and a chaoticist: experts in, respectively, the universe's surface appearance and its underlying causes. They tutored me at home until I passed their competence at age ten and was admitted to UCLA. Mom was a Buddhist and Dad a Taoist. No other sort of background could have prepared me so well to be a relativist—that's why there are so few of us, which is why we're so absurdly well paid—and if I hadn't been a relativist I would not have met my beloved husband Teodor (whose name means "gift of God").

In case you missed it, I've just defined an ascending curve from

First Luck to Best Luck…because a good marriage is one of the most worthwhile things a human can make.

The proof of that statement lurks within the proximate cause of the prayer I was being as I hurtled down the highway that night. Just before I'd left our home to drive to work, Ted had given me a series of orgasms so exquisite and intense that it was a good thing the act of driving is these days essentially finished once you've defined your destination to the car…and furthermore, he had declined my offer to return the favor. ("Sometimes I just like to make my Iris dilate," he'd said.)

Do you see why that was so special? One of the hardest things a person can learn is to forgive herself for the massive extent of her own selfishness—and such selfishness is necessary, because you can't love anyone else until you love yourself utterly. I'd always had trouble in that area until I met Ted; thank the Nameless, he was able to persuade me that he enjoyed my sexual greediness as much as I did…which freed me to appreciate *his* sexual greediness, whenever the wind blew from that direction, and all the other kinds of delicious mutual greediness as well.

My smug contentment at owning a marriage so good that we didn't feel the need to keep books on each other was so pervasive that evening that there was no room left in my heart for frustration at how poorly my work was going—

—until my car, counting off broken-white-lines traversed, concluded it had reached its required coordinates, shut itself down, scanned the area for unfriendlies, and unlocked my door. At the sight of my lab, sitting amid endless hectares of cemetery like the millionaire's mausoleum it might yet become one day, I did an instant emotional one-eighty and became depressed.

What use, I asked myself, are genius, wealth, fame, and one of the great marriages of the Solar System…if your work won't work? I actually tried to slam the car door.

This funk persisted while I persuaded the lab door I was me, entered the building, stripped in the antechamber (unlike most people these days, I dislike driving in the nude), and entered the lab proper— whereupon sadness vanished.

Standing at the far end of the room was someone I recognized at once. I part my hair in the middle, so it was the breasts that confirmed the identification: right noticeably larger than the left. This was no mirror-reversed image.

My visitor was me.

"Thank the Nameless," I cried happily, and then, "What *took* me so long?"

Me grinned at I.

When Ikimono-roshi (whose name means "life," "living creatures," "farm products," or "uncooked food") discovered the star-drive in 1995, he thereby also created the profession called "relativist." The best definition ever offered to the layman of what a relativist does is (naturally) the Roshi's: he said we meditate on and with the engine, in order to make it happy enough to function. He held back the part about how we dissuade the star-drive from becoming a star…until humankind had become utterly economically dependent on star travel. Fortunately that took only a couple of decades: the Roshi's only significant character flaw was reluctance to keep a joke to himself. (A great pity: it finally killed him…a joke he must have loved.)

The profession he created was ideal for me. It paid the highest salary in human history—in return for which I was required to spend days at a time meditating on the imaginary distinctions between mathematics, physical philosophy and religion. In itself, that should have contented any supergenius…but one relativistic "day," as I was contemplating the second of Ikimono-roshi's three splendid 4-D *jukugo*, drugged to the eyeballs with don't-sleep (somewhere between Sol and Sirius A/B—going to the dogs, that is), I achieved the insight that should have made time-travel practical.

Which caused me to shut down the engine, forfeiting my pay for that trip, and go look up a passenger named Teodor I'd met during turnover and drag him off to bed with me, which helped us finish beginning to fall in love, which inspired him to write a song so good it forced us to get married—yes, he's *that* Teodor—but these are other stories. Another time.

It took Ted and me four agonizing years to force the government to let me retire—hell, I understand their position; there were only forty-six relativists alive and sane at that time—but finally I was free to chase my chimera full-time. Perhaps my motivation will seem inadequate to you, especially if you're one of the hundreds who debarked at the Sirius System two weeks later than you expected, but it was sufficient for me: I wanted to go backward in time and meet my biological (as opposed to my "real") mother. Emotional considerations aside, it would have been useful to know rather than deduce my medical and genetic history. But only a fool puts emotional considerations aside: above all, I needed to know whether I forgave her.

In any case, there finally came a time when I was able to enter my ideal laboratory/zendo and put my all attention on time travel for ten hours a night. (I wish the biophyzzle folks would buckle down and solve immortality; 200-odd years just isn't enough time for a person to get any serious thinking done. There's always *something*, you know?)

What ensued was two solid months of frustration…which got worse as time passed. The question that kept digging around under my skin like a burrowing parasite was: *where the hell was I?*

(Am I going too fast? Brunner tells the story of a prof scrawling equations on the lecture-hall blackboard who declaimed, "It is therefore obvious—"…frowned, scratched his head, left the hall amid growing murmurs, and returned ten minutes later to announce triumphantly, "I was right: it *is* obvious!" I often have the same trouble communicating with those more fortunate than myself. Hyperintelligence is a very mixed blessing.)

My antinomy was this: if I were to succeed in inventing…oh, let's give in and call it a time machine…I was sure the first thing I would *do* with it (after testing it for safety) would be to come back and tell me I was going to succeed. Naturally I would not have told myself *how* I'd done it—don't you hate it when someone tells you how the book is going to come out?—but I'm so cocky I didn't see how it could hurt to have my cleverness confirmed in advance.

So the fact that I had not met me during my first two months of work had been unnerving. No: maddening!

And now, at last, here me was. The sense of relief was overwhelming.

"Eventually," me said, "we'll either have to restructure English, or speak math. But for now, let's try to keep this as simple as possible. You can call me Jay, eh?"

I believed I understood. Jay is what comes after Eye-for-Iris in the alphabet, and the way Jay phrased it raised resonances of another old-time comedian we both loved because he had only a single joke to his name. I forgot what sort of bird a jay is.

"I…Jay…'kay," I said, and had the satisfaction of seeing my self smile at one of my own puns. No one else but Teodor ever does.

But there was something about that smile I recognized all to well, even without the usual mirror-reversal.

Jay was *miserable*, through and through. So saturated with sadness, I think even another person could have seen it.

"What's wrong?" I cried…and then remembered what had once made me look that sad, and what had cured me. My yo-yo heart plummeted again. "Oh, *no*! Ted's—"

"No," Jay said at once. "It's almost worse than that, Iris. He's still alive. But we're divorced. Bitterly."

I screamed. First time in my life. Then: "WHY?"

"Do you really want to know?"

"Hell. Of course not. Thank you. Any…any hope at all?"

"I don't think so," she said.

Despair. "Ah Jay, Jay—why did you *tell*…cancel, I asked you. Oh, damn me! And my cursed curiosity…."

I had never in my life wished more fervently that I'd been born a normal human being, able to *not* think things through if I chose. Can you imagine how fervently that is? I wasted ten whole silent seconds feeling sorry for myself—a lifetime record—before I was able to turn my attention to feeling sorry for my *other* self…who had been in this pain for much longer than I had. That selfishness I mentioned earlier. "Is there anything I can do to help you, Jay?"

"Yes."

"What?"

Jay didn't answer. In a second, I got it. If you'd lost your life's one love, wouldn't you give anything to be with him one last time if you could! "Here," I said, and gave her my key ring.

A fraction of her sadness seemed to lift from her. "Thank you, Iris!"

"He'll be pleasantly surprised," I told her, trying to make this sad consolation-prize as happy as possible. "He's ready for some loving, and not expecting to get it sooner than dawn at the earliest. Just tell him your selfish need to hear him groan with joy overcame your need to work; it'll flatter the hell out of him. Uh…if you think of it, afterward, kiss him once for me."

"I will," she promised. "I should be back by dawn. If…if you could use some consolation yourself, then…"

The concept was horridly hilarious, mind-boggling; I groped in vain for a response.

She turned and left hastily.

My pain was so great that I could not contemplate it. Greater, in other words, than the fire at the heart of a star-drive. My choices were to go mad, or to drown myself in my work.

After all, I knew now that I could succeed. That I had…would have had…done so.

First invent the time machine, Iris. Then revamp English to fit the new facts.

I booted up my computer and got started. Somewhere in the back of my mind as I worked was the mad, less-than-half-believed hope that somehow I might employ a completed time machine to avert the disaster in my future, to use an "undo" key on reality. It was illogical, but so is all hope.

An hour later I roared with frustrated rage and pounded on my keyboard. Zero progress.

No. Less than zero. I had succeeded in *proving* that the line of attack I'd been using was a dead end. And I could see no other.

I wished I'd cheated, and pumped Jay for hints before letting her go.

Why hadn't I? In too much of a hurry, yes…but *why*?

It hit me like a slap. One small component of the eagerness with which I'd agreed to Jay's pitiful request has been…oh, shit…relief. Relief from a minor nagging guilt. At having accepted Ted's gift of unreciprocated pleasure earlier that night.

I had welcomed Jay's intervention because it would help me balance a set of books I prided myself on not keeping.

Why? Because now that I knew I was going to be divorced from Ted some day, I was subconsciously operating in accordance with one of the basic principles of star-travel: "When the ship lifts, all bills are paid." I had been able to live with unbalanced books because I'd believed the ship was never going to lift. But if Ted and I *were* going to separate, my selfish subconscious did not want to leave owing him any debt—even one as trivial as an unreciprocated orgasm.

…which implied that the separation was *imminent* …

The second insight hit with the force of a death-blow, although my subconscious seemed to have known it for an hour.

Oh, Nameless! All she has to do, in the heat of passion, is to make the slightest slip, offer the most harmless of hints. Ted's quick: he'll pick up on it at once, even in the heat of passion, and then he'll get the whole story out of her—

—*and what will he think of me then!*

What would you think? Suppose you learned that your spouse had conspired with her divorced future-self to take advantage of you…to steal from you love and affection *which you would have withheld if you'd been in possession of all the facts!*

Future-Ted presumably had what seemed to him good and sufficient reasons to withhold his love from Future-Iris, from Jay. Therefore Jay's actions constituted rape, seduction-by-guile. Ted would see that at once if he learned the truth—

—and I, present-I, Iris, his trusted wife, had collaborated in his rape—

Dear Nameless—had I destroyed my own marriage? No wonder

he was going to divorce me: I had betrayed his trust. In order to do a favor for Jay, for my self. Without thinking...

Only a supergenius could have been so stupid!

To confirm the awful inevitable, I phoned home.

There was no answer—the answer I'd half-expected—so I punched in my override code to activate the home-camera anyway. It showed our...what had been our...bedroom, empty, sheets snarled by illicit love. There was something visible on the floor; I zoomed in on it.

It was a sheet of paper, handwritten; dear Ted was so old fashioned. At max magnification I could read what was written on it.

The best song he'd written in his life. So good that even the best melody could not have added much to it. More than a song: a poem. I can reproduce it from memory:

> *Afterglow (Iris's Song)*
> by Ted Rowe
>
> Tending to tension by conscious intent,
> declining declension, disdaining dissent,
> into the dementia dimension we are sent:
> we are our content, and we are content.
>
> Incandescent invention and blessed event;
> tumescent distention, tumultuous descent;
> our bone of convention again being spent,
> I am your contents, and I am content
>
> to be living...to be trying...
> to be crying...to be dying—l want
> to be giving...to be making...
> to be shaking...to be taking all you have
>
> Assuming Ascension, Assumption, assent
> all of our nonsense is finally non-sent...

with honorable mention for whatever we meant;
you are my content, and I am content.

How glorious, to see such a song, with my name on it.

How terrible, to see that the sheet of paper on which it was written had been torn nearly in half and flung to the floor.

Jay had made some slip; he had guessed.

I broke the connection and buried my head in my hands.

My next conscious thought, an indeterminate time later, was: *How could me do this to I?*

How could Jay, my very own self, have done this horrid thing—when she had to have known it would blow up in our face, that it would precipitate all our mutual misery?

With that thought, my brain woke up and began to think for the first time that night.

My line of work had required me to study a little astronomy—an interesting field for a mathematician—and one of the few anecdotes from the history of astronomy which had stuck in my mind was the story of Fritz Zwicky's "Method of Negation and Subsequent Construction." Zwicky said he *began* with the absolute certainty that dwarf galaxies must exist, *because Edwin Hubble said they could not*...and thus certain, was able to prove their existence. This form of reasoning had amused me, so I'd remembered it.

I employed it now.

I wanted so badly to believe that Jay could not be me—that not even time and sustained pain could make me so stupid as to cause that pain—that I *assumed* it.

And that single axiom made all anomalies disappear, caused things to fall into place with an almost audible click. I came close to shouting aloud the word, "Eureka!"

I'll take you through it step by step.

Postulate that my unknown biological mother was at least highly intelligent. Not a supergenius like me, necessarily, but I can't see her as a dummy. Even now, no one knows for sure how much of genius is hereditary and how much is environmental, but grant me the premise.

Admittedly, she lived most of her life during the dark ages just ended. Provisionally accept the current theory that genius and genius-plus children tend to be borne by mothers over 30, and say that Mother (as opposed to Mom, who raised me) was born around 1955. The Stone Age as far as women were concerned.

But even if you assume her luck was minimal, that she was a poverty stricken handicapped ugly single-parent in an era which treated single-parents barbarically…still and even so, it would *seem* that she ought to have been able to cope with parenthood, at least for longer than the week or two she stuck it out.

But suppose she birthed *twins*….

Suppose further that my hypothetical identical twin—let's call her, for the sake of the argument, "Jay"—had even fractionally less than my own good luck in foster parents. Not hard to believe.

Endless studies have uncovered cases in which identical twins raised separately, unaware that a twin existed, had astonishingly similar lives, down to their professions, IQs, favorite swear words and the names of their spouses and children.

But with even a slight wrinkle in the blueprint, Jay might have grown to maturity without ever having learned the most crucial life-lesson I had learned: that it's okay to be selfish.

Supergeniuses who lack that realization cannot love themselves fully. This must surely inhibit, twist their intelligence. Such a crippled supergenius might well cause her own marriage to self-destruct, to drive away a loving husband because of her inevitable contempt for anyone stupid enough to give unconditional love to a monster like herself.

That list of great comedians I started with? One I left out was *marx*, who said, "I could never belong to a club that would have me as a member." He went through quite a few broken relationships before merciful death eased his magnificent, needless suffering.

How might such a self-contemptuous woman punish herself for hurting and driving away a good and loving man?

Well, if she knew or somehow learned that she had a twin, she might be moved to research her. And if that twin's life was turning out infuriatingly better than her own, she might just construct an elaborate and cruel hoax to wreck her sister's marriage too....

As far as I was concerned the thing was proved. Yet I turned to my terminal. I intended to finally use some of the awesome clout and access even an ex-relativist can command to smash through all the bureaucratic barriers against my learning the name of my mother and the circumstances of my birth and adoption. I had not planned to do so until I had a working time machine and could act on the information...but I was aware that Negation and Subsequent Construction is a ladder of dubious strength, and I wanted this nailed down.

But as my modem program came up on the screen, the door to the lab opened and Ted came in. He was pushing Jay along before him; she was swearing brilliantly in Russian, my own favorite language for cursing. He locked the door behind them with his coded card and stepped past her to face me.

"I'm sorry, darling," I blurted, springing to my feet. "I wasn't thinking clearly—"

"In your place I think I might have done the same thing," he interrupted. "It was a sweet, selfish, human thing to do. Nothing worth losing a mate like you over. Very few things warp your judgment, my love: I'm flattered that the prospect of losing me is one of them." He smiled, and burst into tears.

So I did too. We embraced fiercely.

"I know how I figured it out," I said when I could. "But how did you figure it out?"

"You'll like it," he promised. "Nothing I could think of could have suddenly made you so bad a lover."

One of many reasons I love my Ted: he keeps his promises. I tightened my embrace.

"You can't hold me," Jay snarled. "This can't be construed as a citizen's arrest: nothing I've done is a felony." She poked futilely at the locked door.

"You seem to know me pretty well, sister," I said. "How much do I care for law?"

She paled. "What are you going to do to me?" she asked us.

"Your privilege, love," Ted said to me.

I nodded. "The nastiest, most sadistic, most poetically appropriate thing I can think of," I told my twin. "We're going to try to heal you." She looked shocked. "You're crippled with self-hatred, and I think we're just the two people who can fix that."

"Without my consent? That's...immoral."

"If you were anyone else," I said, "I would agree with you. I believe people have a general right to keep their neuroses as long as they think they need them. But in this special case, I cannot accept the risk. You're damn near as clever as me, and as long as you remain damaged you will mean harm to Ted and me. I decline to spend the rest of my life burning energy to stay a step ahead of you. Out of raw self-interest, I propose to teach you things you don't want to learn, and keep you prisoner until you've learned them." I smiled wickedly. "And make you like it. You'll thank me when I'm done—isn't that *awful*? Just remember: you asked for it."

She tried to attack me, but my husband is very quick and very strong. She ended up with one arm wrenched up behind her.

"And if we can manage to fix the kink in your heart," he went on while she cursed and struggled, "we're all going to track down your ex-husband—Russian, like me, isn't he?—and try to heal your marriage."

She was struck speechless. She went limp in his grip.

"It's certainly worth thinking about," I agreed—and suddenly it was as if two continental plates had slipped inside my skull: a massive realignment that was over in an instant. "Now if the two of you will excuse me," I said dizzily, "I've got a time machine to invent. It just now came to me: *two* fields, almost but not quite identical, just out of phase. If it works, I'll be waiting for you both at home when you get there." I caught Ted's eye. "We'll lock her up in the guest room for the night, and make other arrangements tomorrow. I'm going to make you write that song to me retroactively, darling. Very retro, very actively."

"Yes, dear," he said mildly, and got the hell out of my lab, dragging Jay with him.

That's another reason I love him. He doesn't try to top my puns.

And as I turned back to my workstation, there was a small clap of thunder, and a pressure change that made my ears pop, and my *real* future-self winked into being a meter away, wearing a grid of wires, a headband, a plastic backpack that hummed softly, and a smile.

"Congratulations," me said.

After a moment's hesitation—it had been a *long* night—I returned my smile.

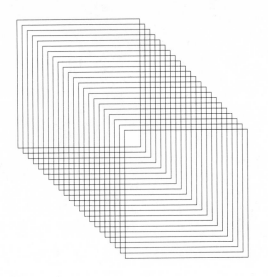

TIMESKIP

BY CHARLES DE LINT

Every time it rains a ghost comes walking.

He goes up by the stately old houses that line Stanton Street, down Henratty Lane to where it leads into the narrow streets and crowded backalleys of Crowsea, and then back up Stanton again in an unvarying routine.

He wears a worn tweed suit—mostly browns and greys with a faint rosy touch of heather. A shapeless cap presses down his brown curls. His features give no true indication of his age, while his eyes are both innocent and wise. His face gleams in the rain, slick and wet as that of a living person. When he reaches the streetlamp in front of the old Hamill estate, he wipes his eyes with a brown hand. Then he fades away.

Samantha Rey knew it was true because she'd seen him.

More than once.

She saw him every time it rained.

⚛

"So, have you asked her out yet?" Jilly wanted to know.

We were sitting on a park bench, feeding pigeons the leftover crusts from our lunches. Jilly had worked with me at the post office, that Christmas they hired outside staff instead of letting the regular employees work the overtime, and we'd been friends ever since. These days she worked three nights a week as a waitress, while I made what I could busking on the Market with my father's old Czech fiddle.

Jilly was slender, with a thick tangle of brown hair and pale blue eyes, electric as sapphires. She had a penchant for loose clothing and fingerless gloves when she wasn't waitressing. There were times, when I met her on the streets in the evening, that I mistook her for a baglady: skulking in an alleyway, gaze alternating between the sketchbook held in one hand and the faces of the people on the streets as they walked by. She had more sketches of me playing my fiddle than had any right to exist.

"She's never going to know how you feel until you talk to her about it," Jilly went on when I didn't answer.

"I know."

I'll make no bones about it: I was putting the make on Sam Rey and had been ever since she'd started to work at Gypsy Records half a year ago. I never much went in for the blonde California beach girl type, but Sam had a look all her own. She had some indefinable quality that went beyond her basic cheerleader appearance. Right. I can hear you already. Rationalizations of the North American libido. But it was true. I didn't just want Sam in my bed; I wanted to know we were going to have a future together. I wanted to grow old with her. I wanted to build up a lifetime of shared memories.

About the most Sam knew about all this was that I hung around and talked to her a lot at the record store.

"Look," Jilly said. "Just because she's pretty, doesn't mean she's having a perfect life or anything. Most guys look at someone like her and they won't even approach her because they're sure she's got men coming out of her ears. Well, it doesn't always work that way. For instance—" she touched her breastbone with a narrow hand and smiled "—consider yours truly."

I looked at her long fingers. Paint had dried under her nails

"You've started a new canvas," I said.

"And you're changing the subject," she replied. "Come on, Geordie. What's the big deal? The most she can say is no."

"Well, yeah. But…"

"She intimidates you, doesn't she?"

I shook my head. "I talk to her all the time."

"Right. And that's why I've got to listen to your constant mooning over her." She gave me a sudden considering look, then grinned. "I'll tell you what, Geordie, me lad. Here's the bottom line: I'll give you twenty-four hours to ask her out. If you haven't got it together by then, I'll talk to her myself."

"Don't even joke about it."

"Twenty-four hours," Jilly said firmly. She looked at the chocolate chip cookie in my hand. "Are you eating that?" she added in that certain tone of voice of hers that plainly said, all previous topics of conversation have been dealt with and completed. We are now changing topics.

So we did. But all the while we talked, I thought about going into the record store and asking Sam out, because if I didn't, Jilly would do it for me. Whatever else she might be, Jilly wasn't shy. Having her go in to plead my case would be as bad as having my mother do it for me. I'd never be able to show my face in there again.

❊

Gypsy Records is on Williamson Street, one of the city's main arteries. The street begins as Highway 14 outside the city, lined with a sprawl of fast food outlets, malls and warehouses. On its way downtown, it begins to replace the commercial properties with ever-increasing handfuls of residential blocks, until it reaches the downtown core, where shops and low-rise apartments mingle in gossiping crowds.

The store gets its name from John Butler, a short round-bellied man without a smidgen of Romany blood, who began his business out of the back of a hand-drawn cart that gypsied its way through the city's streets for years, always keeping just one step ahead of the municipal licensing board's agents. While it carries the usual bestsellers, the lifeblood of its sales are more obscure titles—imports and albums published by independent record labels. Albums, singles and compact discs of punk, traditional folk, jazz, heavy metal and alternative music line its shelves. Barring Sam, most of those who work there would look just as at home in the fashion pages of the most current British alternative fashion magazines.

Sam was wearing a blue cotton dress today, embroidered with silver threads. Her blonde hair was cut in a short shag on the top, hanging down past her shoulders at the back and sides. She was dealing with a defect when I came in. I don't know if the record in question worked or not, but the man returning it was definitely defective.

"It sounds like there's a radio broadcast right in the middle of the song," he was saying as he tapped the cover of the Pink Floyd album on the counter between them.

"It's supposed to be there," Sam explained. "It's *part* of the song." The tone of her voice told me that this conversation was going into its twelfth round or so.

"Well, I don't like it," the man told her. "When I buy an album of music, I expect to get just music on it."

"You still can't return it."

I worked in a record shop one Christmas—two years before the post office job. The best defect I got was from someone returning an in concert album by Marcel Marceau. Each side had thirty minutes of silence, with applause at the end—I kid you not.

I browsed through the Celtic records while I waited for Sam to finish with her customer. I couldn't afford any of them, but I liked to see what was new. Blasting out of the store's speakers was the new Beastie Boys album. It sounded like a cross between heavy metal and bad rap and was about as appealing as being hit by a car. You couldn't deny its energy, though.

By the time Sam was free I'd located five records I would have bought in more flush times. Leaving them in the bin, I drifted over to the front cash register just as the Beastie Boys' last cut ended. Sam replaced them with a tape of New Age piano music.

"What's the new Oyster Band like?" I asked.

Sam smiled. "It's terrific. My favorite cut's 'The Old Dance'. It's sort of an allegory based on Adam and Eve and the serpent that's got a great hook in the chorus. Telfer's fiddling just sort of skips ahead, pulling the rest of the song along."

That's what I like about alternative record stores like Gypsy's— the people working in them actually know something about what they're selling.

"Have you got an open copy?" I asked.

She nodded and turned to the bin of opened records behind her to find it. With her back to me, I couldn't get lost in those deep blue eyes of hers. I seized my opportunity and plunged ahead.

"Areyouworkingtonight,wouldyouliketogooutwithmesomewhere?"

I'd meant to be cool about it, except the words all blurred together as they left my throat. I could feel the flush start up the back of my neck as she turned and looked back at me with those baby blues.

"Say what?" she asked.

Before my throat closed up on me completely, I tried again, keeping it short. "Do you want to go out with me tonight?"

Standing there with the Oyster Band album in her hand, I thought she'd never looked better. Especially when she said, "I thought you'd never ask."

※

I put in a couple of hours of busking that afternoon, down in Crowsea's Market, the fiddle humming under my chin to the jingling rhythm of the coins that passers-by threw into the case lying open in front of me. I came away with twenty-six dollars and change—not the best of days, but enough to buy a halfway decent dinner and a few beers.

I picked up Sam after she finished work and we ate at The Monkey Woman's Nest, a Mexican restaurant on Williamson just a couple of blocks down from Gypsy's. I still don't know how the place got its name. Emestina Verdad, the Mexican woman who owns the place, looks like a showgirl and not one of her waitresses is even vaguely simian in appearance.

It started to rain as we were finishing our second beer, turning Williamson Street slick with neon reflections. Sam got a funny look on her face as she watched the rain through the window. Then she turned to me.

"Do you believe in ghosts?" she asked.

The serious look in her eyes stopped the half-assed joke that two beer brewed in the carbonated swirl of my mind. I never could hold my alcohol. I wasn't drunk, but I had a buzz on.

"I don't think so," I said carefully. "At least I've never seriously stopped to think about it."

"Come on," she said, getting up from the table. "I want to show you something."

I let her lead me out into the rain, though I didn't let her pay anything towards the meal. Tonight was my treat. Next time I'd be happy to let her do the honours.

"Every time it rains," she said, "a ghost comes walking down my street...."

She told me the story as we walked down into Crowsea. The rain was light and I was enjoying it, swinging my fiddle case in my right hand, Sam hanging onto my left as though she'd always walked there. I felt like I was on top of the world, listening to her talk, feeling the pressure of her arm, the bump of her hip against mine.

She had an apartment on the third floor of an old brick and frame building on Stanton Street. It had a front porch that ran the length of the house, dormer windows—two in the front and back, one on each side—and a sloped mansard roof. We stood on the porch, out of the rain which was coming down harder now. An orange and white tom was sleeping on the cushion of a white wicker chair by the door. He twitched a torn ear as we shared his shelter, but didn't bother to open his eyes. I could smell the mint that was growing up alongside the porch steps, sharp in the wet air.

Sam pointed down the street to where the yellow glare of a streetlamp glistened on the rain-slicked cobblestone walk that led to the Hamill estate. The Hamill house itself was separated from the street by a low wall and a dark expanse of lawn, bordered by the spreading boughs of huge oak trees.

"Watch the street," she said. "Just under the streetlight."

I looked, but I didn't see anything. The wind gusted suddenly, driving the rain in hard sheets along Stanton Street, and for a moment we lost all visibility. When it cleared, he was standing there, Sam's ghost, just like she'd told me. As he started down the street, Sam gave my arm a tug. I stowed my fiddle case under the tom's wicker chair, and we followed the ghost down Henratty Lane.

By the time he returned to the streetlight in front of the Hamill estate, I was ready to argue that Sam was mistaken. There was nothing in the least bit ghostly about the man we were following. When he returned up Henratty Lane, we had to duck into a doorway to let him pass. He never looked at us, but I could see the rain hitting him. I could hear the sound of his shoes on the pavement. He had to have come out of the bordered walk that led up to the estate's house, at the same time as that sudden gust of wind-driven rain. It had been a simple coincidence, nothing more. But when he returned to the streetlight, he lifted a hand to wipe his face, and then he was gone.

He just winked out of existence. There was no wind. No gust of rain. No place he could have gone. A ghost.

"Jesus," I said softly as I walked over to the pool of light cast by the streetlamp. There was nothing to see. But there had been a man there. I was sure of that much.

"We're soaked," Sam said. "Come on up to my place and I'll make us some coffee."

The coffee was great and the company was better. Sam had a small clothes drier in her kitchen. I sat in the living room in an over-sized housecoat while my clothes tumbled and turned, the machine creating a vibration in the floorboards that I'm sure Sam's downstairs neighbours must have just loved. Sam had changed into a dark blue sweatsuit—she looked best in blue, I decided—and dried her hair while she was making the coffee. I'd prowled around her living room while she did, admiring her books, her huge record collection, her sound system, and the mantle above a working fireplace that was crammed with knick-knacks.

All her furniture was the kind made for comfort—they crouched like sleeping animals about the room. Fat sofa in front of the fireplace, an old pair of matching easy chairs by the window. The bookcases, record cabinet, side tables and trim were all natural wood, polished to a shine with furniture oil.

We talked about a lot of things, sitting on the sofa, drinking our coffees, but mostly we talked about the ghost.

"Have you ever approached him?" I asked at one point.

Sam shook her head. "No. I just watch him walk. I've never even talked about him to anybody else." That made me feel good. "You know, I can't help but feel that he's waiting for something, or someone. Isn't that the way it usually works in ghost stories?"

"This isn't a ghost story," I said.

"But we didn't imagine it did we? Not both of us at the same time?"

"I don't know."

But I knew someone who probably did. Jilly. She was into every sort of strange happening, taking all kinds of odd things seriously. I could remember her telling me that Bramley Dapple—one of her professors at Butler U. and a friend of my brother's—was really a wizard who had a brown-skinned goblin for a valet, but the best thing I remembered about her was her talking about that scene in Disney's *101 Dalmatians*, where the dogs are all howling to send a message across town, one dog sending it out, another picking it up and passing it along, all the way across town and out into the country.

"That's how they do it," she'd said. "Just like that."

And if you walked with her at night and a dog started to howl—if no other dog picked it up, then she'd pass it on. She could mimic any dog's bark or howl so perfectly it was uncanny. It could also be embarrassing, because she didn't care who was around or what kinds of looks she got. It was the message that had to be passed on that was important.

When I told Sam about Jilly, she smiled, but there wasn't any mockery in her smile. Emboldened, I related the ultimatum that Jilly had given me this afternoon.

Sam laughed aloud. "Jilly sounds like my kind of person," she said. "I'd like to meet her."

When it started to get late, I collected my clothes and changed in the bathroom. I didn't want to start anything, not yet, not this soon, and I knew that Sam felt the same way, though neither of us had spoken of it. She kissed me at the door, a long warm kiss that had me buzzing again.

"Come see me tomorrow?" she asked. "At the store?"

"Just try and keep me away," I replied.

I gave the old tom on the porch a pat and whistled all the way home to my own place on the other side of Crowsea.

Jilly's studio was its usual organized mess. It was an open loft-like affair that occupied half of the second floor of a four-story brown brick building on Yoors Street where Foxville's low rentals mingle with Crowsea's shops and older houses. One half of the studio was taken up with a Murphy bed that was never folded back into the wall, a pair of battered sofas, a small kitchenette, storage cabinets and a tiny box-like bathroom obviously designed with dwarves in mind.

Her easel stood in the other half of the studio, by the window where it could catch the morning sun. All around it were stacks of sketchbooks, newspapers, unused canvases and art books. Finished canvases leaned face front, five to ten deep, against the back wall. Tubes of paint covered the tops of old wooden orange crates—the new ones lying in neat piles like logs by a fireplace, the used ones in a haphazard scatter, closer to hand. Brushes sat waiting to be used in mason jars. Others were in liquid waiting to be cleaned. Still more, their brushes stiff with dried paint, lay here and there on the floor like discarded pick-up-sticks.

The room smelled of oil paint and turpentine. In the corner furthest from the window was a life-sized fabric maché sculpture of an artist at work that bore an uncanny likeness to Jilly herself, complete with Walkman, one paintbrush in hand, another sticking out of its mouth. When I got there that morning, Jilly was at her new canvas, face scrunched up as she concentrated. There was already paint in her hair. On the windowsill behind her a small ghetto blaster was playing a Bach fugue, the piano notes spilling across the room like a light rain. Jilly looked up as I came in, a frown changing liquidly into a smile as she took in the foolish look on my face.

"I should have thought of this weeks ago," she said. "You look like the cat who finally caught the mouse. Did you have a good time?"

"The best."

Leaving my fiddle by the door, I moved around behind her so that I could see what she was working on. Sketched out on the white canvas was a Crowsea street scene. I recognized the corner— McKennitt and Lee. I'd played there from time to time, mostly in the spring. Lately a rockabilly band called the Broken Hearts had taken over the spot.

"Well?" Jilly prompted.

"Well what?"

"Aren't you going to give me all the lovely sordid details?"

I nodded at the painting. She'd already started to work in the background with oils.

"Are you putting in the Hearts?" I asked.

Jilly jabbed at me with her paint brush, leaving a smudge the colour of a Crowsea red brick tenement on my jean jacket.

"I'll thump you if you don't spill it all, Geordie, me lad. Just watch if I don't."

She was liable to do just that, so I sat down on the ledge behind her and talked while she painted. We shared a pot of her cowboy coffee which was what Jilly called the foul brew she made from used coffee grounds. I took two spoons of sugar to my usual one, just to cut back on the bitter taste it left in my throat. Still beggars couldn't be choosers. That morning I didn't even have used coffee grounds at my own place.

"I like ghost stories," she said when I was finished telling her about my evening. She'd finished roughing out the buildings by now and bent closer to the canvas to start working on some of the finer details before she lost the last of the morning light.

"Was it real?" I asked.

"That depends. Bramley says—"

"I know, I know," I said breaking in.

If it wasn't Jilly telling me some weird story about him, it was my brother. What Jilly liked best about him was his theory of consensual reality, the idea that things exist *because* we agree that they exist.

"But think about it," Jilly went on. "Sam sees a ghost—maybe because she expects to see one—and you see the same ghost because you care about her, so you're willing to agree that there's one there where she says it will be."

"Say it's not that, then what could it be?"

"Any number of things. A timeslip—a bit of the past slipping into the present. It could be a restless spirit with unfinished business. From what you say Sam's told you, though, I'd guess that it's a case of a timeskip."

She turned to grin at me which let me know that the word was one of her own coining. I gave her a dutifully admiring look, then asked, "A what?"

"A timeskip. It's like a broken record, you know? It just keeps playing the same bit over and over again, only unlike the record it needs something specific to cue it in."

"Like rain."

"Exactly." She gave me a sudden sharp look. "This isn't for one of your brother's stories, is it?"

My brother Christy collects odd tales just like Jilly does, only he writes them down. I've heard some grand arguments between the two of them comparing the superior qualities of the oral versus written traditions.

"I haven't seen Christy in weeks," I said.

"All right, then."

"So how do you go about handling this sort of thing?" I asked. "Sam thinks he's waiting for something."

Jilly nodded. "For someone to lift the tone arm of time." At the pained look on my face, she added, "Well, have you got a better analogy?"

I admitted that I didn't. "But how do you do that? Do you just go over and talk to him, or grab him, or what?"

"Any and all might work. But you have to be careful about that kind of thing."

"How so?"

"Well," Jilly said, turning from the canvas to give me a serious look, "sometimes a ghost like that can drag you back to whenever it is that he's from and you'll be trapped in his time. Or you might end up taking his place in the timeskip."

"Lovely."

"Isn't it?" She went back to the painting. "What colour's that sign Duffy has over his shop on McKennitt?" she asked.

I closed my eyes, trying to picture it, but all I could see was the face of last night's ghost, wet with rain.

It didn't rain again for a couple of weeks. They were good weeks. Sam and I spent the evenings and weekends together. We went out a few times, twice with Jilly, once with a couple of Sam's friends. Jilly and Sam got along just as well as I'd thought they would—and why shouldn't they? They were both special people. I should know.

The morning it did rain it was Sam's day off from Gypsy's. The previous night was the first I'd stayed over all night. The first we made love. Waking up in the morning with her warm beside me was everything I thought it would be. She was sleepy-eyed and smiling, more than willing to nestle deep under the comforter while I saw about getting some coffee together.

When the rain started, we took our mugs into the living room and watched the street in front of the Hamill estate. A woman came by walking one of those fat white bull terriers that look like they're more pig than dog. The terrier didn't seem to mind the rain but the woman at the other end of the leash was less than pleased. She alternated between frowning at the clouds and tugging him along. About five minutes after the pair had rounded the corner, our ghost showed up, just winking into existence out of nowhere. Or out of a slip in time. One of Jilly's timeskips.

We watched him go through his routine. When he reached the streetlight and vanished again, Sam leaned her head against my shoulder. We were cozied up together in one of the big comfy chairs, feet on the windowsill.

"We should do something for him," she said.

"Remember what Jilly said," I reminded her.

Sam nodded. "But I don't think this he's out to hurt anybody. It's not like he's calling out to us or anything. He's just there, going through the same moves, time after time. The next time it rains…"

"What're we going to do?"

Sam shrugged. "Talk to him, maybe?"

I didn't see how that could cause any harm. Truth to tell, I was feeling sorry for the poor bugger myself.

"Why not?" I said.

About then Sam's hands got busy and I quickly lost interest in the ghost. I started to get up, but Sam held me down in the chair.

"Where you going?" she asked.

"Well, I thought the bed would be…"

"We've never done it in a chair before."

"There's a lot of places we haven't done it yet," I said.

Those deep blue eyes of hers, about five inches from my own, just about swallowed me.

"We've got all the time in the world," she said.

It's funny how you remember things like that later.

❀

The next time it rained, Jilly was with us. The three of us were walking home from Your Second Home, a sleazy bar on the other side of Foxville where the band of a friend of Sam's was playing. None of us looked quite right for the bar when we walked in. Sam was still the perennial California beach girl, all blonde and curves in a pair of tight jeans and a white T-shirt, with a faded jean jacket overtop. Jilly and I looked like the scruffs we were.

The bar was a place for serious drinking during the day, serving mostly unemployed blue-collar workers spending their welfare cheques on a few hours of forgetfulness. By the time the band started around nine, though, the clientele underwent a drastic transformation. Scattered here and there through the crowd was the odd individual who still dressed for volume—all the colours turned up loud—but mostly we were outnumbered thirty-to-one by spike-haired punks in their black leathers and blue jeans. It was like being on the inside of a bruise.

The band was called the Wang Boys and ended up being pretty good—especially on their original numbers—if a bit loud. My ears were ringing when we finally left the place sometime after midnight. We were having a good time on the walk home. Jilly was in rare form, half-dancing on the street around us, singing the band's closing number, making up the words, turning the piece into a punk gospel number. She kept bouncing around in front of us, skipping backwards as she tried to get us to sing along.

The rain started as a thin drizzle as were making our way through Crowsea's narrow streets. Sam's fingers tightened on my arm and Jilly stopped fooling around as we stepped into Henratty Lane, the rain coming down in earnest now. The ghost was just turning in the far end of the lane.

"Geordie," Sam said, her fingers tightening more.

I nodded. We brushed by Jilly and stepped up our pace, aiming to connect with the ghost before he made his turn and started back towards Stanton Street.

"This is not a good idea," Jilly warned us, hurrying to catch up. But by then it was too late.

We were right in front of the ghost. I could tell he didn't see Sam or me and I wanted to get out of his way before he walked right through us—I didn't relish the thought of having a ghost or a timeskip or whatever he was going through me. But Sam wouldn't move. She put out her hand, and as her fingers brushed the wet tweed of his jacket, everything changed.

The sense of vertigo was strong. Henratty Lane blurred. I had the feeling of time flipping by like the pages of a calendar in an old movie, except each page was a year, not a day. The sounds of the city around us—sounds we weren't normally aware of—were noticeable by their sudden absence. The ghost jumped at Sam's touch. There was a bewildered look in his eyes and he backed away. That sensation of vertigo and blurring returned until Sam caught him by the arm and everything settled down again. Quiet, except for the rain and a far-off voice that seemed to be calling my name.

"Don't be frightened," Sam said keeping her grip on the ghost's arm. "We want to help you."

"You should not be here," he replied. His voice was stiff and a little formal. "You were only a dream—nothing more. Dreams are to be savoured and remembered, not walking the streets."

Underlying their voices I could still hear the faint sound of my own name being called. I tried to ignore it, concentrating on the ghost and our surroundings. The lane was cleaner than I remembered it—no trash littered against the walls, no graffiti scrawled across the bricks. It seemed darker, too. It was almost possible to believe that we'd been pulled back into the past by the touch of the ghost.

I started to get nervous then, remembering what Jilly had told us. Into the past. What if we *were* in the past and we couldn't get out again? What if we got trapped in the same timeskip as the ghost and were doomed to follow his routine each time it rained?

Sam and the ghost were still talking but I could hardly hear what they were saying. I was thinking of Jilly. We'd brushed by her to reach the ghost, but she'd been right behind us. Yet when I looked back, there was no one there. I remembered that sound of my name, calling faintly across some great distance. I listened now, but heard only a vague unrecognizable sound. It took me long moments to realize that it was a dog barking.

I turned to Sam, tried to concentrate on what she was saying to the ghost. She was starting to pull away from him, but now it was his hand that held her arm. As I reached forward to pull her loose, the barking suddenly grew in volume—not one dog's voice, but those of hundreds, echoing across the years that separated us from our own time. Each year caught and sent on its own dog's voice, the sound building into a cacophonous chorus of yelps and barks and howls.

The ghost gave Sam's arm a sharp tug and I lost my grip on her, stumbling as the vertigo hit me again. I fell through the sound of all those barking dogs, through the blurring years, until I dropped to my knees on the wet cobblestones, my hands reaching for Sam. But Sam wasn't there.

"Geordie?"

It was Jilly, kneeling by my side, hand on my shoulder. She took my chin and turned my face to hers, but I pulled free.

"Sam!" I cried.

A gust of wind drove rain into my face, blinding me, but not before I saw that the lane was truly empty except for Jilly and me. Jilly, who'd mimicked the barking of dogs to draw us back through time. But only I'd returned. Sam and the ghost were both gone.

"Oh, Geordie," Jilly murmured as she held me close. "I'm so sorry."

I don't know if the ghost was ever seen again, but I saw Sam one more time after that night. I was with Jilly in Moore's Antiques in Lower Crowsea, flipping through a stack of old sepia-toned photographs, when a group shot of a family on their front porch stopped me cold. There, amongst the somber faces, was Sam. She looked different. Her hair was drawn back in a tight bun and she wore a plain unbecoming dark dress, but it was Sam all right. I turned the photograph over and read the photographer's date on the back. 1912.

Something of what I was feeling must have shown on my face, for Jilly came over from a basket of old earrings that she was looking through.

"What's the matter, Geordie, me lad?" she asked.

Then she saw the photograph in my hand. She had no trouble recognizing Sam either. I didn't have any money that day, but Jilly bought the picture and gave it to me. I keep it in my fiddle case.

I grow older each year, building up a lifetime of memories, only I've no Sam to share them with. But often when it rains, I go down to Stanton Street and stand under the streetlight in front of the old Hamill estate. One day I know she'll be waiting there for me.

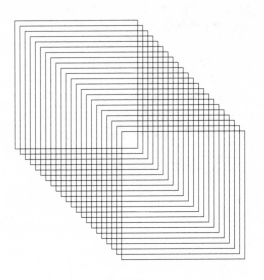

A SOUND OF THUNDER

BY RAY BRADBURY

The sign on the wall seemed to quaver under a film of sliding warm water. Eckels felt his eyelids blink over his stare, and the sign burned in this momentary darkness:

TIME SAFARI, INC.
SAFARIS TO ANY YEAR IN THE PAST.
YOU NAME THE ANIMAL.
WE TAKE YOU THERE.
YOU SHOOT IT.

A warm phlegm gathered in Eckels's throat; he swallowed and pushed it down. The muscles around his mouth formed a smile as he put his hand slowly out upon the air, and in that hand waved a check for ten thousand dollars to the man behind the desk.

"Does this safari guarantee I come back alive?"

"We guarantee nothing," said the official, "except the dinosaurs." He turned. "This is Mr. Travis, your Safari Guide in the Past. He'll tell you what and where to shoot. If he says no shooting, no shooting. If you disobey instructions, there's a stiff penalty of another ten thousand dollars, plus possible government action, on your return."

Eckels glanced across the vast office at a mass and tangle, a snaking and humming of wires and steel boxes, at an aurora that flickered now orange, now silver, now blue. There was a sound like a gigantic bonfire burning all of Time, all the years and all the parchment calendars, all the hours piled high and set aflame.

A touch of the hand and this burning would, on the instant, beautifully reverse itself. Eckels remembered the wording in the advertisements to the letter. Out of chars and ashes, out of dust and coals, like golden salamanders, the old years, the green years, might leap; roses sweeten the air, white hair turn Irish-black, wrinkles vanish; all, everything fly back to seed, flee death, rush down to their beginnings, suns rise in western skies and set in glorious easts, moons eat themselves opposite to the custom, all and everything cupping one in another like Chinese boxes, rabbits into hats, all and everything returning to the fresh death, the seed death, the green death, to the rime before the beginning. A touch of a hand might do it, the merest touch of a hand.

"Hell and damn," Eckels breathed, the light of the Machine on his thin face. "A real Time Machine." He shook his head. "Makes you think. If the election had gone badly yesterday, I might be here now running away from the results. Thank God Keith won. He'll make a fine president of the United States."

"Yes," said the man behind the desk. "We're lucky. If Deutscher had gotten in, we'd have the worst kind of dictatorship. There's an anti-everything man for you, a militarist, anti-Christ, anti-human, anti-intellectual. People called us up, you know, joking but not joking. Said if Deutscher became President they wanted to go live in 1492. Of course it's not our business to conduct Escapes, but to form Safaris. Anyway, Keith's President now. All you got to worry about is—"

"Shooting my dinosaur," Eckels finished it for him.

"A *Tyrannosaurus rex*. The Thunder Lizard, the damnedest monster in history. Sign this release. Anything happens to you, we're not responsible. Those dinosaurs are hungry."

Eckels flushed angrily. "Trying to scare me!"

"Frankly, yes. We don't want anyone going who'll panic at the first shot. Six Safari leaders were killed last year, and a dozen hunters. We're here to give you the damnedest thrill a *real* hunter ever asked for. Traveling you back sixty million years to bag the biggest damned game in all Time. Your personal check's still there. Tear it up."

Mr. Eckels looked at the check for a long time. His fingers twitched.

"Good luck," said the man behind the desk. "Mr. Travis, he's all yours."

They moved silently across the room, taking their guns with them, toward the Machine, toward the silver metal and the roaring light.

First a day and then a night and then a day and then a night, then it was day-night-day-night-day. A week, a month, a year, a decade! A.D. 2055. A.D. 2019. 1999! 1957! Gone! The Machine roared.

They put on their oxygen helmets and tested the intercoms.

Eckels swayed on the padded seat, his face pale, his jaw stiff. He felt the trembling in his arms and he looked down and found his hands tight on the new rifle. There were four other men in the Machine. Travis, the Safari Leader, his assistant, Lesperance, and two other hunters, Billings and Kramer. They sat looking at each other, and the years blazed around them.

"Can these guns get a dinosaur cold?" Eckels felt his mouth saying.

"If you hit them right," said Travis on the helmet radio. "Some dinosaurs have two brains, one in the head, another far down the spinal column. We stay away from those. That's stretching luck. Put your first two shots into the eyes, if you can, blind them, and go back into the brain."

The Machine howled. Time was a film run backward. Suns fled and ten million moons fled after them. "Good God," said Eckels. "Every hunter that ever lived would envy us to-day. This makes Africa seem like Illinois."

The Machine slowed; its scream fell to a murmur. The Machine stopped.

The sun stopped in the sky.

The fog that had enveloped the Machine blew away and they were in an old time, a very old time indeed, three hunters and two Safari Heads with their blue metal guns across their knees.

"Christ isn't born yet," said Travis. "Moses has not gone to the mountain to talk with God. The Pyramids are still in the earth, waiting to be cut out and put up. *Remember* that. Alexander, Caesar, Napoleon, Hitler—none of them exists."

The men nodded.

"That,"—Mr. Travis pointed—"is the jungle of sixty million two thousand and fifty-five years before President Keith."

He indicated a metal path that struck off into green wilderness, over swamp, among giant ferns and palms.

"And that," he said, "is the Path, laid by Time Safari for your use. It floats six inches above the earth. Doesn't touch so much as one grass blade, flower, or tree. It's an anti-gravity metal. Its purpose is to keep you from touching this world of the past in any way. Stay on the Path. Don't go off it. I repeat. *Don't go off.* For *any* reason! If you fall off, there's a penalty. And don't shoot any animal we don't okay."

"Why?" asked Eckels.

They sat in the ancient wilderness. Far birds' cries blew on a wind, and the smell of tar and an old salt sea, moist grasses, and flowers the color of blood.

"We don't want to change the Future. We don't belong here in the Past. The government doesn't *like* us here. We have to pay big graft to keep our franchise. A Time Machine is damn finicky business. Not knowing it, we might kill an important animal, a small bird, a roach, a flower even, thus destroying an important link in a growing species."

"That's not clear." said Eckels.

"All right," Travis continued, "say we accidentally kill one mouse here. That means all the future families of this one particular mouse are destroyed, right?"

"Right."

"And all the families of the families of the families of that one mouse! With a stamp of your foot, you annihilate first one, then a dozen, then a thousand, a million, a *billion* possible mice!"

"So they're dead," said Eckels. "So what?"

"So what?" Travis snorted quietly. "Well, what about the foxes that'll need those mice to survive! For want of ten mice, a fox dies. For want of ten foxes, a lion starves. For want of a lion, all manner of insects, vultures, infinite billions of life forms are thrown into chaos and destruction. Eventually it all boils down to this: fifty-nine million years later, a cave man, one of a dozen on the *entire world*, goes hunting wild boar or sabre-tooth tiger for food. But you, friend, have *stepped* on all the tigers in that region. By stepping on *one* single mouse. So the cave man starves. And the cave man, please note, is not just *any* expendable man, no! He is an *entire future nation*. From his loins would have sprung ten sons. From *their* loins one hundred sons, and thus onward to a civilization. Destroy this one man, and you destroy a race, a people, an entire history of life. It is comparable to slaying some of Adam's grandchildren. The stomp of your foot, on one mouse, could start an earthquake, the effects of which could shake our earth and destinies down through Time, to their very foundations. With the death of that one cave man, a billion others yet unborn are throttled in the womb. Perhaps Rome never rises on its seven hills.

Perhaps Europe is forever a dark forest, and only Asia waxes healthy and teeming. Step on a mouse and you crush the Pyramids. Step on a mouse and you leave your print, like a Grand Canyon, across Eternity. Queen Elizabeth might never be born, Washington might not cross the Delaware, there might never be a United States at all. So be careful. Stay on the Path. *Never* step off!"

"I see," said Eckels. "Then it wouldn't pay for us to even touch the *grass?*"

"Correct. Crushing certain plants could add up infinitesimally. A little error here would multiply in sixty million years, all out of proportion. Of course maybe our theory is wrong. Maybe Time *can't* be changed by us. Or maybe it can be changed only in little subtle ways. A dead mouse here makes an insect imbalance there, a population disproportion later, a bad harvest further on, a depression, mass starvation, and, finally, a change in *social* temperament in far-flung countries. Something much more subtle, like that. Perhaps only a soft breath, a whisper, a hair, pollen on the air, such a slight, slight change that unless you looked close you wouldn't see it. Who knows? Who really can say he knows? We don't know. We're guessing. But until we do know for certain whether our messing around in Time *can* make a big roar or a little rustle in history, we're being damned careful. This Machine, this Path, your clothing and bodies, were sterilized, as you know, before the journey. We wear these oxygen helmets so we can't introduce our bacteria into an ancient atmosphere."

"How do we know which animals to shoot?"

"They're marked with red paint," said Travis. "Today, before our journey, we sent Lesperance here back with the Machine. He came to this particular era and followed certain animals."

"Studying them?"

"Right," said Lesperance. "I track them through their entire existence, noting which of them lives longest. Very few. How many times they mate. Not often. Life's short. When I find one that's going to die when a tree falls on him, or one that drowns in a tar pit, I note the exact hour, minute, and second. I shoot a paint bomb. It leaves a red patch on his side. We can't miss it. Then I correlate our arrival in the Past so that we meet the Monster not more than two minutes before he would have died anyway. This way, we kill only animals with no future, that are never going to mate again. You see how *careful* we are!"

"But if you came back this morning in Time," said Eckels eagerly, "you must've bumped into *us*, our Safari! How did it turn out? Was it successful? Did all of us get through—alive?"

Travis and Lesperance gave each other a look.

"That'd be a paradox," said the latter. "Time doesn't permit that sort of mess—a man meeting himself. When such occasions threaten, Time steps aside. Like an airplane hitting an air pocket. You felt the Machine jump just before we stopped? That was us passing ourselves on the way back to the Future. We saw nothing. There's no way of telling *if* this expedition was a success, *if we* got our monster, or whether all of us—meaning *you*, Mr. Eckels—got out alive."

Eckels smiled palely.

"Cut that," said Travis sharply. "Everyone on his feet!"

They were ready to leave the Machine.

The jungle was high and the jungle was broad and the jungle was the entire world forever and forever. Sounds like music and sounds like flying tents filled the sky, and those were pterodactyls soaring with cavernous gray wings, gigantic bats out of delirium and a night fever. Eckels, balanced on the narrow Path, aimed his riffle playfully.

"Stop that!" said Travis. "Don't even aim for fun, damn it! If your guns should go off—"

Eckels flushed. "Where's our *Tyrannosaurus?*"

Lesperance checked his wrist watch. "Up ahead. We'll bisect his trail in sixty seconds. Look for the red paint, for Christ's sake. Don't shoot till we give the word. Stay on the Path. *Stay on the Path!*"

They moved forward in the wind of morning.

"Strange," murmured Eckels. "Up ahead, sixty million years, Election Day over. Keith made President. Everyone celebrating. And here we are, a million years lost, and they don't exist. The things we worried about for months, a lifetime, not even born or thought about yet."

"Safety catches off, everyone!" ordered Travis. "You, first shot, Eckels. Second, Billings. Third, Kramer."

"I've hunted tiger, wild boar, buffalo, elephant, but Jesus, this is it," said Eckels. "I'm shaking like a kid."

"Ah," said Travis.

Everyone stopped.

Travis raised his hand. "Ahead," he whispered. "In the mist. There he is. There's His Royal Majesty now."

The jungle was wide and full of twitterings, rustlings, murmurs, and sighs.

Suddenly it all ceased, as if someone had shut a door.

Silence.

A sound of thunder.

Out of the mist, one hundred yards away, came Tyrannosaurus rex.

"Jesus God," whispered Eckels.

"Sh!"

It came on great oiled, resilient, striding legs. It towered thirty feet above half of the trees, a great evil god, folding its delicate watchmaker's claws close to its oily reptilian chest. Each lower leg was a piston, a thousand pounds of white bone, sunk in thick ropes of muscle, sheathed over in a gleam of pebbled skin like the mail of a terrible warrior. Each thigh was a ton of meat, ivory, and steel mesh. And from the great breathing cage of the upper body those two delicate arms dangled out front, arms with hands which might pick up and examine men like toys, while the snake neck coiled. And the head itself, a ton of sculptured stone, lifted easily upon the sky. Its mouth gaped, exposing a fence of teeth like daggers. Its eyes rolled, ostrich eggs, empty of all expression save hunger. It closed its mouth in a death grin. It ran, its pelvic bones crushing aside trees and bushes, its taloned feet clawing damp earth, leaving prints six inches deep wherever it settled its weight. It ran with a gliding ballet step, far too poised and balanced for its ten tons. It moved into a sunlit arena warily, its beautifully reptile hands feeling the air.

"My God!" Eckels twitched his mouth. "It could reach up and grab the moon."

"Sh!" Travis jerked angrily. "He hasn't seen us yet."

"It can't be killed." Eckels pronounced this verdict quietly, as if there could be no argument. He had weighed the evidence and this was his considered opinion. The rifle in his hands seemed a cap gun. "We were fools to come. This is impossible."

"Shut up!" hissed Travis.

"Nightmare."

"Turn around," commanded Travis. "Walk quietly to the Machine. We'll remit one half your fee."

"I didn't realize it would be this *big*," said Eckels. "I miscalculated, that's all. And now I want out."

"It *sees* us!"

"There's the red paint on its chest!"

The Thunder Lizard raised itself. Its armored flesh glittered like a thousand green coins. The coins, crusted with slime, steamed. In the slime, tiny insects wriggled, so that the entire body seemed to twitch and undulate, even while the monster itself did not move. It exhaled. The stink of raw flesh blew down the wilderness.

"Get me out of here," said Eckels. "It was never like this before. I was always sure I'd come through alive. I had good guides, good safaris, and safety. This time, I figured wrong. I've met my match and admit it. This is too much for me to get hold of."

"Don't run," said Lesperance. "Turn around. Hide in the Machine."

"Yes." Eckels seemed to be numb. He looked at his feet as if trying to make them move. He gave a grunt of helplessness.

"Eckels!"

He took a few steps, blinking, shuffling.

"Not *that* way!"

The Monster, at the first motion, lunged forward with a terrible scream. It covered one hundred yards in four seconds. The rifles jerked up and blazed fire. A windstorm from the beast's mouth engulfed them in the stench of slime and old blood. The Monster roared, teeth glittering with sun.

Eckels, not looking back, walked blindly to the edge of the Path, his gun limp in his arms, stepped off the Path, and walked, not knowing it, in the jungle. His feet sank into green moss. His legs moved him, and he felt alone and remote from the events behind.

The rifles cracked again. Their sound was lost in shriek and lizard thunder. The great lever of the reptile's tail swung up, lashed sideways. Trees exploded in clouds of leaf and branch. The Monster twitched its jeweller's hands down to fondle at the men, to twist them in half, to crush them like berries, to cram them into its teeth and its screaming throat. Its boulder-stone eyes leveled with the men. They saw themselves mirrored. They fired at the metallic eyelids and the blazing black iris.

Like a stone idol, like a mountain avalanche, *Tyrannosaurus* fell. Thundering, it clutched trees, pulled them with it. It wrenched and tore the metal Path. The men flung themselves back and away. The body hit, ten tons of cold flesh and stone. The guns fired. The Monster lashed its armored tail, twitched its snake jaws, and lay still. A fount of blood spurted from its throat. Somewhere inside, a sac of fluids burst. Sickening gushes drenched the hunters. They stood, red and glistening.

The thunder faded.

The jungle was silent. After the avalanche, a green peace. After the nightmare, morning.

Billings and Kramer sat on the pathway and threw up. Travis and Lesperance stood with smoking rifles, cursing steadily.

In the Time Machine, on his face, Eckels lay shivering. He had found his way back to the Path, climbed into the Machine.

Travis came walking, glanced at Eckels, took cotton gauze from a metal box, and returned to the others, who were sitting on the Path.

"Clean up."

They wiped the blood from their helmets. They began to curse too. The Monster lay, a hill of solid flesh. Within, you could hear the sighs and murmurs as the furthest chambers of it died, the organs malfunctioning, liquids running a final instant from pocket to sac to spleen, everything shutting off, closing up forever. It was like standing by a wrecked locomotive or a steam shovel at quitting time, all valves being released or levered tight. Bones cracked; the tonnage of its own flesh, off balance, dead weight, snapped the delicate forearms, caught underneath. The meat settled, quivering.

Another cracking sound. Overhead, a gigantic tree branch broke from its heavy mooring, fell. It crashed upon the dead beast with finality.

"There." Lesperance checked his watch. "Right on time. That's the giant tree that was scheduled to fall and kill this animal originally." He glance at the two hunters. "You want the trophy picture?"

"What?"

"We can't take a trophy back to the Future. The body has to stay right here where it would have died originally, so the insects, birds, and bacteria can get at it, as they were intended to. Everything in balance. The body stays. But we *can* take a picture of you standing near it."

The two men tried to think, but gave up, shaking their heads.

They let themselves be led along the metal Path. They sank wearily into the Machine cushions. They gazed back at the ruined Monster, the stagnating mound, where already strange reptilian birds and golden insects were busy at the steaming armor.

A sound on the floor of the Time Machine stiffened them. Eckels sat there, shivering.

"I'm sorry," he said at last.

"Get up!" cried Travis.

Eckels got up.

"Go out on that Path alone," said Travis. He had his rifle pointed. "You're not coming back in the Machine. We're leaving you here!"

Lesperance seized Travis's arm. "Wait—"

"Stay out of this!" Travis shook his hand away. "This son of a bitch nearly killed us. But it isn't *that* so much. Hell, no. It's his *shoes!* Look at them! He ran off the Path. My God, that *ruins* us! Christ knows how much we'll forfeit! Tens of thousands of dollars of insurance! We guarantee no one leaves the Path. He left it. Oh, the damn fool! I'll have to report to the government. They might revoke our license to travel. God knows *what* he's done to Time, to History!"

"Take it easy, all he did was kick up some dirt."

"How do we *know?*" cried Travis. "We don't know anything! It's all a damn mystery! Get out here, Eckels!"

Eckels fumbled his shirt. "I'll pay anything. A hundred thousand dollars!"

Travis glared at Eckels's cheque book and spat. "Go out there. The Monster's next to the Path. Stick your arms up to your elbows in his mouth. Then you can come back with us."

"That's unreasonable!"

"The Monster's dead, you yellow bastard. The bullets! The bullets can't be left behind. They don't belong in the Past; they might change something. Here's my knife. Dig them out!"

The jungle was alive again, full of the old tremorings and bird cries. Eckels turned slowly to regard that primeval garbage dump, that hill of nightmares and terror. After a long time, like a sleepwalker, he shuffled out along the Path.

He returned, shuddering, five minutes later, his arms soaked and red to the elbows. He held out his hands. Each held a number of steel bullets. Then he fell. He lay where he fell, not moving.

"You didn't have to make him do that," said Lesperance.

"Didn't I? It's too early to tell." Travis nudged the still body. "He'll live. Next time he won't go hunting game like this. Okay." He jerked his thumb wearily at Lesperance. "Switch on. Let's go home."

1492. 1776. 1812.

They cleaned their hands and faces. They changed their caking shirts and pants. Eckels was up and around again, not speaking. Travis glared at him for a full ten minutes.

"Don't look at me," cried Eckels. "I haven't done anything."

"Who can tell?"

"Just ran off the Path, that's all, a little mud on my shoes—what do you want me to do—get down and pray?"

"We might need it. I'm warning you, Eckels, I might kill you yet. I've got my gun ready."

"I'm innocent. I've done nothing!"

1999. 2000. 2055.

The Machine stopped.

"Get out," said Travis.

The room was there as they had left it. But not the same as they had left it. The same man sat behind the same desk. But the same man did not quite sit behind the same desk.

Travis looked around swiftly. "Everything okay here?" he snapped.

"Fine. Welcome home!"

Travis did not relax. He seemed to be looking at the very atoms of the air itself, at the way the sun poured through the one high window.

"Okay, Eckels, get out. Don't ever come back."

Eckels could not move.

"You heard me," Travis said. "What are you *staring* at?"

Eckels stood smelling of the air, and there was a thing to the air, a chemical taint so subtle, so slight, that only a faint cry of his sublimal senses warned him it was there. The colors, white, gray, blue, orange, in the wall, in the furniture, in the sky beyond the window, were...were... And there was a *feel*. His flesh twitched. His hands twitched. He stood drinking the oddness with the pores of his body. Somewhere, someone must have been screaming one of those whistles that only a dog can hear. His body screamed silence in return. Beyond this room, beyond this wall, beyond this man who was not quite the same man seated at this desk that was not quite the same desk...lay an entire world of streets and people. What sort of world it was now, there was no telling. He could feel them moving there, beyond the walls, almost, like so many chess pieces blown in a dry wind....

But the immediate thing was the sign painted on the office wall, the same sign he had read earlier today on first entering.

Somehow, the sign had changed:

> TYME SEFARI INC.
> SEFARIS TU ANY YEER EN THE PAST.
> YU NAIM THE ANIMALL.
> WEE TAEK YU THAIR.
> YU SHOOT ITT.

Eckels felt himself fall into a chair. He fumbled crazily at the thick slime on his boots. He held up a clod of dirt, trembling. "No, it *can't* be. Not a *little* thing like that. No!"

Embedded in the mud, glistening green and gold and black, was a butterfly, very beautiful, and very dead.

"Not a little thing like *that*! Not a butterfly!" cried Eckels.

It fell to the floor, an exquisite thing, a small thing that could upset balances and knock down a line of small dominoes and then big dominoes and then gigantic dominoes, all down the years across Time. Eckels's mind whirled. It *couldn't* change things. Killing one butterfly couldn't be *that* important! Could it?

His face was cold. His mouth trembled, asking: "Who-who won the presidential election yesterday!"

The man behind the desk laughed. "You joking? You know damn well. Deutscher, of course! Who else? Not that damn weakling Keith. We got an iron man now, a man with guts, by God!" The official stopped. "What's wrong?"

Eckels moaned. He dropped to his knees. He scrabbled at the golden butterfly with shaking fingers. "Can't we," he pleaded to the world, to himself, to the officials, to the Machine, "can't we take it *back*, can't we *make* it alive again? Can't we start over? Can't we—"

He did not move. Eyes shut, he waited, shivering. He heard Travis breathe loud in the room; he heard Travis shift his rifle, click the safety catch, and raise the weapon.

There was a sound of thunder.

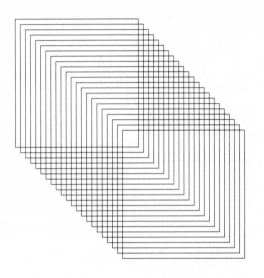

WHAT WE LEARNED FROM THIS MORNING'S NEWSPAPER

BY ROBERT SILVERBERG

1

I got home from the office as usual at 6:47 this evening and discovered that our peaceful street has been in some sort of crazy uproar all day. The newsboy it seems came by today and delivered the New York *Times* for Wednesday December 1 to every house on Redbud Crescent. Since today is Monday November 22 it follows therefore that Wednesday December 1 is the middle of next week. I said to my wife are you sure that this really happened? Because I looked at the newspaper myself before I went off to work this morning and it seemed quite all right to me.

At breakfast time the newspaper could be printed in Albanian and it would seem quite all right to you my wife replied. Here look at this. And she took the newspaper from the hall closet and handed it all folded up to me. It looked just like any other edition of the New York *Times* but now I saw what I had failed to notice at breakfast time, that it said Wednesday December 1.

Is today the 22nd of November I asked? Monday?

It certainly is my wife told me. Yesterday was Sunday and tomorrow is going to be Tuesday and we haven't even come to Thanksgiving yet. Bill what are we going to do about this?

I glanced through the newspaper. The front page headlines were nothing remarkable I must admit, just the same old New York *Times* stuff that you get any day when there hasn't been some event of cosmic importance. NIXON, WITH WIFE, TO VISIT 3 CHINESE CITIES IN 7 DAYS. Yes. 10 HURT AS GUNMEN SHOOT WAY INTO AND OUT OF BANK. All right. GROUP OF 10, IN ROME, BEGINS NEGOTIATING REALIGNMENT OF CURRENCIES. Okay. The same old New York *Times* stuff and no surprises. But the paper was dated Wednesday December 1 and that was a surprise of sorts I guess.

This is only a joke I told my wife.

Who would do such a thing for a joke? To print up a whole newspaper? It's impossible Bill.

It's also impossible to get next week's newspaper delivered this week you know or hadn't you considered what I said?

She shrugged and I picked up the second section. I opened to page 50 which contained the obituary section and I admit I felt quite queasy for a moment since after all this might not be any joke and what would it be like to find my own name there? To my relief the people whose obituaries I saw were Harry Rogoff, Terry Turner, Dr M. A. Feinstein and John Millis. I will not say that the deaths of these people gave me any pleasure but better them than me of course. I even looked at the death notices in smaller type but there was no listing for me. Next I turned to the sports section and saw KNICKS' STREAK ENDED, 110-109. We had been talking about going to get tickets for that game at the office and my first thought now was that it isn't worth bothering to see it. Then I remembered you can bet on basketball games and I knew who was going to win and that made me feel very strange. So also I felt odd to look at the bottom of page 64 where they had the results of the racing at Yonkers Raceway and then quickly flip flip flip I was on page 69 and the financial section lay before my eyes. DOW INDEX RISES BY 1-61 to 831-34 the headline said. National Cash Register was the most active stock closing at 27 3/8 off 1/4. Then Eastman Kodak 88 7/8 down 1 1/8. By this time I was starting to sweat very hard and I gave my wife the paper and took off my jacket and tie.

I said how many people have this newspaper?

Everybody on Redbud Crescent she said that's eleven houses altogether.

And nowhere beyond our street?

No the others got the ordinary paper today we've been checking on that.

Who's we I asked?

Marie and Cindy and I she said. Cindy was the one who noticed about the paper first and called me and then we all got together and talked about it. Bill what are we going to do? We have the stock market prices and everything Bill.

If it isn't a joke I told her.

It looks like the real paper doesn't it Bill?

I think I want a drink I said. My hands were shaking all of a sudden and the sweat was still coming. I had to laugh because it was just the other Saturday night some of us were talking about the utter predictable regularity of life out here in the suburbs the dull smooth sameness of it all. And now this. The newspaper from the middle of next week. It's like God was listening to us and laughed up His sleeve and said to Gabriel or whoever it's time to send those stuffed shirts on Redbud Crescent a little excitement.

2

After dinner Jerry Wesley called and said we're having a meeting at our place tonight Bill can you and your lady come ?

I asked him what the meeting was about and he said it's about the newspaper.

Oh yes I said. The newspaper. What about the newspaper?

Come to the meeting he said I really don't want to talk about this on the phone.

Of course we'll have to arrange a sitter Jerry.

No you won't we've already arranged it he told me. The three Fischer girls are going to look after all the kids on the block. So just come over around quarter to nine.

Jerry is an insurance broker very successful at that he has the best house on the Crescent, two-story Tudor style with almost an acre of land and a big paneled rumpus room in the basement. That's where the meeting took place. We were the seventh couple to arrive and soon after us the Maxwells the Bruces and the Thomasons came in. Folding chairs were set out and Cindy Wesley had done her usual great trays of canapes and such and there was a lot of liquor, self-service at the bar. Jerry stood up in front of everybody and grinned and said I guess you've all been wondering why I called you together this evening. He held up his copy of the newspaper. From where I was sitting I could make out only one headline clearly it was 10

HURT AS GUNMEN SHOOT WAY INTO AND OUT OF BANK
but that was enough to enable me to recognize it as the newspaper.

Jerry said did all of you get a copy of this paper today?

Everybody nodded.

You know Jerry said that this paper gives us some extraordinary opportunities to improve our situation in life. I mean if we can accept it as the real December 1 edition and not some kind of fantastic hoax then I don't need to tell you what sort of benefits we can get from it, right ?

Sure Bob Thomason said but what makes anybody think it isn't a hoax? I mean next week's newspaper who could believe that?

Jerry looked at Mike Nesbit. Mike teaches at Columbia Law and is more of an intellectual than most of us.

Mike said well of course the obvious conclusion is that somebody's playing a joke on us. But have you looked at the newspaper closely? Every one of those stories has been written in a perfectly legitimate way. There aren't any details that ring false. It isn't like one of those papers where the headlines have been cooked up but the body of the text is an old edition. So we have to consider the probabilities. Which sounds more fantastic? That someone would take the trouble of composing an entire fictional edition of the *Times* setting it in type printing it and having it delivered or that through some sort of fluke of the fourth dimension we've been allowed a peek at next week's newspaper? Personally I don't find either notion easy to believe but I can accept fourth-dimensional hocus-pocus more readily than I can the idea of a hoax. For one thing unless you've had a team the size of the *Times'* own staff working on this newspaper it would take months and months to prepare it and there's no way that anybody could have begun work on the paper more than a few days in advance because there are things in it that nobody could have possibly known as recently as a week ago. Like the Phase Two stuff and the fighting between India and Pakistan.

But how could we get next week's newspaper Bob Thomason still wanted to know?

I can't answer that said Mike Nesbit. I can only reply that I am willing to accept it as genuine. A miracle if you like.

So am I, said Tim McDermott and a few others said the same.

We can make a pile of money out of this thing said Dave Bruce.

Everybody began to smile in a strange strained way. Obviously everybody had looked at the stock market stuff and the racetrack stuff and had come to the same conclusions.

Jerry said there's one important thing we ought to find out first. Has anybody here spoken about this newspaper to anybody who isn't currently in this room?

People said nope and uh-uh and not me.

Good said Jerry. I propose we keep it that way. We don't notify the *Times* and we don't tell Walter Cronkite and we don't even let our brother-in-law on Dogwood Lane know, right? We just put our newspapers away in a safe place and quietly do whatever we want to do about the information we've got. Okay? Let's put that to a vote. All in favor of stamping this newspaper top secret raise your right hand.

Twenty-two hands went up.

Good said Jerry. That includes the kids you realize. If you let the kids know anything they'll want to bring the paper to school for show and tell for Christ's sake. So cool it you hear?

Sid Fischer said are we going to work together on exploiting this thing or do we each act independently?

Independently said Dave Bruce.

Right independently said Bud Maxwell.

It went all around the room that way. The only one who wanted some sort of committee system was Charlie Harris. Charlie has bad luck in the stock market and I guess he was afraid to take any risks even with a sure thing like next week's paper. Jerry called for a vote and it came out ten to one in favor of individual enterprise. Of course if anybody wants to team up with anybody else I said there's nothing stopping anybody.

As we started to adjourn for refreshments Jerry said remember you only have a week to make use of what you've been handed. By the first of December this is going to be just another newspaper and a million other people will have copies of it. So move fast while you've got an advantage.

The trouble is when they give you only next week's paper you don't ordinarily have a chance to make a big killing in the market. I mean stocks don't generally go up 50% or 80% in just a few trading sessions. The really broad swings take weeks or months to develop. Still and all I figured I could make out all right with the data I had. For one thing there evidently was going to be a pretty healthy rally over the next few days. According to the afternoon edition of the *Post* that I brought home with me the market had been off seven on the 22nd, closing with the Dow at 803.15, the lowest all year. But the December 1 *Times* mentioned a stunning two-day advance and the average finished at 831-34 on the 30th. Not bad. Then too I could work on margin and other kinds of leverage to boost my return. We're going to make a pile out of this I told my wife.

If you can trust that newspaper she said.

I told her not to worry. When we got home from Jerry's I spread out the *Post* and the *Times* in the den and started hunting for stocks that moved up at least 10% between Nov. 22 and Nov. 30. This is the chart I made up:

Stock Nov 22 close Nov 30 high

Levitz Furniture 89 1/2103 3/4
Bausch & Lomb 133 3/8 149
Natomas ' 45 1/457
Disney 99 7/8116 3/4
EG&G19 1/423 3/4

Spread your risk Bill I told myself. Don't put all your eggs in one basket. Even if the newspaper was phony I couldn't get hurt too badly if I bought all five. So at 9:30 the next morning I phoned my broker and told him I wanted to do some buying in the margin account at the opening. He said don't be in a hurry Bill the market's in lousy shape. Look at yesterday there were 201 new lows this market's going to be under 750 by Christmas. You can see from this that he's an unusual kind of brother since most of them will never try to discourage you from placing an order that'll bring them a commission. But I said no I'm playing a hunch I want to go all out on this and I put in buys on Levitz Bausch Natomas Disney and EG&G. I used the margin right up to the hilt and then some. Okay I told myself if this works out the way you hope it will you've just bought yourself a vacation in Europe and a new Chrysler and a mink for the wife and a lot of other goodies. And if not ? If not you just lost yourself a hell of a lot of money Billy boy.

Also I made some use out of the sports pages.

At the office I looked around for bets on the Knicks vs. the SuperSonics next Tuesday at the Garden. A couple of guys wondered why I was interested in action so far ahead but I didn't bother to answer and finally I got Eddie Martin to take the Knicks by 11 points. Also I got Marty Felks to take Milwaukee by 8 over the Warriors that same night. Felks thinks Abdul-Jabbar is the best center the game ever had and he'll always bet the Bucks but my paper had it that the Warriors would cop it, 10-103. At lunch with the boys from Leclair & Anderson I put down $250 with Butch Hunter on St Louis over the Giants on Sunday. Next I stopped off at the friendly neighborhood Off Track Betting office and entered a few wagers on the races at Aqueduct. My handy guide to the future told me that the Double paid $54-20 and the third Exacta paid $62-20, so I spread a little cash on each. Too bad there were no $2500 payoffs that way but you can't be picky about your miracles can you?

5

Tuesday night when I got home I had a drink and asked my wife what's new and she said everybody on the block had been talking about the newspaper all day and some of the girls had been placing bets and phoning their brokers. A lot of the women here play the market and even the horses though my wife is not like that, she leaves the male stuff strictly to me.

What stocks were they buying I asked?

Well she didn't know the names. But a little while later Joni Bruce called up for a recipe and my wife asked her about the market and Joni said she had bought Winnebago Xerox and Transamerica. I was relieved at that because I figured it might look really suspicious if everybody on Redbud Crescent suddenly phoned in orders the same day for Levitz Bausch Disney Natomas and EG&G. On the other hand what was I worrying about nobody would draw any conclusions and if anybody did we could always say we had organized a neighborhood investment club. In any case I don't think there's any law against people making stock market decisions on the basis of a peek at next week's newspaper. Still and all who needs publicity and I was glad we were all buying different stocks.

I got the paper out after dinner to check out Joni's stocks. Sure enough Winnebago moved up from 33 1/8 to 38~ 1/8, Xerox from 105 3/4 to 111 7/8, and Transamerica from 14 7/8 to 17 5/8. I thought it was dumb of Joni to bother with Xerox getting only a 6% rise since it's the percentages where you pay off but Winnebago was up better than 10% and Transamerica close to 20%. I wished I had noticed Transamerica at least although no sense being greedy, my own choices would make out all right.

Something about the paper puzzled me. The print looked a little blurry in places and on some pages I could hardly read the words. I didn't remember any blurry pages. Also the paper it's printed on seemed a different colour, darker grey, older-looking. I compared it with the newspaper that came this morning and the December 1 issue was definitely darker. A paper shouldn't get old-looking that fast, not in two days.

I wonder if something's happening to the paper I said to my wife.

What do you mean?

Like it's deteriorating or anyway starting to change.

Anything can happen said my wife. It's like a dream you know and in dreams things change all the time without warning.

6

Wed. Nov. 24. I guess we just have to sweat this thing out so far the market in general isn't doing much one way or the other. This afternoon's *Post* gives the closing prices there was a rally in the morning but it all faded by the close and the Dow is down to 798.63. However my own five stocks all have had decent upward moves Tues. and Wed. so maybe I shouldn't worry. I have four points profit in Bausch already two in Natomas five in Levitz two in Disney three-quarters in EG&G and even though that's a long way from the quotations in the Dec. 1 newspaper it's better than having losses, also there's still that 'stunning two-day' advance due at the end of the month. Maybe I'm going to make out all right. Winnebago Transamerica and Xerox are also up a little bit. Market's closed tomorrow on account of Thanksgiving.

7

Thanksgiving Day. We went to the Nesbits in the afternoon. It used to be that people spent Thanksgiving with their own kin their aunts uncles grandparents cousins et cetera but you can't do that out here in a new suburb where everybody comes from someplace else far away so we eat the turkey with neighbors instead. The Nesbits invited the Fischers the Harrises the Thomasons and us with all the kids of course too. A big noisy gathering. The Fischers came very late so late that we were worried and thinking of sending someone over to find out what was the matter. It was practically time for the turkey when they showed up and Edith Fischer's eyes were red and puffy from crying.

My God my god she said I just found out my older sister is dead.

We started to ask the usual meaningless consoling questions like was she a sick woman and where did she live and what did she die of? And Edith sobbed and said I don't mean she's dead yet I mean she's going to die next Tuesday.

Next Tuesday Tammy Nesbit asked? What do-you mean I don't understand how you can know that now. And then she thought a moment and she did understand and so did all the rest of us. Oh Tammy said the newspaper.

The newspaper yes Edith said. Sobbing harder.

Edith was reading the death notices Sid Fischer explained God knows why she was bothering to look at them just curiosity I guess and all of a sudden she lets out this terrible cry and says she sees her sister's name. Sudden passing, a heart attack,

Her heart is weak Edith told us. She's had two or three bad attacks this year.

Lois Thomason went to Edith and put her arms around her the way Lois does so well and said there there Edith it's a terrible shock to you naturally but you know it must have been inevitable sooner or later and at least the poor woman isn't suffering any more.

But don't you see Edith cried she's still alive right now maybe if I phone and say go to the hospital right away they can save her? They might put her under intensive care and get ready for the attack before it even comes. Only I can't say that can I? Because what can I tell her? That I read about her death in next week's newspaper? She'll think I'm crazy and she'll laugh and she won't pay any attention to me. Or maybe she'll get very upset and drop dead right on the spot all on account of me. What can I do oh God what can I do?

You could say it was a premonition my wife suggested. A very vivid dream that had the ring of truth to you. If your sister puts any faith at all in things like that maybe she'll decide it can't hurt to see her doctor and then—

No Mike Nesbit broke in you mustn't do any such thing Edith. Because they can't save her. No way. They didn't save her when the time came.

The time hasn't come yet said Edith.

So far as we're concerned said Mike the time has already come because we have the newspapers that describe the events of Nov. 30 in the past tense. So we know your sister is going to die and to all intents and purposes is already dead. It's absolutely certain because it's in the newspaper and if we accept the newspaper as authentic then it's a record of actual events beyond any hope of changing.

But my sister Edith said.

Your sister's name is already on the roll of the dead. If you interfere now it'll only bring unnecessary aggravation to her family and it won't change a thing.

How do you know it won't Mike?

The future mustn't be changed Mike said. For us the events of that one day in the future are permanent as any event in the past. We don't dare play around with changing the future not when it's already signed sealed and delivered in that newspaper. For all we know the future's like a house of cards. If we pull one card out say your sister's life we might bring the whole house tumbling down. You've got to accept the decree of fate Edith. You've got to. Otherwise there's no telling what might happen.

My sister Edith said. My sister's going to die and you won't let me do anything to save her.

Edith carrying on like that put a damper on the whole Thanksgiving celebration. After a while she pulled herself together more or less but she couldn't help behaving like a woman in mourning and it was hard for us to be very jolly and thankful with her there choking back the sobs. The Fischers left right after dinner and we all hugged Edith and told her how sorry we were. Soon afterwards the Thomasons and the Harrises left too.

Mike looked at my wife and me and said I hope you aren't going to run off also.

No I said not yet there's no hurry is there?

We sat around some while longer. Mike talked about Edith and her sister. The sister can't be saved he kept saying. And it might be very dangerous for everybody if Edith tries to interfere with fate.

To get the subject away from Edith we started talking about the stock market. Mike said he had bought Natomas Transamerica and Electfbnic Data Systems which he said was due to rise from 36 3/4 on Nov 22nd to 47 by the 30th. I told him I had bought Natomas too and I told him my other stocks and pretty soon he had his copy of the December 1 paper out so we could check some of the quotations. Looking over his shoulder I observed that the print was even blurrier than it had seemed to me Tuesday night which was the last occasion I had examined my paper and also the pages seemed very grey and rough.

What do you think is going on I said? The paper definitely seems to be deteriorating.

It's entropic creep he said.

Entropic creep?

Entropy you know is the natural tendency of everything in the universe to come apart at the seams as time goes along. These newspapers must be subject to unusually strong entropic strain because of their anomalous position out of their proper place in time. I've been noticing how the print is getting harder to read and I wouldn't be surprised if it became completely illegible in another couple of days.

We hunted up the prices of my stocks in his paper and the first one we saw was Bausch & Lomb hitting a high of 149 3/4 on November 30.

Wait a second I said I'm sure the high is supposed to be 149 even.

Mike thought it might be an effect of the general blurriness but no it was still quite clear on that page of stock market quotations and it said 149 3/4. I looked up Natomas and the high that was listed was 56 7/8. I said I'm positive it's 57. And so on with several other stocks. The figures didn't jibe with what I remembered. We had a friendly little discussion about that and then it became not so friendly as Mike implied my memory was faulty and in the end I jogged down the street to my place and got my own copy of the paper. We spread them both out side by side and compared the quotes. Sure enough the two were different. Hardly any quote in his paper matched those in mine, all of them off an eighth here, a quarter there. What was even worse the figures didn't quite match the ones I had noted down on the first day. My paper now gave the Bausch high for November 30 as 149 1/2 and Natomas as 56 1/2 and Disney as 117. Levitz 104, EG&G 23 5/8. Everything seemed to be sliding around.

It's a bad case of entropic creep Mike said.

I wonder if the newspapers were ever identical to each other I said. We should have compared them on the first day. Now we'll never know whether we all had the same starting point.

Let's check out the other pages Bill.

We compared things. The front page headlines were all the same but there were little differences in the writing. The classified ads had a lot of rearrangements. Some of the death notices were different. All in all the papers were similar but not anything like identical.

How can this be happening I asked? How can on a printed page be different one day from another ?

How can a newspaper from the future get delivered in the first place Mike asked?

We phoned some of the others and asked about stock prices. Just trying to check something out we explained. Charlie Harris said Natomas was quoted at 56 and Jerry Wesley said it was 57 1/4 and Bob Thomason found that the whole stock market page was too blurry to read although he thought the Natomas quote was 57 1/2. And so on. Everybody's paper slightly different.

Entropic creep. It's hitting hard.

What can we trust? What's real?

Saturday afternoon Bob Thomason came over very agitated. He had his newspaper under his arm. He showed it to me and said look at this Bill how can it be? The pages were practically falling apart and they were completely blank. You could make out little dirty traces where there once had been words but that was all. The paper looked about a million years old.

I got mine out of the closet. It was in bad shape but not that bad. The print was faint and murky yet I could still make some things out clearly. Natomas 56 1/4. Levitz Furniture 103 1/2. Disney 117 1/4. New numbers all the time.

Meanwhile out in the real world the market has been rallying for a couple of days right on schedule and all my stocks are going up. I may go crazy but it looks at least like I'm not going to take a financial beating.

11

Monday night Nov. 29. One week since this whole thing started. Everybody's newspaper is falling apart. I can read patches of print on two or three pages of mine and the rest is pretty well shot. Dave Bruce says his paper is completely blank the way Bob's was on Saturday. Mike's is in better condition but it won't last long. They're all getting eaten up by entropy. The market rallied strongly again this afternoon. Yesterday the Giants got beaten by St. Louis and at lunch today I collected my winnings from Butch Hunter. Yesterday also Sid and Edith Fischer left suddenly for a vacation in Florida. That's where Edith's sister lives, the one who's supposed to die tomorrow.

12

I can't help wondering whether Edith did something about her sister after all despite the things Mike said to her Thanksgiving.

13

So now it's Tuesday night November 30 and I'm home with the *Post* and the closing stock prices. Unfortunately I can't compare them with the figures in my copy of tomorrow's *Times* because I don't have the paper any more it turned completely to dust and so did everybody else's but I still have the notes I took the first night when I was planning my market action. And I'm happy to say everything worked out perfectly despite the effects of entropic creep. The Dow Industrials closed at 831-34 today which is just what my record says. And look at this list of highs for the day where my broker sold me out on the nose:

Levitz Furniture103 3/4
Bausch & Lomb149
Natomas57
Disney116 3/4
EG&G23 3/4

So whatever this week has cost me in nervous aggravation it's more than made up in profits.

Tomorrow is December 1 finally and it's going to be funny to see that newspaper again. With the headlines about Nixon going to

China and the people wounded in the bank robbery and the currency negotiations in Rome. Like an old friend coming home.

14

I suppose everything has to balance out. This morning before breakfast I went outside as usual to get the paper and it was sitting there in the bushes but it wasn't the paper for Wednesday December 1 although this is in fact Wednesday December 1. What the newsboy gave me this morning was the paper for Monday November 22 which I never actually received the day of the first mix-up.

That in itself wouldn't be so bad. But this paper is full of stuff I don't remember from last Monday. As though somebody has reached into last week and switched everything around, making up a bunch of weird events. Even though I didn't get to see the *Times* that day I'm sure I would have heard about the assassination of the Governor of Missouri. And the earthquake in Peru that killed ten thousand people. And Mayor Lindsay resigning to become Nixon's new Secretary of State. Especially about Mayor Lindsay resigning to become Nixon's new Secretary of State. This paper *has* to be a joke.

But what about the one we got last week? How about those stock prices and the sports results?

When I get into the city this morning I'm going to stop off first thing at the New York Public Library and check the file copy of the November 22 Times. I want to see if the library's copy in anything like the one I just got.

What kind of newspaper am I going to get tomorrow?

15

Don't think I'm going to get to work at all today. Went out after breakfast to get the car and drive to the station and the car wasn't there nothing was there just grey everything grey no lawn no shrubs no trees none of the other houses in sight just grey like a thick fog swallowing everything up at ground level. Stood there on the front step afraid to go into that grey. Went back into the house woke up my wife told her. What does it mean Bill she asked what does it mean why is it all grey? I don't know I said. Let's turn on the radio. But there was no sound out of the radio nothing on the TV not even a test pattern the phone line dead too everything dead and I don't know what's happening or where we are I don't understand any of this except that this must be a very bad case of entropic creep. All of time must have looped back on itself in some crazy way and I don't know anything I don't understand a thing.

Edith what have you done to us?

I don't want to live here any more I want to cancel my newspaper subscription I want to sell my house I want to get away from here back into the real world but how how I don't know it's all grey grey everything grey nothing out there just a lot of grey.

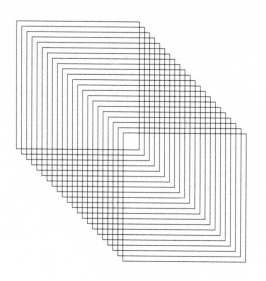

JEFFTY IS FIVE

FIVE

BY HARLAN ELLISON

When I was five years old, there was a little kid I played with: Jeffty. His real name was Jeff Kinzer, and everyone who played with him called him Jeffty. We were five years old together, and we had good times playing together.

When I was five, a Clark Bar was as fat around as the gripping end of a Louisville Slugger, and pretty nearly six inches long, and they used real chocolate to coat it, and it crunched very nicely when you bit into the center, and the paper it came wrapped in smelled fresh and good when you peeled off one end to hold the bar so it wouldn't melt onto your fingers. Today, a Clark Bar is as thin as a credit card, they use something artificial and awful-tasting instead of pure chocolate, the thing is soft and soggy, it costs fifteen or twenty cents instead of a decent, correct nickel, and they wrap it so you think it's the same size it was twenty years ago, only it isn't; it's slim and ugly and nasty tasting and not worth a penny, much less fifteen or twenty cents.

When I was that age, five years old, I was sent away to my Aunt Patricia's home in Buffalo, New York, for two years. My father was going through "bad times" and Aunt Patricia was very beautiful, and had married a stockbroker. They took care of me for two years. When I was seven, I came back home and went to find Jeffty, so we could play together.

I was seven. Jeffty was still five. I didn't notice any difference. I didn't know: I was only seven.

When I was seven years old, I used to lie on my stomach in front of our Atwater-Kent radio and listen to swell stuff. I had tied the ground wire to the radiator, and I would lie there with my coloring books and my Crayolas (when there were only sixteen colors in the big box), and listen to the NBC Red network: Jack Benny on the *Jell-O Program*, *Amos 'n' Andy*, Edgar Bergen and Charlie McCarthy on the *Chase and Sanbom Program*, *One Man's Family*, *First Nighter*; the NBC Blue network: *Easy Aces*, the *Jergens Program* with Walter Winchell, *Information Please*, *Death Valley Days*; and best of all, the Mutual Network with *The Green Hornet*, *The Lone Ranger*, *The Shadow*, and *Quiet, Please*. Today, I turn on my car radio and go from one end of the dial to the other and all I get is 100 strings orchestras, banal housewives and insipid truckers discussing their kinky sex lives with arrogant talk show hosts, country and western drivel and rock music so loud it hurts my ears.

When I was ten, my grandfather died of old age and I was "a troublesome kid," and they sent me off to military school, so I could be "taken in hand."

I came back when I was fourteen. Jeffty was still five.

When I was fourteen years old, I used to go to the movies on Saturday afternoons and a matinee was ten cents and they used real butter on the popcorn and I could always be sure of seeing a western like Lash LaRue, or Wild Bill Elliott as Red Ryder with Bobby Blake as Little Beaver, or Roy Rogers, or Johnny Mack Brown; a scary picture like *House of Horrors* with Rondo Hatton as the Strangler, or *The Cat People*, or *The Mummy*, or *I Married a Witch* with Fredric March and Veronica Lake; plus an episode of a great serial like *The Shadow* with Victor Jory, or *Dick Tracy* or *Flash Gordon*; and three cartoons; a James Fitzpatrick TravelTalk; Movietone News; and a singalong and, if I stayed on till evening, Bingo or Keeno; and free dishes. Today, I go to movies and see Clint Eastwood blowing people's heads apart like ripe cantaloupes.

At eighteen, I went to college. Jeffty was still five. I came back during the summers, to work at my Uncle Joe's jewelry store. Jeffty hadn't changed. Now I knew there was something different about him, something wrong, something weird. Jeffty was still five years old, not a day older.

At twenty-two, I came home for keeps. To open a Sony television franchise in town, the first one. I saw Jeffty from time to time. He was five.

Things are better in a lot of ways. People don't die from some of the old diseases any more. Cars go faster and get you there more quickly on better roads. Shirts are softer and silkier. We have paperback books even though they cost as much as a good hardcover used to. When I'm running short in the bank I can live off credit cards till things even out. But I still think we've lost a lot of good stuff. Did you know you can't buy linoleum any more, only vinyl floor covering? There's no such thing as oilcloth any more; you'll never again smell that special, sweet smell from your grandmother's kitchen. Furniture isn't made to last thirty years or longer because they took a survey and found that young homemakers like to throw their furniture out and bring in all new, color-coded, borax every seven years. Records don't feel right; they're not thick and solid like the old ones, they're thin and you can bend them...that doesn't seem right to me. Restaurants don't serve cream in pitchers any more, just that artificial glop in little plastic tubs, and one is never enough to get coffee the right color. You can make a dent in a car fender with only a sneaker. Everywhere you go, all the towns look the same with Burger Kings and McDonald's and 7-Elevens and Taco Bells and motels and shopping centers. Things may be better, but why do I keep thinking about the past?

What I mean by five years old is not that Jeffty was retarded. I don't think that's what it was. Smart as a whip for five years old; very bright, quick, cute, a funny kid.

But he was three feet tall, small for his age, and perfectly formed: no big head, no strange jaw, none of that. A nice, normal-looking five-year-old kid. Except that he was the same age as I was: twenty-two.

When he spoke it was with the squeaking, soprano voice of a five-year-old; when he walked it was with the little hops and shuffles of a five-year-old; when he talked to you it was about the concerns of a five-year-old...comic books, playing soldier, using a clothes pin to attach a stiff piece of cardboard to the front fork of his bike so the sound it made when the spokes hit was like a motorboat, asking questions like *why does that thing do that like that*, how high is up, how old is old, why is grass green, what's an elephant look like? At twenty-two, he was five.

Jeffty's parents were a sad pair. Because I was still a friend of Jeffty's, still let him hang around with me in the store, sometimes took him to the county fair or to the miniature golf or the movies, I wound up spending time with *them*. Not that I much cared for them, because they were so awfully depressing. But then, I suppose one couldn't expect much more from the poor devils. They had an alien thing in their home, a child who had grown no older than five in twenty-two years, who provided the treasure of that special childlike state indefinitely, but who also denied them the joys of watching the child grow into a normal adult.

Five is a wonderful time of life for a little kid...or it *can* be, if the child is relatively free of the monstrous beastliness other children indulge in. It is a time when the eyes are wide open and the patterns are not yet set; a time when one has not yet been hammered into accepting everything as immutable and hopeless; a time when the hands cannot do enough, the mind cannot learn enough, the world is infinite and colorful and filled with mysteries. Five is a special time before they take the questing, unquenchable, quixotic soul of the young dreamer and thrust it into dreary schoolroom boxes. A time before they take the trembling hands that want to hold everything, touch everything, figure everything out, and make them lie still on desktops. A time before people begin saying "act your age" and "grow up" or "you're behaving like a baby." It is a time when a child who acts adolescent is still cute and responsive and everyone's pet. A time of delight, of wonder, of innocence.

Jeffty had been stuck in that time, just five, just so.

But for his parents it was an ongoing nightmare from which no one—not social workers, not priests, not child psychologists, not teachers, not friends, not medical wizards, not psychiatrists, no one— could slap or shake them awake. For seventeen years their sorrow had grown through stages of parental dotage to concern, from concern to worry, from worry to fear, from fear to confusion, from confusion to anger, from anger to dislike, from dislike to naked hatred, and finally, from deepest loathing and revulsion to a stolid, depressive acceptance.

John Kinzer was a shift foreman at the Balder Tool & Die plant. He was a thirty-year man. To everyone but the man living it, his was a spectacularly uneventful life. In no way was he remarkable...save that he had fathered a twenty-two-year-old five-year-old.

John Kinzer was a small man; soft, with no sharp angles; with pale eyes that never seemed to hold mine for longer than a few seconds. He continually shifted in his chair during conversations, and seemed to see things in the upper corners of the room, things no one else could see…or wanted to see. I suppose the word that best suited him was *haunted*. What his life had become…well, *haunted* suited him.

Leona Kinzer tried valiantly to compensate. No matter what hour of the day I visited, she always tried to foist food on me. And when Jeffty was in the house she was always at *him* about eating: "Honey, would you like an orange? A nice orange? Or a tangerine? I have tangerines. I could peel a tangerine for you." But there was clearly such fear in her, fear of her own child, that the offers of sustenance always had a faintly ominous tone.

Leona Kinzer had been a tall woman, but the years had bent her. She seemed always to be seeking some area of wallpapered wall or storage niche into which she could fade, adopt some chintz or rose-patterned protective coloration and hide forever in plain sight of the child's big brown eyes, pass her a hundred times a day and never realize she was there, holding her breath, invisible. She always had an apron tied around her waist, and her hands were red from cleaning. As if by maintaining the environment immaculately she could pay off her imagined sin: having given birth to this strange creature.

Neither of them watched television very much. The house was usually dead silent, not even the sibilant whispering of water in the pipes, the creaking of timbers settling, the humming of the refrigerator. Awfully silent, as if time itself had taken a detour around that house.

As for Jeffty, he was inoffensive. He lived in that atmosphere of gentle dread and dulled loathing, and if he understood it, he never remarked in any way. He played, as a child plays, and seemed happy. But he must have sensed, in the way of a five-year-old, just how alien he was in their presence.

Alien. No, that wasn't right. He was *too* human, if anything. But out of phase, out of synch with the world around him, and resonating to a different vibration than his parents, God knows. Nor would other children play with him. As they grew past him, they found him at first childish, then uninteresting, then simply frightening as their perceptions of aging became clear and they could see he was not affected by time as they were. Even the little ones, his own age, who might wander into the neighborhood, quickly came to shy away from him like a dog in the street when a car backfires.

Thus, I remained his only friend. A friend of many years. Five years. Twenty-two years. I liked him; more than I can say. And never knew exactly why. But I did, without reserve.

But because we spent time together, I found I was also—polite society—spending time with John and Leona Kinzer. Dinner, Saturday afternoons sometimes, an hour or so when I'd bring Jeffty back from a movie. They were grateful: slavishly so. It relieved them of the embarrassing chore of going out with him, or having to pretend before the world that they were loving parents with a perfectly normal, happy, attractive child. And their gratitude extended to hosting me. Hideous, every moment of their depression, hideous.

I felt sorry for the poor devils, but I despised them for their inability to love Jeffty, who was eminently lovable.

I never let on, of course, even during the evenings in their company that were awkward beyond belief.

We would sit there in the darkening living room—*always* dark or darkening, as if kept in shadow to hold back what the light might reveal to the world outside through the bright eyes of the house— we would sit and silently stare at one another. They never knew what to say to me.

"So how are things down at the plant?" I'd say to John Kinzer.

He would shrug. Neither conversation nor life suited him with any ease or grace. "Fine, just fine," he would say, finally.

And we would sit in silence again.

"Would you like a nice piece of coffee cake?" Leona would say. "I made it fresh just this morning." Or deep dish green apple pie. Or milk and tollhouse cookies. Or a brown betty pudding.

"No, no, thank you, Mrs. Kinzer; Jeffty and I grabbed a couple of cheeseburgers on the way home." And again, silence.

Then, when the stillness and the awkwardness became too much even for them (and who knew how long that total silence reigned when they were alone, with that thing they never talked about any more hanging between them), Leona Kinzer would say, "I think he's asleep."

John Kinzer would say, "I don't hear the radio playing."

Just so, it would go on like that, until I could politely find excuse to bolt away on some flimsy pretext. Yes, that was the way it would go on, every time, just the same...except once.

"I don't know what to do any more," Leona said. She began crying. "There's no change, not one day of peace."

Her husband managed to drag himself out of the old easy chair and went to her. He bent and tried to soothe her, but it was clear from the graceless way in which he touched her graying hair that the ability to be compassionate had been stunned in him. "Shhh, Leona, it's all right. Shhh." But she continued crying. Her hands scraped gently at the antimacassars on the arms of the chair.

Then she said, "Sometimes I wish he had been stillborn."

John looked up into the corners of the room. For the nameless shadows that were always watching him? Was it God he was seeking in those spaces? "You don't mean that," he said to her, softly, pathetically, urging her with body tension and trembling in his voice to recant before God took notice of the terrible thought. But she meant it; she meant it very much.

I managed to get away quickly that evening. They didn't want witnesses to their shame. I was glad to go.

And for a week I stayed away. From them, from Jeffty, from their street, even from that end of town.

I had my own life. The store, accounts, suppliers' conferences, poker with friends, pretty women I took to well-lit restaurants, my own parents, putting anti-freeze in the car, complaining to the laundry about too much starch in the collars and cuffs, working out at the gym, taxes, catching Jan or David (whichever one it was) stealing from the cash register. I had my own life.

But not even *that* evening could keep me from Jeffty. He called me at the store and asked me to take him to the rodeo. We chummed it up as best a twenty-two-year-old with other interests *could*...with a five-year-old. I never dwelled on what bound us together; I always thought it was simply the years. That, and affection for a kid who could have been the little brother I never had. (Except I *remembered* when we had played together, when we had both been the same age; I *remembered* that period, and Jeffty was still the same.)

And then, one Saturday afternoon, I came to take him to a double feature, and things I should have noticed so many times before, I first began to notice only that afternoon.

I came walking up to the Kinzer house, expecting Jeffty to be sitting on the front porch steps, or in the porch glider, waiting for me. But he was nowhere in sight.

Going inside, into that darkness and silence, in the midst of May sunshine, was unthinkable. I stood on the front walk for a few moments, then cupped my hands around my mouth and yelled, "Jeffty? Hey, Jeffty, come on out, let's go. We'll be late."

His voice came faintly, as if from under the ground.

"Here I am, Donny."

I could hear him, but I couldn't see him. It was Jeffty, no question about it: as Donald H. Horton, President and Sole Owner of The Horton TV & Sound Center, no one but Jeffty called me Donny. He had never called me anything else.

(Actually, it isn't a lie. I *am*, as far as the public is concerned, Sole Owner of the Center. The partnership with my Aunt Patricia is only to repay the loan she made me, to supplement the money I came into when I was twenty-one, left to me when I was ten by my grandfather. It wasn't a very big loan, only eighteen thousand, but I asked her to be a silent partner, because of when she had taken care of me as a child.)

"Where are you, Jeffty?"

"Under the porch in my secret place."

I walked around the side of the porch, and stooped down and pulled away the wicker grating. Back in there, on the pressed dirt, Jeffty had built himself a secret place. He had comics in orange crates, he had a little table and some pillows, it was lit by big fat candles, and we used to hide there when we were both...five.

"What'cha up to?" I asked, crawling in and pulling the grate closed behind me. It was cool under the porch, and the dirt smelled comfortable, the candles smelled clubby and familiar. Any kid would feel at home in such a secret place: there's never been a kid who didn't spend the happiest, most productive, most deliciously mysterious times of his life in such a secret place.

"Playin'," he said. He was holding something golden and round. It filled the palm of his little hand.

"You forget we were going to the movies?"

"Nope. I was just waitin' for you here."

"Your mom and dad home?"

"Momma."

I understood why he was waiting under the porch. I didn't push it any further. "What've you got there?"

"Captain Midnight Secret Decoder Badge," he said, showing it to me on his flattened palm.

I realized I was looking at it without comprehending what it was for a long time. Then it dawned on me what a miracle Jeffty had in his hand. A miracle that simply could *not* exist.

"Jeffty," I said softly, with wonder in my voice, "where'd you get that?"

"Came in the mail today. I sent away for it."

"It must have cost a lot of money."

"Not so much. Ten cents an' two inner wax seals from two jars of Ovaltine."

"May I see it?" My voice was trembling, and so was the hand I extended. He gave it to me and I held the miracle in the palm of my hand. It was *wonderful*.

You remember. *Captain Midnight* went on the radio nationwide in 1940. It was sponsored by Ovaltine. And every year they issued a Secret Squadron Decoder Badge. And every day at the end of the program, they would give you a clue to the next day's installment in a code that only kids with the official badge could decipher. They stopped making those wonderful Decoder Badges in 1949. I remember the one I had in 1945: it was beautiful. It had a magnifying glass in the center of the code dial. *Captain Midnight* went off the air in 1950, and though I understand it was a short-lived television series in the mid-Fifties, and though they issued Decoder Badges in 1955 and

1956, as far as the *real* badges were concerned, they never made one after 1949.

The Captain Midnight Code-O-Graph I held in my hand, the one Jeffty said he had gotten in the mail for ten cents (*ten cents!!!*) and two Ovaltine labels, was brand new, shiny gold metal, not a dent or a spot of rust on it like the old ones you can find at exorbitant prices in collectible shoppes from time to time…it was a *new* Decoder. And the date on it was *this* year.

But *Captain Midnight* no longer existed. Nothing like it existed on the radio. I'd listened to the one or two weak imitations of old-time radio the networks were currently airing, and the stories were dull, the sound effects bland, the whole feel of it wrong, out of date, cornball. Yet I held a *new* Code-O-Graph.

"Jeffty, tell me about this," I said.

"Tell you what, Donny? It's my new Capt'n Midnight Secret Decoder Badge. I use it to figger out what's gonna happen tomorrow."

"Tomorrow how?"

"On the program."

"*What* program?!"

He stared at me as if I was being purposely stupid. "On Capt'n Midnight! Boy!" I was being dumb.

I still couldn't get it straight. It was right there, right out in the open, and I still didn't know what was happening. "You mean one of those records they made of the old-time radio programs? Is that what you mean, Jeffty?"

"What records?" he asked. He didn't know what *I* meant.

We stared at each other, there under the porch. And then I said, very slowly, almost afraid of the answer, "Jeffty, how do you hear *Captain Midnight?*"

"Every day. On the radio. On my radio. Every day at five-thirty."

News. Music, dumb music, and news. That's what was on the radio every day at 5:30. Not *Captain Midnight*. The Secret Squadron hadn't been on the air in twenty years.

"Can we hear it tonight?" I asked.

"Boy!" he said. I was being dumb. I knew it from the way he said it; but I didn't know *why*. Then it dawned on me: this was Saturday.

Captain Midnight was on Monday through Friday. Not on Saturday or Sunday.

"We goin' to the movies?"

He had to repeat himself twice. My mind was somewhere else. Nothing definite. No conclusions. No wild assumptions leapt to. Just off somewhere trying to figure it out, and concluding—as *you* would have concluded, as *any*one would have concluded rather than accepting the truth, the impossible and wonderful truth—just finally concluding there was a simple explanation I didn't yet perceive. Something mundane and dull, like the passage of time that steals all good, old things from us, packratting trinkets and plastic in exchange. And all in the name of Progress.

"We goin' to the movies, Donny?"

"You bet your boots we are, kiddo," I said. And I smiled. And I handed him the Code-O-Graph. And he put it in his side pants pocket. And we crawled out from under the porch. And we went to the movies. And neither of us said anything about *Captain Midnight* all the rest of that day. And there wasn't a ten-minute stretch, all the rest of that day, that I didn't think about it.

It was inventory all that next week. I didn't see Jeffty till late Thursday. I confess I left the store in the hands of Jan and David, told them I had some errands to run, and left early. At 4:00. I got to the Kinzers' right around 4:45. Leona answered the door, looking exhausted and distant. "Is Jeffty around?" She said he was upstairs in his room...

...listening to the radio.

I climbed the stairs two at a time.

All right, I had finally made that impossible, illogical leap. Had the stretch of belief involved anyone but Jeffty, adult or child, I would have reasoned out more explicable answers. But it *was* Jeffty, clearly another kind of vessel of life, and what he might experience should not be expected to fit into the ordered scheme.

I admit it: I *wanted* to hear what I heard.

Even with the door closed, I recognized the program:

"*There he goes, Tennessee! Get him!*"

There was the heavy report of a rifle shot and the keening whine of the slug ricocheting, and then the same voice yelled triumphantly, "*Got him! D-e-a-a-a-d center!*"

He was listening to the American Broadcasting Company, 790 kilocycles, and he was hearing *Tennessee Jed*, one of my most favorite programs from the Forties, a western adventure I had not heard in twenty years, because it had not existed for twenty years.

I sat down on the top step of the stairs, there in the upstairs hall of the Kinzer home, and I listened to the show. It wasn't a rerun of an old program, because there were occasional references in the body of the drama to current cultural and technological developments, and phrases that had not existed in common usage in the Forties: aerosol spray cans, laserasing of tattoos, Tanzania, the word "uptight."

I could not ignore the fact. Jeffty was listening to a *new* segment of *Tennessee Jed*.

I ran downstairs and out the front door to my car. Leona must have been in the kitchen. I turned the key and punched on the radio and spun the dial to 790 kilocycles. The ABC station. Rock music.

I sat there for a few moments, then ran the dial slowly from one end to the other. Music, news, talk shows. No *Tennessee Jed*. And it was a Blaupunkt, the best radio I could get. I wasn't missing some perimeter station. It simply was not there!

After a few moments I turned off the radio and the ignition and went back upstairs quietly. I sat down on the top step and listened to the entire program. It was *wonderful*.

Exciting, imaginative, filled with everything I remembered as being most innovative about radio drama. But it was modern. It wasn't an antique, re-broadcast to assuage the need of that dwindling listenership who longed for the old days. It was a new show, with all the old voices, but still young and bright. Even the commercials were for currently available products, but they weren't as loud or as insulting as the screamer ads one heard on radio these days.

And when *Tennessee Jed* went off at 5:00, I heard Jeffty spin the dial on his radio till I heard the familiar voice of the announcer Glenn Riggs proclaim, "*Presenting Hop Harrigan! America's ace of the airwaves!*" There was the sound of an airplane in flight. It was a prop plane, *not* a jet! Not the sound kids today have grown up with, but the sound *I* grew up with, the *real* sound of an airplane, the growling, revving, throaty sound of the kind of airplanes G-8 and His Battle Aces flew, the kind Captain Midnight flew, the kind Hop Harrigan flew. And then I heard Hop say, "*CX-4 calling control tower. CX-4 calling control tower. Standing by!*" A pause, then, "*Okay, this is Hop Harrigan...coming in!*"

And Jeffty, who had the same problem all of us kids had had in the Forties with programming that pitted equal favorites against one another on different stations, having paid his respects to Hop Harrigan and Tank Tinker, spun the dial and went back to ABC, where I heard the stroke of a gong, the wild cacophony of nonsense Chinese chatter, and the announcer yelled, "*T-e-e-e-rry and the Pirates!*"

I sat there on the top step and listened to Terry and Connie and Flip Corkin and, so help me God, Agnes Moorehead as The Dragon Lady, all of them in a new adventure that took place in a Red China that had not existed in the days of Milton Caniff's 1937 version of the Orient, with river pirates and Chiang Kai-shek and warlords and the naïve Imperialism of American gunboat diplomacy.

Sat, and listened to the whole show, and sat even longer to hear *Superman* and part of *Jack Armstrong, The All American Boy* and part of *Captain Midnight*, and John Kinzer came home and neither he nor Leona came upstairs to find out what had happened to me, or where Jeffty was, and sat longer, and found I had started crying, and could not stop, just sat there with tears running down my face, into the corners of my mouth, sitting and crying until Jeffty heard me and opened his door and saw me and came out and looked at me in childish confusion as I heard the station break for the Mutual Network and they began the theme music of *Tom Mix*, "When It's Round-up Time in Texas and the Bloom Is on the Sage," and Jeffty touched my shoulder and smiled at me, with his mouth and his big brown eyes, and said, "Hi, Donny. Wanna come in an' listen to the radio with me?"

Hume denied the existence of an absolute space, in which each thing has its place; Borges denies the existence of one single time, in which all events are linked.

Jeffty received radio programs from a place that could not, in logic, in the natural scheme of the space-time universe as conceived by Einstein, exist. But that wasn't all he received. He got mail order premiums that no one was manufacturing. He read comic books that had been defunct for three decades. He saw movies with actors who had been dead for twenty years. He was the receiving terminal for endless joys and pleasures of the past that the world had dropped along the way. On its headlong suicidal flight toward New Tomorrows, the world had razed its treasurehouse of simple happinesses, had poured concrete over its playgrounds, had abandoned its elfin stragglers, and all of it was being impossibly, miraculously shunted back into the present through Jeffty. Revivified, updated, the traditions maintained but contemporaneous. Jeffty was the unbidding Aladdin whose very nature formed the magic lampness of his reality.

And he took me into his world with him.

Because he trusted me.

We had breakfast of Quaker Puffed Wheat Sparkies, and warm Ovaltine that we drank out of *this* year's Little Orphan Annie Shake-Up Mugs. We went to the movies and while everyone else was seeing a comedy starring Goldie Hawn and Ryan O'Neal, Jeffty and I were enjoying Humphrey Bogart as the professional thief Parker in John Huston's brilliant adaptation of the Donald Westlake novel SLAYGROUND. The second feature was Spencer Tracy, Carole Lombard and Laird Cregar in the Val Lewton-produced film of *Leiningen Versus the Ants*.

Twice a month we went down to the newsstand and bought the current pulp issues of *The Shadow*, *Doc Savage* and *Startling Stories*. Jeffty and I sat together and I read to him from the magazines. He particularly liked the new short novel by Henry Kuttner, "The Dreams of Achilles," and the new Stanley G. Weinbaum series of short stories set in the subatomic particle universe of Redurna. In September we enjoyed the first installment of the new Robert E. Howard Conan novel, ISLE OF THE BLACK ONES, in *Weird Tales*; and in August we were only mildly disappointed by Edgar Rice Burroughs's fourth novella in the Jupiter series featuring John Carter of Barsoom—"Corsairs of Jupiter." But the editor of *Argosy All-Story Weekly* promised there would be two more stories in the series, and it was such an unexpected revelation for Jeffty and me that it dimmed our disappointment at the lessened quality of the current story.

We read comics together, and Jeffty and I both decided—separately, before we came together to discuss it—that our favorite characters were Doll Man, Airboy and The Heap. We also adored the George Carlson strips in *Jingle Jangle Comics*, particularly the Pie-Face Prince of Old Pretzleburg stories, which we read together and laughed over, even though I had to explain some of the esoteric puns to Jeffty, who was too young to have that kind of subtle wit.

How to explain it? I can't. I had enough physics in college to make some offhand guesses, but I'm more likely wrong than right. The laws of the conservation of energy occasionally break. These are laws that physicists call "weakly violated." Perhaps Jeffty was a catalyst for the weak violation of conservation laws we're only now beginning to realize exist. I tried doing some reading in the area—muon decay of the "forbidden" kind: gamma decay that doesn't include the muon neutrino among its products—but nothing I encountered, not even the latest readings from the Swiss Institute for Nuclear Research near Zurich gave me an insight. I was thrown back on a vague acceptance of the philosophy that the real name for "science" is *magic*.

No explanations, but enormous good times.

The happiest time of my life.

I had the "real" world, the world of my store and my friends and my family, the world of profit&loss, of taxes and evenings with young women who talked about going shopping or the United Nations, or the rising cost of coffee and microwave ovens. And I had Jeffty's world, in which I existed only when I was with him. The things of the past he knew as fresh and new, I could experience only when in his company. And the membrane between the two worlds grew ever thinner, more luminous and transparent. I had the best of both worlds.

And knew, somehow, that I could carry nothing from one to the other.

Forgetting that, for just a moment, betraying Jeffty by forgetting, brought an end to it all.

Enjoying myself so much, I grew careless and failed to consider how fragile the relationship between Jeffty's world and my world really was. There is a reason why the present begrudges the existence of the past. I never really understood. Nowhere in the beast books, where survival is shown in battles between claw and fang, tentacle and poison sac, is there recognition of the ferocity the present always brings to bear on the past. Nowhere is there a detailed statement of how the present lies in wait for What-Was, waiting for it to become Now-This-Moment so it can shred it with its merciless jaws.

Who could know such a thing…at any age…and certainly not at my age…who could understand such a thing?

I'm trying to exculpate myself. I can't. It was my fault.

It was another Saturday afternoon.

"What's playing today?" I asked him, in the car, on the way downtown.

He looked up at me from the other side of the front seat and smiled one of his best smiles. "Ken Maynard in *Bullwhip Justice* an' *The Demolished Man*." He kept smiling, as if he'd really put one over on me. I looked at him with disbelief.

"You're *kidding*!" I said, delighted. "Bester's THE DEMOLISHED MAN?" He nodded his head, delighted at my being delighted. He knew it was one of my favorite books. "Oh, that's super!"

"Super *duper*," he said.

"Who's in it?"

"Franchot Tone, Evelyn Keyes, Lionel Barrymore and Elisha Cook, Jr." He was much more knowledgeable about movie actors than I'd ever been. He could name the character actors in any movie he'd ever seen. Even the crowd scenes.

"And cartoons?" I asked.

"Three of 'em: a *Little Lulu*, a *Donald Duck* and a *Bugs Bunny*. An' a *Pete Smith Specialty* an' a *Lew Lehr Monkeys is da C-r-r-r-aziest Peoples.*"

"Oh boy!" I said. I was grinning from ear to ear. And then I looked down and saw the pad of purchase order forms on the seat. I'd forgotten to drop it off at the store.

"Gotta stop by the Center," I said. "Gotta drop off something. It'll only take a minute."

"Okay," Jeffty said. "But we won't be late, will we?"

"Not on your tintype, kiddo," I said.

When I pulled into the parking lot behind the Center, he decided to come in with me and we'd walk over to the theater. It's not a large town. There are only two movie houses, the Utopia and the Lyric. We were going to the Utopia and it was only three blocks from the Center.

I walked into the store with the pad of forms, and it was bedlam. David and Jan were handling two customers each, and there were people standing around waiting to be helped. Jan turned a look on me and her face was a horror-mask of pleading. David was running from the stockroom to the showroom and all he could murmur as he whipped past was "Help!" and then he was gone.

"Jeffty," I said, crouching down, "listen, give me a few minutes. Jan and David are in trouble with all these people. We won't be late, I promise. Just let me get rid of a couple of these customers." He looked nervous, but nodded okay.

I motioned to a chair and said, "Just sit down for a while and I'll be right with you."

He went to the chair, good as you please, though he knew what was happening, and he sat down.

I started taking care of people who wanted color television sets. This was the first really substantial batch of units we'd gotten in— color television was only now becoming reasonably priced and this was Sony's first promotion—and it was bonanza time for me. I could see paying off the loan and being out in front for the first time with the Center. It was business.

In my world, good business comes first.

Jeffty sat there and stared at the wall. Let me tell you about the wall.

Stanchion and bracket designs had been rigged from floor to within two feet of the ceiling. Television sets had been stacked artfully on the wall. Thirty-three television sets. All playing at the same time. Black and white, color, little ones, big ones, all going at the same time.

Jeffty sat and watched thirty-three television sets, on a Saturday afternoon. We can pick up a total of thirteen channels including the UHF educational stations. Golf was on one channel; baseball was on a second; celebrity bowling was on a third; the fourth channel was a religious seminar; a teenage dance show was on the fifth; the sixth was a rerun of a situation comedy; the seventh was a rerun of a police show; eighth was a nature program showing a man flycasting endlessly; ninth was news and conversation; tenth was a stock car race; eleventh was a man doing logarithms on a blackboard; twelfth was a woman in a leotard doing setting-up exercises; and on the thirteenth channel was a badly animated cartoon show in Spanish. All but six of the shows were repeated on three sets. Jeffty sat and watched that wall of television on a Saturday afternoon while I sold as fast and as hard as I could, to pay back my Aunt Patricia and stay in touch with my world. It was business.

I should have known better. I should have understood about the present and the way it kills the past. But I was selling with both hands. And when I finally glanced over at Jeffty, half an hour later, he looked like another child.

He was sweating. That terrible fever sweat when you have stomach flu. He was pale, as pasty and pale as a worm, and his little hands were gripping the arms of the chair so tightly I could see his knuckles in bold relief. I dashed over to him, excusing myself from the middle-aged couple looking at the new 21" Mediterranean model.

"Jeffty!"

He looked at me, but his eyes didn't track. He was in absolute terror. I pulled him out of the chair and started toward the front door with him, but the customers I'd deserted yelled at me, "Hey!"

The middle-aged man said, "You wanna sell me this thing or don't you?"

I looked from him to Jeffty and back again. Jeffty was like a zombie. He had come where I'd pulled him. His legs were rubbery and his feet dragged. The past, being eaten by the present, the sound of something in pain.

I clawed some money out of my pants pocket and jammed it into Jeffty's hand. "Kiddo...listen to me...get out of here right now!" He still couldn't focus properly. "*Jeffty*," I said as tightly as I could, "*listen* to me!" The middle-aged customer and his wife were walking toward us. "Listen, kiddo, get out of here right this minute. Walk over to the Utopia and buy the tickets. I'll be right behind you." The middle-aged man and his wife were almost on us. I shoved Jeffty through the door and watched him stumble away in the wrong direction, then stop as if gathering his wits, turn and go back past the front of the Center and in the direction of the Utopia. "Yes sir," I said, straightening up and facing them, "yes, ma'am, that is one terrific set with some sensational features! If you'll just step back here with me..."

There was a terrible sound of something hurting, but I couldn't tell from which channel, or from which set, it was coming.

Most of it I learned later, from the girl in the ticket booth, and from some people I knew who came to me to tell me what had happened. By the time I got to the Utopia, nearly twenty minutes later, Jeffty was already beaten to a pulp and had been taken to the Manager's office.

"Did you see a very little boy, about five years old, with big brown eyes and straight brown hair...he was waiting for me?"

"Oh, I think that's the little boy those kids beat up?"

"What!?! *Where is he?*"

"They took him to the Manager's office. No one knew who he was or where to find his parents—"

A young girl wearing an usher's uniform was kneeling down beside the couch, placing a wet paper towel on his face.

I took the towel away from her and ordered her out of the office.

She looked insulted and snorted something rude, but she left. I sat on the edge of the couch and tried to swab away the blood from the lacerations without opening the wounds where the blood had caked. Both his eyes were swollen shut. His mouth was ripped badly. His hair was matted with dried blood.

He had been standing in line behind two kids in their teens. They started selling tickets at 12:30 and the show started at 1:00. The doors weren't opened till 12:45. He had been waiting, and the kids in front of him had had a portable radio. They were listening to the ball game. Jeffty had wanted to hear some program, God knows what it might have been, *Grand Central Station*, *Let's Pretend*, *Land of the Lost*, God only knows which one it might have been.

He had asked if he could borrow their radio to hear the program for a minute, and it had been a commercial break or something, and the kids had given him the radio, probably out of some malicious kind of courtesy that would permit them to take offense and rag the little boy. He had changed the station…and they'd been unable to get it to go back to the ball game. It was locked into the past, on a station that was broadcasting a program that didn't exist for anyone but Jeffty.

They had beaten him badly…as everyone watched.

And then they had run away.

I had left him alone, left him to fight off the present without sufficient weaponry. I had betrayed him for the sale of a 21" Mediterranean console television, and now his face was pulped meat. He moaned something inaudible and sobbed softly.

"Shhh, it's okay, kiddo, it's Donny. I'm here. I'll get you home, it'll be okay."

I should have taken him straight to the hospital. I don't know why I didn't. I should have. I should have done that.

When I carried him through the door, John and Leona Kinzer just stared at me. They didn't move to take him from my arms. One of his hands was hanging down. He was conscious, but just barely. They stared, there in the semi-darkness of a Saturday afternoon in the present. I looked at them. "A couple of kids beat him up at the theater." I raised him a few inches in my arms and extended him. They stared at me, at both of us, with nothing in their eyes, without movement. "Jesus Christ," I shouted, "he's been beaten! He's your son! Don't you even want to touch him? What the hell kind of people are you?!"

Then Leona moved toward me very slowly. She stood in front of us for a few seconds, and there was a leaden stoicism in her face that was terrible to see. It said, *I have been in this place before, many times, and I cannot bear to be in it again; but I am here now.*

So I gave him to her. God help me, I gave him over to her.

And she took him upstairs to bathe away his blood and his pain.

John Kinzer and I stood in our separate places in the dim living room of their home, and we stared at each other. He had nothing to say to me.

I shoved past him and fell into a chair. I was shaking.

I heard the bath water running upstairs.

After what seemed a very long time Leona came downstairs, wiping her hands on her apron. She sat down on the sofa and after a moment John sat down beside her. I heard the sound of rock music from upstairs.

"Would you like a piece of nice pound cake?" Leona said.

I didn't answer. I was listening to the sound of the music. Rock music. On the radio. There was a table lamp on the end table beside the sofa. It cast a dim and futile light in the shadowed living room.

Rock music from the present, on a radio upstairs? I started to say something, and then *knew*...Oh, God...no!

I jumped up just as the sound of hideous crackling blotted out the music, and the table lamp dimmed and dimmed and flickered. I screamed something, I don't know what it was, and ran for the stairs.

Jeffty's parents did not move. They sat there with their hands folded, in that place they had been for so many years.

I fell twice rushing up the stairs.

There isn't much on television that can hold my interest. I bought an old cathedral-shaped Philco radio in a second-hand store, and I replaced all the burnt-out parts with the original tubes from old radios

I could cannibalize that still worked. I don't use transistors or printed circuits. They wouldn't work. I've sat in front of that set for hours sometimes, running the dial back and forth as slowly as you can imagine, so slowly it doesn't look as if it's moving at all sometimes.

But I can't find *Captain Midnight* or *The Land of the Lost* or *The Shadow* or *Quiet, Please.*

So she did love him, still, a little bit, even after all those years. I can't hate them: they only wanted to live in the present world again. That isn't such a terrible thing.

It's a good world, all things considered. It's much better than it used to be, in a lot of ways. People don't die from the old diseases any more. They die from new ones, but that's Progress, isn't it?

Isn't it?

Tell me.

Somebody please tell me.

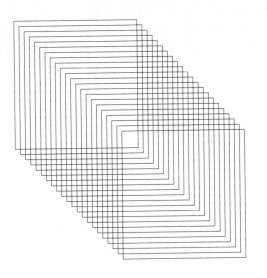

THE
ISOLINGUALS

BY L. SPRAGUE DE CAMP

Nick looked at the cop, and the cop looked at Nick. The fruit vendor's friendly smile suddenly froze. The cop didn't know it, but something had gone *ping* inside Nick's head. He wasn't Niccolo Franchetti any longer. He was Decimus Agricola, engineering officer of the good old XXXIInd Legion. He had been standing behind his ballista, laying it for the Parthians' next charge. Of the crew, only he and two privates had not been struck down by the Asiatics' terrible arrows.

Then something awful had happened: the vast red rock desert of Mesopotamia had vanished, and with it the swirling masses of hostile cavalry, the heaps of dead and wounded, and everything else. One of the ballista crew was gone likewise; the other had metamorphosed into this fat fellow in the tight clothes. His catapult had, in the same twinkling, become a little two-wheeled wagon piled with fruit. He was standing on a paved street, lined with buildings of fantastic height.

Decimus blinked incredulously. Sorcery! Those Parthians were said to be good at it. The man looking at him *must* be Cartoricus, the Gaulish replacement. "*Onere*" he shouted. "Load!"

The man in dark blue just stared. Decimus lost his temper.

"What's the matter, don't you understand good Latin? They'll be at us again in a minute!" The man did nothing. Decimus felt for his sword. It wasn't there. He was wearing queer, uncomfortable clothes like the other. He snatched an apple; at the touch of it his mind reeled. It felt like a real apple, not a sorcerer's illusion. He bit into it. Then stark terror seized him. He threw the apple at the fat man and started to run.

Arthur Lindsley picked up the hand set. "Hello? ... Oh, it's you, Pierre. How's the esteemed son-in-law this morning!"

"Fairish," replied the instrument. "I'm up at Rockefeller Med. Bill Jenkins has a case that might interest you. None of their high-powered psychiatrists have been able to do a thing with it. Want to come up?"

Lindsley looked at his watch. "Let's see—my elementary biology class lets out at two thirty. I can come up then."

"Fine. And could you round up a couple of good linguists and bring 'em along!"

"Huh! What for?"

"Take too long to explain over the phone. Can you bring them?"

"Well, there's Van Wyck over at Barnard, and Squier's office is down the hall. Say, are you and Elsa going to have Christmas dinner with us?"

"Sorry, but we promised my folks to have it with them this year. Yeah, we're taking the train for Quebec next Thursday. Thanks anyway. Now please bring some really good language sharks. It might be important."

Professor Lindsley sighed as he hung up. He didn't look forward with much pleasure to the undiluted company of his two sons all day Christmas. Hugh would talk interminably about the vacuum-cleaner business. Malcolm would drape himself over the furniture and make languid remarks in his newly acquired college voice about how art is all. What did Pierre mean by dragging Elsa off to spend Christmas with his Canuck parents? They were the only intelligent members of the family, besides himself—

Lindsley took the new Tenth Avenue Subway up to the Medical Center, with his two linguists in tow. Squier had been in, but not Van Wyck. A search of the language department had unearthed a Dr. Fedor Jevsky, who said he'd be ver-r-ry glad to come. Lindsley was a smallish man, very erect, with snapping eyes and a diminutive white beard. He looked odd, leading the rangy Squier and the obese Jevsky like a couple of puppies.

Dr. Jenkins' office was jammed. The thickset, shabby man was speaking: "It's just like I told the guys down at the hospital, doc; Mrs. Garfinkle and I been married ten years, and she never showed no symptoms or nothin'. We're just poor woiking people—"

Jenkins' bedside voice suddenly recovered its normal snap. "Come in, Arthur; I take it these are your linguists. I've got a queer job for them."

Pierre Lamarque's broad, coppery face ginned at his father-in-law from across the room. Jenkins was explaining: "—and all at once her normal personality went out like a light. She began talking this gibberish, and didn't know her husband or the city or anything else. That's just the trouble; we can't locate a single physical paranoiac symptom, and aphasia won't work either. Split personality, yes, but it doesn't explain her making up what seems to be a whole new language of her own. But that's not all. She's the third of these cases the hospital has received in twenty-four hours. Sure, naturally we gave 'em all the routine tests."

The telephone rang. "Yes! Oh, Lord!…Yes…. No…. Glad you let me know." Jenkins hung up. "Twelve more cases. Seems to be an epidemic."

Jevsky had inclined his globular form—it was impossible for him to bend—in front of the plain-looking woman on the chair. She seemed to be so earnestly trying to tell him something with that rush of strange syllables. He suddenly seemed to catch something, for he barked at her what sounded like "Haybye-ded-yow?"

The rush of sound stopped, and the woman's face broke into a grateful smile. Then the torrent began again

Jevsky wasn't listening. He spoke to Jenkins, "What foreign languages has Meesez Garfinkle studied?"

"None at all; she was born in New York City; both parents spoke English, at least of a sort; she left school at the end of the eighth grade. What do you think you've got Dr. Jevsky?"

"I'm not sure, but it might be Gothic."

"What!"

The vast shoulders shrugged. "I know it sounds crazy, but *habai-dêdjau* means 'if I had' in Gothic. I don't really know the language, except for a few fragments like that; nor, I theenk, will many of my colleagues. You, Dr. Squier?"

The other linguist shook his head. "The Celtic languages are my specialty. But I suppose there's at least one Gothic scholar in New York City. There's at least one of everything else."

Jenkins shook *his* head. "No, gentlemen, it's hardly worth trying to dig one up on such a fantastic hypothesis. Guess we have a new form of dementia here. Sorry I hauled you up; she acted so rational that I thought you might find something. By the way, what *is* Gothic?"

Squier answered: "The language of the ancient Goths; it's more or less the common ancestor of English, Dutch, and German. A complicated affair with about nine thousand useless inflections. We have only a partial knowledge of it."

The telephone rang again. When Jenkins had hung up, he swore. "More cases. They're coming in regularly now. They've got one who seems to be talking some kind of English dialect, and they're bringing him up here. Suppose you all stick around for a while."

They stood or sat on the floor. Lindsley argued with one of the Rockefeller psychiatrists about politics. The biologist thought Slidell and his so-called Union Party were a real menace, that they were aiming for a dictatorship and were pretty good shots. The psychiatrist didn't; he admitted that Slidell was a fanatical demagogue and all that, but said that if the other parties would stop trying to cut each other's throats they could squash the would-be dictator overnight.

At last the hospital men brought in a slim, blond youth with a harassed expression. Jenkins rose. "I understand you're—"

The young man interrupted. He spoke a peculiar English, rather like a strong Irish brogue. "If thou're going to ask me who I be, like the rest of these knaves, my name is Sergeant Ronald Blake, of the theerd company of Noll Croomle's foot, and a mor-r-rtal enemy of ahl Papists! Now are ye satisfied?"

Squier said, "Whose foot? I mean, how do you spell him?"

The youth frowned. "I'm no clerk, but I bethink me 'tis C-r-o-m-w-e-l-l, Croomle."

Lindsley spoke up, "What year is it?"

"Certainly, 'tis the year of our Lord sixteen forty-eight."

The scientists looked at one another.

Jenkins said, "We seem to be getting somewhere, but I'm not sure just where. Young man, suppose you tell us just what happened."

"Well, I had gone home on leave, and my wife asked me to go down to the butcher's, and I had just toorned on the main street o' the village when I spied my old friend Hawks. 'Hoy, Ronald,' he says, 'how's the brave soldyer lad? And is't true thou wert as Naseby?' So I began to tell him ahl about the great battle, and how at the end the Cavaliers fled like rabbits, with their long hair streamin' out behind—" The voice from the past, if such it was, rolled on and on. Sergeant Blake was evidently a man who believed in getting in all the details.

Later, Lindsley and his son-in-law sat in the former's office. Tobacco smoke crawled bluely up through the rays of the desk lamp.

"Something's gone haywire," said the professor. "I can't believe this is an ordinary form of insanity, or any extraordinary form, either. How can you explain how Mike Watrous, package dispatcher at a department store, a young man of little learning and few talents, not only gets the idea that he's a sergeant in the Parliamentary army in the English Civil War, but also acquires a complete biography, personality, and accent to go with it? How many literate people, let alone those of Mike's background and tastes, know that Oliver Cromwell pronounced his name 'Croomle'? In most cases of this kind the victim thinks he's Napoleon or Julius Caesar, but after the delusion has come on he doesn't know any more about Napoleon or Caesar, really, than he did before."

Lamarque shrugged. "Any other hypothesis I can think of seems equally crazy, unless you're going to admit the transmigration of souls, or some such nonsense. Suppose I caught this disease, or whatever it is, and thought I was the first Lamarque, who came over to Canada in 1746, or thereabouts. I wouldn't have the vaguest idea of how to go about talking eighteenth-century French."

Lindsley sighed. "And now they want us to drop everything we're doing and try to help them out. I wish they made these psychiatrists—and that includes our friend Jenkins—learn enough advanced biology so they wouldn't come running to us when they get stumped. But I suppose we'll have to go through the motions, anyway. The worm of it is that I haven't the foggiest notion of where to start—"

Hans Rumpel was making a speech. He was in fine form. His Yorktown audience drank in his flood of words, his piercing yells, his windmill gestures. "Red plot...Jewish assassins...Destruction of civilization—" he screeched.

Hans faltered; his oratory died away to a mumble. His audience was mildly surprised to see him going through the motions of stroking an imaginary beard. Then his voice rose again, this time not in

English, but in mournful Hebrew. He was, in fact, reciting a Hebrew service, just as he—not Hans Rumpel, but Levi ben Eliezar, a respected rabbi of the Hasidim—had been reciting it in a Krakow synagogue in the year 1784. The would-be saviors of civilization from the horrors of democratic government looked at one another. Was he another of those cases they had been reading about? Hans mopped his chant, gaped at his audience, and fell on his knees. He was praying with mountain-moving fervor.

Professor Lindsley emerged from behind the tarn of books and papers and threw his eye shade in the corner. "Pierre! Let's cut this damn nonsense and get some breakfast. It's seven o'clock."

Lamarque appeared. "Any luck? None here, either. Can't find anything definite, although Minakuchi's paper on ancestral memory in rats might be worth following up."

Lindsley frowned. "Something you said the day before yesterday gave me an idea, but it popped out of my mind like a watermelon seed, before I could grab it. I've been trying to think of it ever since. Must be getting old."

Later, Lamarque made a face. "With all the advances in our modern civilization, nobody has yet found how to make a drug store serve good coffee. Oh, remind me to wire Quebec and tell the folks the Christmas dinner is off. That's the latest from Jenkins?"

"More of the same. At the present rate every hospital in New York will be full in a couple of days, and all the medicos in town are running around in circles, and the psychiatrists are just dithering. Bill says they're fairly sure it isn't infectious, from what case histories they've been able to trace. And *we* aren't any further than when we started—"

Sunday, in the new church on Tremont Avenue, the Bronx, H. Perkins rolled his eyes around so that he could see the congregation. Pretty miserable showing. Why had the vestry wanted to build this church, anyway? He'd heard a lot about the "return to religion" since 1950, but they didn't seem to be returning to *his* denomination. Such a worried looking lot, too! Between the threat of a dictatorship by that bellowing mountebank, Slidell, and the strange plague of insanity, he didn't wonder. What would happen if Slidell got in?

H. Perkins passed down the aisle with his most seraphic expression.

The "plate"—a most unplatelike object, when you thought of it— was coming toward him again, giving forth a pleasant clink as each coin went into it. He reached over and took it from Mrs. Dinwiddie— and it was as though H. Perkins had never been. He, Joshua Hardy, had been standing on a heaving deck yelling to the verminous crew the commands from "Old Pegleg." They'd just sighted Spaniard, and were cracking on sail to have a closer look. Might be the monthly treasure ship from Colon. And here he was, in the aisle of a church, surrounded by people in strange clothes, and holding a little velvet bag with two dark wood handles.

Josh was too impulsive to make a really tap-notch pirate. He shook the bag; to his ears came that sweetest of sounds, the clink of coin. Better grab the loot and run, boys. "Avast, ye lubbers," he roared "*Give* me that!" He snatched the other little bag. "Ho, you over there, stand and deliver! *Where* in fifteen thousand bloody hells is my cutlass?" He raced down the aisle to cut off the fellow with the remaining bag. Too late! The chase pounded out into the street—

Professor Lindsley slammed down his brief case. "I'm about ready to give up and go in for the transmigration of souls after all" he said wrathfully to Lamarque, who was peering into a microscope. On the microscope slide was a bit of nerve tissue of one of the cases who had gotten him- self killed by an automobile.

Lindsley continued: "They're going to mart a concentration camp for new cases, as every institution for miles around is full. The roads leading out of New York are jammed; people are leaving. Glad we sent our women folks off to Quebec while you could still buy transportation. A driver of a Madison Avenue bus had a seizure and ran his bus into a hydrant between Fifty-third and Fifty-fourth Streets. What's new around here?"

"If you mean research, nothing. But the first case in the university faculty has happened."

"Huh? Tell me about it, quick!"

"It was in the lunch room. You know Calderwood, the mathematician? As sane and sober a man as you'll find. Well, at lunch to-day he jumped up with a howl and began throwing things.

Then he got into the kitchen and chased everybody out with a carving knife.

"But the best part happened next. Some of them watched him around a corner. He marched into the dining room, took off his pants, pulled a tablecloth off one of the tables, and wound it around his waist like a skirt. Then he stuck the knife through one of his garters.

"He must have been a sketch. Wish I'd been there to see. He strutted up and down for a while, apparently challenging the people, in his own lingo, to come back and fight.

"Well, our friend Squier heard the fuss and came up. Squier had a bright idea. He talked Gaelic to Calderwood, and he calmed down right away. Seems he wasn't Graham Calderwood any more, but the terrible Gavin MacTaggart, a wild Highlander looking for a MacDonald throat to cut. If he couldn't have a MacDonald, a Gordon would do. They got him rounded up eventually."

Lindsley took off his glasses and rubbed his red-rimmed eyes. "You're an unfeeling young devil. How'd you like to be a member of poor Graham's family! Did you see about my classes!"

"Yeah. One of your students in advanced biology is down too! Arne Holmgren. Know him? He thinks he's a Viking.

"When they took him away he was roaring some early Scandinavian battle-song; at least, that's what I suppose it was. Say, hadn't you better get some sleep? You can't work efficiently if you don't, you know."

Lindsley started to snap back an irritated reply, but checked himself. "Maybe you're right, Pierre. When my normally saintly disposition starts to go sour there's something wrong. If anybody 'phones, tell 'em you don't know when I'll be back "

Chase Burge lay on his back with his eyes closed, enjoying the last moment of his doze. His conscience, which woke up a little more slowly than the rest of him, showed signs of stirring. He shouldn't have lost his temper yesterday in that argument. But, damn it, Hobart was so rabid on the subject.

Then he sat up suddenly, the last vapors of sleep gone from his brain. How had he gotten into this strange room? He'd gone to bed perfectly sober. He'd been snatched! He sprang from the bed.

The door opened and a man in a dressing gown walked into the room. Chase tensed himself to spring; but, no, the man might have a gun. Better find out what it was all about.

"Morning, son," said the kidnapper. "I think one of my shirts strayed into your bureau—"

"Where am I?" snarled Chase.

"Where—Oh, my Lord—" The gray-haired man looked at him with a horrified expression. "You've got it, too!"

"Got what! What did you kidnap me for? My folks haven't any dough to speak of!"

The other man composed himself with an effort. "Who do you think you are! No, I mean that as a serious question."

"I'm Chase Burge, of 351 West 55th Street, and I demonstrate automobiles for a living. Who are *you?*"

"I'm Chase Burge. Senior, that is. You're Chase Burge, Junior, and I'm your father."

"No, you're not. My father's dead, and he didn't look like you anyway. Is this a funny way of adopting me, or what?"

Chase Burge, Senior, sat down with a perplexed expression. "Let me explain. You just think you're me. But you're really me—no, I mean you're you. You're your own son, really; that is, you're the son of the man you think you are, but who is really me. Oh dear, I wish I could explain! It's this way: you're suffering a delusion that you're your own father—"

Chase interrupted. "You sound like something out of Gilbert and Sullivan. If anybody has delusions around here it's—uk!" His hand touched his chin. In a flash he was at the mirror.

"Holy Moses, where did I get this D'Arragnan effect! Have I been unconscious long"

"Why, you've been wearing that goatee for five years. Lots of the young men wear them."

Chase Burge, Junior, began to laugh hysterically. "Oh, Lord, I guess I am crazy! I know; this is a loony bin that I've been shut up in. I'm crazy, and so are you, unless you're one of the keepers."

Pierre Lamarque threw down *his* brief case. "I think I have something, but I'm not sure."

"Let's have it, quick!" barked Lindsley.

"Let me begin at the beginning. I was down at the hospital I ~ looking over the new cases. They had one who they said was an Englishman of about 1300. I couldn't understand him at all, never realized how fan the language changes. He told us we were a 'pock of foals,' which didn't make much sense, until a professor told me it meant 'pack of fools.'

"But the prize exhibit was one of the new cases from out of town— a Mrs. Rhodes of White Plains. They told me she was—or had been— one of the outstanding uplifters of her community; during the revival of prohibition agitation twelve years ago she was one of the leading lights in the movement.

"Well, you ought to see her now! She chatters in Renaissance Italian, and slinks around with a snaky glide you wouldn't believe possible for a lady prohibitionist in her forties. She'd made a dead set for all the doctors in the place, until they're scared to be alone with her. Says she's Elena della Colleoni.

"That gave me an idea, so I stopped in at the library, and found that there really was such a person as Elena della Colleoni." Lamarque grinned wickedly. "She was a notorious strumpet at the court of Cesare Borgia."

Lindsley polished his glasses slowly. Lamarque knew that meant an idea coming, and kept still.

"I-think-l-begin-to see," said the older biologist. "First, the cases, when we catch them, all act scared to death, but otherwise perfectly sane, except that they've acquired the personality of some one, real or imaginary, who lived before them.

"Secondly; the pseudopsyche is always an individual who might conceivably have been the case's direct ancestor, as in the case of the redcap over in the jersey Heights Terminal who thought he was a Zulu warrior and tried to use a traveler's umbrella as an assagai. Sometimes the descent would be difficult to trace, as in the case of Mrs. Rhodes Colleoni, but you go back enough generations and you could be almost anybody's descendant. In one case—that of the young man who thought he was his own father—we know the phylogenic relationship of the case and its pseudopsyche for a fact.

"Thirdly, in at least some cases, and conceivably in all, the pseudopsyche corresponds to a person who really lived."

"But," objected Lamarque, "if they are real, how come the fact hasn't been noted before this?"

"Hm-m-m. Well, consider the ratio between the total number of people who've lived in the last couple of millennia and the number who were prominent enough to leave a historical record of their doings. You'll see how small the chances are of turning up any big shots.

"Fourthly, the average age of the pseudopsyche is around thirty. That doesn't prove anything by itself. Jerry Plotnik's revising the average to include the latest data now. But the age figures are much too closely grouped for a random distribution: no children, and hardly any elderly people.

"Now suppose—just suppose—that the pseudopsyche is a piece of ancestral memory that's gotten carried along in the germ cells, like a piece of ultra-microscopic motion-picture film, and suppose that something happens to substitute this carried-over memory for the case's real one. You'd think you're the ancestor whose memory you've been carrying around. For obvious reasons. It would end at a point before the time when the said ancestor's child from whom you're descended was conceived. Suppose we call the phenomenon genotropism. That's not a very good name, but it'll do until think of a better one."

Lamarque whistled. "I hope if it happens to me that I'll be one of my French ancestors and not one of my aboriginal ones. I might be sort of unmanageable as an Ojibiway Indian. But say, won't this knock Weismann's theory into a cocked hat?"

"If it's correct, it'll do worse than that. I'll have to eat what I've been saying for thirty years about Lamarkism's being a zombie among evolutionary theories. But remember, this idea of ours is idea just an ideal and we haven't any *positive* evidence whatever yet. More than one scientist has been caught because he assumed that because a theory of his *might* account for certain facts, it therefore *was* the explanation."

THE ISOLINGUALS

"Uh-huh, I get you. But now that we have your theory, what are we going to do with it?"

"Damned if I know," said Lindsley, reaching for his pipe. The manager of the "Venus" looked gloomily at his audience, if you could call it that. Everybody who could scrape up the price of a fare was trying to get out of town, and the rest weren't spending much on entertainment. You didn't feel safe on the streets any more. Still, burlesque was holding up better than any other form of entertainment; a lot of the movie places had closed. Then, too, a merciful providence had decreed that two of the "Venus'" biggest creditors should come down with the plague.

Betty Fiorelli was working up to the climax of her strip tease. A few more grinds and bumps, and more clothing had gone into the wings. He'd told her to give 'em the works. The cops weren't likely to send an inspector around at a time like this. A faint "Ah-h-h!" from the audience. But what was the girl up to? Instead of sidling coyly into the wings, she was standing squarely facing the audience, and her rich voice rolled out in verse after sonorous verse of classic Greek, which was just that to her hearers.

Three minutes later the few strollers on 42nd Street gaped incredulously at the sight of a tall and well-made young woman, clad-precisely in a pair of high-heeled shoes, speeding like an arrow along the sidewalk, while after her panted the manager of the "Venus" and three stage hands. They knew not what they pursued, not Betty Fiorelli, but Thea Tisimicles, the great poetess of Lemnos, whose contemporaries (of the Fifth Century B.C.) thought she surpassed even Sappho.

The fishy-eyed man was talking earnestly to Professor Lindsley: "O.K., but I think you scientific guys are nuts for not getting out while the getting's good. You can stay until we pull out the inner police cordon, and then out you go. There's no use keeping the cordon there when the gangs of iso-isolinguals have begun turning up all over New Joisey and Westchester. What does 'isolingual' mean, anyway?"

"It means they speak the same language. You can see how it is. A case speaks Anglo-Saxon, say. He wanders around until he runs into somebody else who speaks Anglo-Saxon, and they join up for purposes of offense and defense. Pretty soon you have a gang. Come in, Jerry. Dr. Plotnik, Detective Inspector Monahan. Dr. Plotnik's been helping us with the mathematical side of our research."

"You mean he's one of these lightning calculators?"

"Whoop! You'll insult him. He's a mathematical genius, which is something else."

The detective applied another match to his cigar. "Something's fishy about this whole business."

Plotnik gave a sort of gurgle. "You're telling us!"

"No, sonny, I didn't just mean the disease. The National Patriots have been showing all kinds of activity. We've been getting reports from the police all over the country. A lot of them have been filtering into New York, when everybody else is trying to get out. We've caught a few trying to get through the cordons. And the big bug who owns 'em, Slidell, has disappeared."

"What!" exclaimed Lindsley.

"Yeah. You ain't read about it in the papers, because they all been too busy with the plague. But it looks to me-it almost looks-as if there might be a human origin to it."

"But how?" Plotnik stopped.

"I dunno. Maybe they poisoned the water. Thought I'd take a little run down below the cordon and see if we couldn't catch one of these tough babies that Slidel's been sending around to beat up people he don't like. Maybe we could find out why they ain't afraid of the plague. Like to come along?"

Plotnik stood up, almost upsetting his chair. "You get Pierre Lamarque to go instead of me; I just had an idea that'll take a little time to work out."

Snowflakes glided slantwise out of a gray January sky. "Better park here," said the detective, as Lindsley swung his car off roadway at 72nd Street. "Won't do to go too far downtown. Look, there's another!"

Lindsley and Lamarque peered through the windows, and saw a hurrying figure slip into a doorway. There was something odd about the figure. Lamarque spoke: "He's wearing a football helmet!"

"Huh!" said the detective, blinking. "Well, anyways, we're gonna take a closer look at his fancy headpiece. Got your guns, you two?" He slid out of the car, skidded a little on the snow, and steadied himself.

"Town's sure gonna get buried in snow, with nobody to remove it. Keep your eyes peeled for the isos."

The three marched abreast along the deserted street. Professor Lindsley almost stumbled over a body, half buried in the snow. He recognized a State trooper's uniform. He looked about, squinting against the snowflakes, and realized that the half dozen other darkish humps in the snow were also corpses. "Say, Monahan——"

"Sh-h! Want our friend to hear you? Now, Professor Lamarque, you stand on this side of the doorway and tackle him m the legs when he comes out. I'll do the rest."

Lamarque had given up trying to explain that he wasn't a full professor. Moreover, unless something was done about the plague soon, it looked as though he never *would* be a full professor. The university buildings were deserted I save for a few dauntless scientists still trying to get at the cause and cure of the affliction.

"Remember," Monahan was whispering, "the foist guy • that shows a sign of going nutty, one of the others taps him on the head, but gentlelike, see? We don't want no fractured skulls." He flipped his blackjack up and down to illustrate "gentlelike."

The black outline of a man, weaving slowly along the sidewalk, materialized out of the snowflakes. He came up to the ambuscade, saying something in a pleading whine.

"Naw, scram, you!" hissed the detective, flipping his blackjack suggestively.

The man scrammed.

Lindsley looked nervously up and down the street, and at the two younger men beside the doorway, Damn it, he'd been a fool to come! Guerrilla warfare was no occupation for a sixty-year-old biology professor. He'd partly brought it on himself, by being the only man to present a plausible theory to the authorities—well, at least as plausible as any others. With New York City practically lost to civilized control they'd have listened to anybody. At the I present rate, in another month New England and the Middle Atlantic States would be a wilderness, inhabited solely by roving bands of isolinguals who battled each other with clubs, rocks, and the loot of hardware stores.

Suppose some of them came along now? Thinking that they had been translated by magic into a strange and terrifying world, they were as dangerous as wild beasts. Lindsley wondered what it was like to shoot a man. And then the door opened and the man in the football helmet came out.

Lamarque tackled the fellow neatly below the knees. He got out one yell before the detective was all over him, kneeling on his ribs and stuffing snow in his mouth. Then Monahan yanked off the helmet and slapped the man's skull with his blackjack. he snapped, getting up and dragging the "Come on!" body by the coat collar toward the car.

A cluster of figures loomed out of the semi-darkness. Lindsley counted six—no, seven, and felt in his pocket for the pistol. The seven just stared. Monahan brought out his pistol. The seven gave back apprehensively. Evidently they'd had painful experience— perhaps in the Battle of Herald Square, when a National Guard detachment—and a troop of State police had scattered a horde of embattled isolinguals, only to be seized themselves, many of them, and start killing each other.

One of the seven spoke up in what sounded like a Slavonic tongue. The detective tried to smile sweetly. "Can't understand you," he said, wagging his head. The leader's sign was audible above the hiss of the falling flakes, and the seven trudged off.

The detectives stuffed their captive into the car. Lindsley let in the clutch slowly; the right rear wheel spun a few revolutions and then gripped the snow.

Monahan yelled in his ear, "Step on it, doc!"

Lindsley jumped and tried to comply. In the mirror he had a glimpse of people swarming out of the doorway. A submachine gun crackled; a hole the diameter of a finger appeared in the windshield, surrounded by a spider web of cracks. Lindsley heard a gasp from the captive, and a stream of profanity from Monahan. "They got our prisoner, the—"

The car slithered around the corner of West End and 72nd. "Damn good thing this wasn't an old front-engined car," the rasping voice continued. "They'd have let daylight into us sure. Bet the rear end looks like gravel sizer. Take it easy, doc; they can't see to shoot more'n a block or two."

Later Monahan said, "Nope, the stiff didn't have no papers on him, but I still think he's a National Patriot. How you coming along with those helmets?"

"All finished," replied Lindsley. "I've been standing over the analysts with a club for twenty-four hours. The shielding inside the helmet was a lead-bismuth-antimony alloy, with traces of platinum and two of the rare metals. My son-in-law's gone out to wire the specifications to Albany and Washington."

"Hope it ain't too late. We better clear out to-night, before any more of us come down with the plague."

"There's still one telephone wire open," continued Lindsley. "And the man I was talking to told me the first case has been reported from San Francisco. A scrub lady started doing a hula. Must be a Polynesian sailor in her family tree somewhere, I—ah—" The voice trailed off. Professor Arthur Lindsley was asleep.

A lurch and the clash of metal on metal awoke him. "Hey, I wha—"

The detective's heroic cursing left off. "You hurt? Guess we're all right. Hey, Joe, where the hell are we? Poughkeepsie? We're on our way to Albany, professor, or rather we *was* on our way before the truck pushed us into this here lamppost. Guess it was a case driving, from the way he weaved. Maybe I should 'a' tried to hunt up a 'plane."

Lamarque's voice came out of the dark: "Looks as if there's been another battle, from the corpses scattered around. Will that left door still open? Say, Monahan, don't you ever sleep?"

"Yeah, I grab a little now and then. Come on."

The drug store's shattered front gaped at them with a defeated air. Inside, the detective's flashlight dug a pallid clerk out from behind the soda fountain. "Don't stop, please!" he quavered. "You're not isolinguals! A gang of 'em took over the town yesterday, and then this evening a bigger gang came along and drove 'em out. I thought they'd all gone and came down to open up shop, but some more came along just now. Look, quick, there they are again!"

"Stand back there!" roared Monahan. The figure in the doorway shouted something back, and the detective's pistol went off.

"Quick, you guys, pile the—" But the two scientists and the other cop were already furiously building a barricade of chairs and tables. A few stones sailed past their heads and made beautiful crashes among the glassware.

Lindsley peered over the top of the upturned table. A figure, wild in the moonlight, rose from the sidewalk and raised a length of pipe or something. Lindsley fumbled for his pistol. Where the devil was the safety catch on the thing! He pulled the trigger. As his senses cleared after the flash and report, he saw that the figure was still there. He gripped the gun in both hands and tried again. The figure doubled over and went *fthup!* in the slush.

Hours later Lamarque wiped his mouth on his sleeve. "If I drink another malted milk I'll get indigestion. What else have you, Mr. Bloom?"

"Sorry, sir, but the isos cleaned out all the pies and bread and things. And the gas is shut off, so I can't make any coffee. It'll have to be sodas or nothing, unless you want to try some cough drops."

"Ugh! Any luck on the 'phone, Joe'"

"Nope, Unless somebody finds us by dark it'll be just tough. They're waiting for that to rush us."

Unless somebody found them—- There wouldn't be any street lights to shoot by. And four pistols wouldn't stop the horde of isolinguals waiting out of sight around the corners.

Darkness—no moon this time. The voices of the isos wafted into the drug more. The leaders were evidently haranguing their men. Then there was a full-throated yell, and the slopping of many feet in the slush. Bloom, the clerk, was carefully setting a row of bottles on the floor to use as missiles. If you didn't have a gun you had to use something.

Lamarque's pistol cracked. "Got one!"

Then the fusillade. But they came on in a solid mass. Lindsley thought, "These are really good, honest citizens I'm shooting, except for their malady." He realized that he had been squeezing the trigger of an empty gun. How the devil did you load the things' He'd never get it figured out before they swarmed in and finished them off. They were almost in the drug store now—

Monahan stopped his target practice to say, "Now why the hell are they all running one way? What's that noise! If it's a machine gun, boy, we're saved!"

Lindsley never imagined he'd find that implacable hammering the sweetest of sounds. The armored car skidded to a stop, and two football-helmeted soldiers jumped out.

Monahan turned to Lamarque. "What's that! Sorry, but I didn't get you. What? *Hey!*" He flung his arms around the young biologist in a bearlike hug. "Soldier! You got any more helmets?"

Lamarque's muttering rose to a frenzied shriek.

"Yeah, they're in the truck."

"*What* truck?"

"They were right behind us; ought to be along any—Yeah, here they come."

"Well, get one, quick! This guy's gone screwy like the others! "

When the helmet had been forced on Lamarque's unwilling head, Monahan rubbed his shins. "Lord, professor, I didn't know you was that strong. I guess the guy you toined into never loined no Queensbury rules or nothing. But you shouldn't have tried to bite me."

Lamarque was acutely embarrassed. "I—I'm sorry. You know I haven't any recollection of the past few minutes at all, up to the time you put the helmet on me—."

"'S all right; it wasn't your fault. Now let's find some of the isos we winged and put helmets on them. . . ."

Forty-eight hours later, Lindsley rubbed his eyes. "What do you mean by waking me up at this time of day, you young scoundrel? Oh, the paper. What's the news, quick?"

Lamarque seated himself on the bed with his slightly satanic grin. "You guessed right. They sent the army down to surround the area we figured the radiations were coming from, or rather that Plotnik figured they were coming from by finding the mass center of the locations of the cases reported. They were all wearing our cute little helmets, so the radiations didn't affect them.

"When they closed in and started searching houses they rounded up several thousand National Patriots. There was a little shooting, but most of the N.P.'s surrendered quietly enough when they saw what they were up against.

"The military located the cause of the whole works in an old house on Christopher Street. The place was full of radio apparatus from cellar to roof. They found Slidell himself, and his master mind, a Dr. Falk, whom nobody ever heard of, but who modestly describes himself as the greater scientist of the age. Maybe he's right.

"This Falk got scared when he saw bayonets pointed at his stomach, and let out the whole story. Seems he found a complicated combination of harmonics on a long radio wave that would work this ancestral-memory switch, and he and Slidell figured to disorganize the whole country with it. And when his broadcasting set was turned off and everybody became himself again, we'd find Slidell installed as dictator and the H.P.'s running everything. Of course, in the meantime they'd be wearing the helmets and would be shielded from the radiations.

"The army turned the thing off right away, and all our medieval knights and yeomen are now ordinary citizens, and busy picking-up the pieces. Slidell, of course, made a speech. Too bad there wasn't a stenographer there to record it I suppose he and Falk will be shot for murder, treason, and every other crime on the books, though I think suppose every other crime on the books, though I think they could plead insanity with some justice.

"Oh, yes, you're now the head of the department, and I'm a full professor. Also, we're famous, and are about to be intensively photographed and interviewed."

Lindsley scratched his diminutive beard. "Seems to me, Pierre, that we're getting away with murder. Plotnik really figured out the source of those radiations, and Monahan had the idea of suspecting the N.P.'s and setting out to catch one."

"Don't worry about them. They're getting their share of the glory."

"I suppose so. But right now what I want is a vacation from all scientific thought."

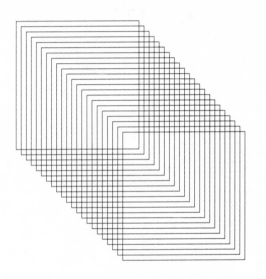

THE MAN WHO WALKED HOME

WALKED HOME

BY JAMES TIPTREE JR.

Transgression! Terror! And he thrust and lost there—punched into impossibility, abandoned never to be known how, the wrong man in the most wrong of all wrong places in that unimaginable collapse of never-to-be-reimagined mechanism—he stranded, undone, his lifeline severed, he in that nanosecond knowing his only tether parting, going away, the longest line to life withdrawing, zoinking out, disappearing forever beyond his grasp—telescoping away from him into the closing vortex beyond which lay his home, his life, his only possibility of being; seeing it sucked back into the deepest maw, melting, leaving him orphaned on what never-to-be-known shore of total wrongness—of beauty beyond joy, perhaps? Of horror? Of nothingness? Of profound otherness only, certainly—whatever it was, that place into which he transgressed, it could not support his life there, his violent and violating aberrance; and he, fierce, brave, crazy—clenched into total protest, one body-fist of utter repudiation of himself there in that place, forsaken there—what did he do? Rejected, exiled, hungering homeward more desperate than any lost beast driving for its unreachable home, his home, his HOME—and no way, no transport, no vehicle, means, machinery, no force but his intolerable resolve aimed homeward along that vanishing vector, that last and only lifeline—he did, what?

He walked.

Home.

Precisely what hashed up in the work of the major industrial lessee of the Bonneville Particle Acceleration Facility in Idaho was never known. Or rather, all those who might have been able to diagnose the original malfunction were themselves obliterated almost at once in the greater catastrophe which followed.

The nature of this second cataclysm was not at first understood either. All that was ever certain was that at 1153.6 of May 2, 1989 Old Style, the Bonneville laboratories and all their personnel were transformed into an intimately disrupted form of matter resembling a high-energy plasma, which became rapidly airborne to the accompaniment of radiating seismic and atmospheric events.

The disturbed area unfortunately included an operational MIRV Watchdog womb.

In the confusion of the next hours the Earth's population was substantially reduced, the biosphere was altered, and the Earth itself was marked with numbers of more conventional craters. For some years thereafter, the survivors were existentially preoccupied and the peculiar dust bowl at Bonneville was left to weather by itself in the changing climatic cycles.

It was not a large crater; just over a kilometer in width and lacking the usual displacement lip. Its surface was covered with a finely divided substance which dried into dust. Before the rains began it was almost perfectly flat. Only in certain lights, had anyone been there to inspect it, a small surface-marking or abraded place could be detected almost exactly at the center.

Two decades after the disaster a party of short brown people appeared from the south, together with a flock of somewhat atypical sheep. The crater at this time appeared as a wide shallow basin in which the grass did not grow well, doubtless from the almost complete lack of soil micro-organisms. Neither this nor the surrounding vigorous grass was found to harm the sheep. A few crude hogans went up at the southern edge and a faint path began to be traced across the crater itself, passing by the central bare spot.

One spring morning two children who had been driving sheep across the crater came screaming back to camp. A monster had burst out of the ground before them, a huge flat animal making a dreadful roar. It vanished in a flash and a shaking of the earth, leaving an evil smell. The sheep had run away.

Since this last was visibly true, some elders investigated. Finding no sign of the monster and no place in which it could hide, they settled for beating the children, who settled for making a detour around the monster-spot, and nothing more occurred for a while.

The following spring the episode was repeated. This time an older girl was present, but she could add only that the monster seemed to be rushing flat out along the ground without moving at all. And there was a scraped place in the dirt. Again nothing was found; an evil-ward in a cleft stick was placed at the spot.

When the same thing happened for the third time a year later, the detour was extended and other charm-wands were added. But since no harm seemed to come of it and the brown people had seen far worse, sheep-tending resumed as before. A few more instantaneous apparitions of the monster were noted, each time in the spring.

At the end of the third decade of the new era a tall old man limped down the hills from the south, pushing his pack upon a bicycle wheel. He camped on the far side of the crater, and soon found the monster-site. He attempted to question people about it, but no one understood him, so he traded a knife for some meat. Although he was obviously feeble, something about him dissuaded them from killing him, and this proved wise because he later assisted the women in treating several sick children.

He spent much time around the place of the apparition and was nearby when it made its next appearance. This excited him very much and he did several inexplicable but apparently harmless things, including moving his camp into the crater by the trail. He stayed on for a full year watching the site and was close by for its next manifestation. After this he spent a few days making a charm-stone for the spot and left northward, hobbling as he had come.

More decades passed. The crater eroded, and a rain-gully became an intermittent streamlet across the edge of the basin. The brown people and their sheep were attacked by a band of grizzled men, after which the survivors went away eastward. The winters of what had been Idaho were now frost-free; aspen and eucalyptus sprouted in the moist plain. Still the crater remained treeless, visible as a flat bowl of grass; and the bare place at the center remained. The skies cleared somewhat.

After another three decades a larger band of black people with ox-drawn carts appeared and stayed for a time, but left again when they too saw the thunderclap-monster. A few other vagrants straggled by.

Five decades later a small permanent settlement had grown up on the nearest range of hills, from which men riding on small ponies with dark stripes down their spines herded humped cattle near the crater. A herdsman's hut was built by the streamlet, which in time became the habitation of an olive-skinned, red-haired family. In due course one of this clan again observed the monster-flash, but these people did not depart. The stone the tall man had placed was noted and left undisturbed.

The homestead at the crater's edge grew into a group of three and was joined by others, and the trail across it became a cart road with a log bridge over the stream. At the center of the still faintly discernible crater the cart road made a bend, leaving a grassy place which bore on its center about a square meter of curiously impacted bare earth and a deeply etched sandstone rock.

The apparition of the monster was now known to occur regularly each spring on a certain morning in this place, and the children of the community dared each other to approach the spot. It was referred to in a phrase that could be translated as "the Old Dragon." The Old Dragon's appearance was always the same: a brief violent thunderburst which began and cut off abruptly, in the midst of which a dragon-like creature was seen apparently in furious motion on the earth, although it never actually moved. Afterward there was a bad smell and the earth smoked. People who saw it from close by spoke of a shivering sensation.

Early in the second century two young men rode into town from the north. Their ponies were shaggier than the local breed, and the equipment they carried included two box-like objects which the young men set up at the monster-site. They stayed in the area a full year, observing two materializations of the Old Dragon, and they provided much news and maps of roads and trading towns in the cooler regions to the north. They built a windmill which was accepted by the community and offered to build a lighting machine, which was refused. Then they departed with their boxes after unsuccessfully attempting to persuade a local boy to learn to operate one.

In the course of the next decades other travelers stopped by and marveled at the monster, and there was sporadic fighting over the mountains to the south. One of the armed bands made a cattle raid into the crater hamlet. It was repulsed, but the raiders left a spotted sickness which killed many. For all this time the bare place at the crater's center remained, and the monster made his regular appearances, observed or not.

The hill-town grew and changed, and the crater hamlet grew to be a town. Roads widened and linked into networks. There were gray-green conifers in the hills now, spreading down into the plain, and chirruping lizards lived in their branches.

At century's end a shabby band of skin-clad squatters with stunted milk-beasts erupted out of the west and were eventually killed or driven away, but not before the local herds had contracted a vicious parasite. Veterinarians were fetched from the market city up north, but little could be done. The families near the crater left, and for some decades the area was empty. Finally cattle of a new strain reappeared in the plain and the crater hamlet was reoccupied. Still the bare center continued annually to manifest the monster, and he became an accepted phenomenon of the area. On several occasions parties came from the distant Northwest Authority to observe it.

The crater hamlet flourished and grew into the fields where cattle had grazed, and part of the old crater became the town park. A small seasonal tourist industry based on the monster-site developed. The townspeople rented rooms for the appearances, and many more-or-less authentic monster-relics were on display in the local taverns.

Several cults now grew up around the monster. One persistent belief held that it was a devil or damned soul forced to appear on Earth in torment to expiate the catastrophe of three centuries back. Others believed that it, or he, was some kind of messenger whose roar portended either doom or hope according to the believer. One very vocal sect taught that the apparition registered the moral conduct of the townspeople over the past year, and scrutinized the annual apparition for changes which could be interpreted for good or ill. It was considered lucky, or dangerous, to be touched by some of the dust raised by the monster. In every generation at least one small boy would try to hit the monster with a stick, usually acquiring a broken arm and a lifelong tavern tale. Pelting the monster with stones or other objects was a popular sport, and for some years people systematically flung prayers and flowers at it. Once a party tried to net it and were left with strings and vapor. The area itself had long since been fenced off at the center of the park.

Through all this the monster made his violently enigmatic annual appearance, sprawled furiously motionless, unreachably roaring.

Only as the fourth century of the new era went by was it apparent that the monster had been changing slightly. He was now no longer on the earth but had an arm and a leg thrust upward in a kicking or flailing gesture. As the years passed he began to change more quickly until at the end of the century he had risen to a contorted crouching pose, arms outflung as if frozen in gyration. His roar, too, seemed somewhat differently pitched, and the earth after him smoked more and more.

It was then widely felt that the man-monster was about to do something, to make some definitive manifestation, and a series of natural disasters and marvels gave support to a vigorous cult teaching this doctrine. Several religious leaders journeyed to the town to observe the apparitions.

However, the decades passed and the man-monster did nothing more than turn slowly in place, so that he now appeared to be in the act of sliding or staggering while pushing himself backward like a creature blown before a gale. No wind, of course, could be felt, and presently the general climate quieted and nothing came of it all.

Early in the fifth century New Calendar three survey parties from the North Central Authority came through the area and stopped to observe the monster. A permanent recording device was set up at the site, after assurances to the townsfolk that no hardscience was involved. A local boy was trained to operate it; he quit when his girl left him but another volunteered. At this time nearly everyone believed that the apparition was a man, or the ghost of one. The record-machine boy and a few others including the school mechanics teacher referred to him as The Man John. In the next decades the roads were greatly improved; all forms of travel increased, and there was talk of building a canal to what had been the Snake River.

One May morning at the end of Century Five a young couple in a smart green mule-trap came jogging up the highroad from the

Sandreas Rift Range to the southwest. The girl was golden-skinned and chatted with her young husband in a language unlike that ever heard by The Man John either at the end or the beginning of his life. What she said to him has, however, been heard in every age and tongue.

"Oh, Serli, I'm so glad we're taking this trip now! Next summer I'll be busy with baby!"

To which Serli replied as young husbands often have, and so they trotted up to the town's inn. Here they left trap and bags and went in search of her uncle, who was expecting them there. The morrow was the day of The Man John's annual appearance, and her Uncle Laban had come from the MacKenzie History Museum to observe it and to make certain arrangements.

They found him with the town school instructor of mechanics, who was also the recorder at the monster-site. Presently Uncle Laban took them all with him to the town mayor's office to meet with various religious personages. The mayor was not unaware of tourist values, but he took Uncle Laban's part in securing the cultists' grudging assent to the MacKenzie authorities' secular interpretation of the monster, which was made easier by the fact that the cults disagreed among themselves. Then, seeing how pretty the niece was, the mayor took them all home to dinner.

When they returned to the inn for the night it was abrawl with holidaymakers.

"Whew," said Uncle Laban. "I've talked myself dry, sister's daughter. What a weight of holy nonsense is that Moksha female! Serli, my lad, I know you have questions. Let me hand you this to read, it's the guidebook we're giving them to sell. Tomorrow I'll answer for it all." And he disappeared into the crowded tavern.

So Serli and his bride took the pamphlet upstairs to bed with them, but it was not until the next morning at breakfast that they found time to read it.

" 'All that is known of John Delgano,' " read Serli with his mouth full, " 'comes from two documents left by his brother Carl Delgano in the archives of the MacKenzie Group in the early years after the holocaust.' Put some honey on this cake, Mira my dove. Verbatim transcript follows, this is Carl Delgano speaking:

" 'I'm not an engineer or an astronaut like John, I ran an electronics repair shop in Salt Lake City. John was only trained as a spaceman, he never got to space; the slump wiped all that out. So he tied up with this commercial group who were leasing part of Bonneville. They wanted a man for some kind of hard vacuum tests, that's all I knew about it. John and his wife moved to Bonneville, but we all got together several times a year, our wives were like sisters. John had two kids, Clara and Paul.

" 'The tests were supposed to be secret, but John told me confidentially they were trying for an antigravity chamber. I don't know if it ever worked. That was the year before.

" 'Then that winter they came down for Christmas and John said they had something far out. He was excited. A temporal displacement, he called it; some kind of time effect. He said their chief honcho was like a real mad scientist. Big ideas. He kept adding more angles every time some other project would quit and leave equipment he could lease. No, I don't know who the top company was—maybe an insurance conglomerate, they had all the cash, didn't they? I guess they'd pay to catch a look at the future, that figures. Anyway, John was go, go, go. Katharine was scared, that's natural. She pictured him like, you know, H. G. Wells—walking around in some future world. John told her it wasn't like that at all. All they'd get would be this flicker, like a second or two. All kinds of complications.'—Yes, yes, my greedy piglet, some brew for me too. This is thirsty work!

"So. 'I remember I asked him, what about Earth moving? I mean, you could come back in a different place, right? He said they had that all figured. A spatial trajectory. Katharine was so scared we dropped it. John told her, don't worry. I'll come home. But he didn't. Not that it makes any difference, of course, everything was wiped out. Salt Lake too. The only reason I'm here is that I went up by Calgary to see Mom, April twenty-ninth. May second it all blew. I didn't find you folks at MacKenzie until July. I guess I may as well stay. That's all I know about John, except that he was a solid guy. If that accident started all this it wasn't his fault.

" 'The second document'—in the name of love, little mother, do I have to read all this? Oh, very well, but you will kiss me first, madam. Must you look so delicious? 'The second document. Dated in the year eighteen, New Style, written by Carl'—see the old handwriting, my plump plump pigeon? Oh, very well, *very* well.

" 'Written at Bonneville Crater: I have seen my brother John Delgano. When I knew I had the rad sickness I came down here to look around. Salt Lake's still hot. So I hiked up here by Bonneville. You can see the crater where the labs were, it's grassed over. It's different, not radioactive; my film's okay. There's a bare place in the middle. Some Indios here told me a monster shows up here every year in the spring. I saw it myself a couple of days after I got here, but I was too far away to see much, except I was sure it's a man. In a vacuum suit. There was a lot of noise and dust, took me by surprise. It was all over in a second. I figured it's pretty close to the day, I mean, May second, old.

" 'So I hung around a year and he showed up again yesterday. I was on the face side, and I could see his face through the visor. It's John, all right. He's hurt. I saw blood on his mouth and his suit is frayed some. He's lying on the ground. He didn't move while I could see him but the dust boiled up, like a man sliding onto base without moving. His eyes are open like he was looking. I don't understand it anyway, but I know it's John, not a ghost. He was in exactly the same position each time and there's a loud crack like thunder and another sound like a siren, very fast. And an ozone smell, and smoke. I felt a kind of shudder.

" 'I know it's John there and I think he's alive. I have to leave here now to take this back while I can still walk. I think somebody should come here and see. Maybe you can help John. Signed, Carl Delgano.

" 'These records were kept by the MacKenzie Group, but it was not for several years'—etcetera, first light-print, etcetera, archives, analysts, etcetera—very good! Now it is time to meet your uncle, my edible one, after we go upstairs for just a moment."

"No, Serli, I will wait for you downstairs," said Mira prudently.

When they came into the town park Uncle Laban was directing

the installation of a large durite slab in front of the enclosure around The Man John's appearance-spot. The slab was wrapped in a curtain to await the official unveiling. Townspeople and tourists and children thronged the walks, and a Ride-for-God choir was singing in the band shell. The morning was warming up fast. Vendors hawked ices and straw toys of the monster and flowers and good-luck confetti to throw at him. Another religious group stood by in dark robes; they belonged to the Repentance church beyond the park. Their pastor was directing somber glares at the crowd in general and Mira's uncle in particular.

Three official-looking strangers who had been at the inn came up and introduced themselves to Uncle Laban as observers from Alberta Central. They went on into the tent which had been erected over the closure, carrying with them several pieces of equipment which the townsfolk eyed suspiciously.

The mechanics teacher finished organizing a squad of students to protect the slab's curtain, and Mira and Serli and Laban went on into the tent. It was much hotter inside. Benches were set in rings around a railed enclosure about twenty feet in diameter. Inside the railing the earth was bare and scuffed. Several bunches of flowers and blooming poinciana branches leaned against the rail. The only thing inside the rail was a rough sandstone rock with markings etched on it.

Just as they came in, a small girl raced across the open center and was yelled at by everybody. The officials from Alberta were busy at one side of the rail, where the light-print box was mounted.

"Oh, no," muttered Mira's uncle, as one of the officials leaned over to set up a tripod stand inside the rails. He adjusted it, and a huge horsetail of fine feathery filaments blossomed out and eddied through the center of the space.

"Oh, *no*," Laban said again. "Why can't they let it be?"

"They're trying to pick up dust from his suit, is that right?" Serli asked.

"Yes, insane. Did you get time to read?"

"Oh, yes," said Serli.

"Sort of," added Mira.

"Then you know. He's falling. Trying to check his—well, call it velocity. Trying to slow down. He must have slipped or stumbled. We're getting pretty close to when he lost his footing and started to fall. What did it? Did somebody trip him?" Laban looked from Mira to Serli, dead serious now. "How would you like to be the one who made John Delgano fall?"

"Ooh," said Mira in quick sympathy. Then she said, "Oh."

"You mean," asked Serli, "whoever made him fall caused all the, caused—"

"Possible," said Laban.

"Wait a minute." Serli frowned. "He did fall. So somebody had to do it—I mean, he has to trip or whatever. If he doesn't fall the past would all be changed, wouldn't it? No war, no—"

"Possible," Laban repeated. "God knows. All *I* know is that John Delgano and the space around him is the most unstable, improbable, highly charged area ever known on Earth, and I'm damned if I think anybody should go poking sticks in it."

"Oh, come now, Laban!" One of the Alberta men joined them, smiling. "Our dust mop couldn't trip a gnat. It's just vitreous monofilaments."

"Dust from the future," grumbled Laban. "What's it going to tell you? That the future has dust in it?"

"If we could only get a trace from that thing in his hand."

"In his hand?" asked Mira. Serli started leafing hurriedly through the pamphlet.

"We've had a recording analyzer aimed at it," the Albertan lowered his voice, glancing around. "A spectroscope. We know there's something there, or was. Can't get a decent reading. It's severely deteriorated."

"People poking at him, grabbing at him," Laban muttered. "You—"

"TEN MINUTES!" shouted a man with a megaphone. "Take your places, friends and strangers."

The Repentance people were filing in at one side, intoning an ancient incantation, "Mi-seri-cordia, Ora pro nobis!"

The atmosphere suddenly became tense. It was now very close and hot in the big tent. A boy from the mayor's office wiggled through the crowd, beckoning Laban's party to come and sit in the guest chairs on the second level on the "face" side. In front of them at the rail one of the Repentance ministers was arguing with an Albertan official over his right to occupy the space taken by a recorder, it being his special duty to look into The Man John's eyes.

"Can he really see us?" Mira asked her uncle.

"Blink your eyes," Laban told her. "A new scene every blink, that's what he sees. Phantasmagoria. Blink-blink-blink—for god knows how long."

"Mi-sere-re, pec-cavi," chanted the penitentials. A soprano neighed "May the red of sin pa-aa-ass from us!"

"They believe his oxygen tab went red because of the state of their souls," Laban chuckled. "Their souls are going to have to stay damned awhile; John Delgano has been on oxygen reserve for five centuries— or rather, he *will be* low for five centuries more. At a half-second per year his time, that's fifteen minutes. We know from the audio trace he's still breathing more or less normally, and the reserve was good for twenty minutes. So they should have their salvation about the year seven hundred, if they last that long."

"FIVE MINUTES! Take your seats, folks. Please sit down so everyone can see. Sit down, folks."

"It says we'll hear his voice through his suit speaker," Serli whispered. "Do you know what he's saying?"

"You get mostly a twenty-cycle howl," Laban whispered back. "The recorders have spliced up something like *ayt*, part of an old word. Take centuries to get enough to translate."

"Is it a message?"

"Who knows? Could be his word for 'date' or 'hate.' 'Too late,' maybe. Anything."

The tent was quieting. A fat child by the railing started to cry and was pulled back onto a lap. There was a subdued mumble of praying. The Holy Joy faction on the far side rustled their flowers.

"Why don't we set our clocks by him?"

"It's changing. He's on sidereal time."

"ONE MINUTE."

In the hush the praying voices rose slightly. From outside a chicken cackled. The bare center space looked absolutely ordinary. Over it the recorder's silvery filaments eddied gently in the breath from a hundred lungs. Another recorder could be heard ticking faintly.

For long seconds nothing happened.

The air developed a tiny hum. At the same moment Mira caught a movement at the railing on her left.

The hum developed a beat and vanished into a peculiar silence and suddenly everything happened at once.

Sound burst on them, raced shockingly up the audible scale. The air cracked as something rolled and tumbled in the space. There was a grinding, wailing roar and—

He was there.

Solid, huge—a huge man in a monster-suit, his head was a dull bronze transparent globe, holding a human face, a dark smear of open mouth. His position was impossible, legs strained forward thrusting himself back, his arms frozen in a whirlwind swing. Although he seemed to be in frantic forward motion nothing moved, only one of his legs buckled or sagged slightly—

—And then he was gone, utterly and completely gone in a thunderclap, leaving only the incredible afterimage in a hundred pairs of staring eyes. Air boomed, shuddering; dust rolled out mixed with smoke.

"Oh! Oh, my god," gasped Mira, unheard, clinging to Serli. Voices were crying out, choking. "He saw me, he saw me!" a woman shrieked. A few people dazedly threw their confetti into the empty dust-cloud, most had failed to throw at all. Children began to howl. "He *saw* me!" the woman screamed hysterically. "Red, oh, Lord have mercy!" a deep male voice intoned.

Mira heard Laban swearing furiously and looked again into the space. As the dust settled she could see that the recorder's tripod had tipped over into the center. There was a dusty mound lying against it—flowers. Most of the end of the stand seemed to have disappeared or been melted. Of the filaments nothing could be seen.

"Some damn fool pitched flowers into it. Come on, let's get out."

"Was it under, did it trip him?" asked Mira, squeezed in the crowd.

"It was still red, his oxygen thing," Serli said over her head. "No mercy this trip, eh, Laban?"

"Shsh!" Mira caught the Repentance pastor's dark glance. They jostled through the enclosure gate and were out in the sunlit park, voices exclaiming, chattering loudly in excitement and relief.

"It was terrible," Mira cried softly. "Oh, I never thought it was a real live man. There he is, he's *there*. Why can't we help him? Did we trip him?"

"I don't know, I don't think so," her uncle grunted. They sat down near the new monument, fanning themselves. The curtain was still in place.

"Did we change the past?" Serli laughed, looked lovingly at his little wife. For a moment he wondered why she was wearing such odd earrings; then he remembered he had given them to her at that Indian pueblo they'd passed.

"But it wasn't just those Alberta people," said Mira. She seemed obsessed with the idea. "It was the flowers really." She wiped at her forehead.

"Mechanics or superstition," chuckled Serli. "Which is the culprit, love or science?"

"Shsh." Mira looked about nervously. "The flowers were love, I guess. I feel so strange. It's hot. Oh, thank you." Uncle Laban had succeeded in attracting the attention of the iced-drink vendor.

People were chatting normally now, and the choir struck into a cheerful song. At one side of the park a line of people were waiting to sign their names in the visitors' book. The mayor appeared at the park gate, leading a party up the bougainvillea alley for the unveiling of the monument.

"What did it say on that stone by his foot?" Mira asked. Serli showed her the guidebook picture of Carl's rock with the inscription translated below: WELCOME HOME JOHN.

"I wonder if he can see it."

The mayor was about to begin his speech.

Much later when the crowd had gone away the monument stood alone in the dark, displaying to the moon the inscription in the language of that time and place:

ON THIS SPOT THERE APPEARS ANNUALLY THE FORM OF MAJOR JOHN DELGANO, THE FIRST AND ONLY MAN TO TRAVEL IN TIME.

MAJOR DELGANO WAS SENT INTO THE FUTURE SOME HOURS BEFORE THE HOLOCAUST OF DAY ZERO. ALL KNOWLEDGE OF THE MEANS BY WHICH HE WAS SENT IS LOST, PERHAPS FOREVER. IT IS BELIEVED THAT AN ACCIDENT OCCURRED WHICH SENT HIM MUCH FARTHER THAN WAS INTENDED. SOME ANALYSTS SPECULATE THAT HE MAY HAVE GONE AS FAR AS FIFTY THOUSAND YEARS AHEAD. HAVING REACHED THIS UNKNOWN POINT MAJOR DELGANO APPARENTLY WAS RECALLED, OR ATTEMPTED TO RETURN, ALONG THE COURSE IN SPACE AND TIME THROUGH WHICH HE WAS SENT. HIS TRAJECTORY IS THOUGHT TO START AT THE POINT WHICH OUR SOLAR SYSTEM WILL OCCUPY AT A FUTURE TIME AND IS TANGENT TO THE COMPLEX HELIX WHICH OUR EARTH DESCRIBES AROUND THE SUN.

HE APPEARS ON THIS SPOT IN THE ANNUAL INSTANTS IN WHICH HIS COURSE INTERSECTS OUR PLANET'S ORBIT, AND HE IS APPARENTLY ABLE TO TOUCH THE GROUND IN THOSE INSTANTS. SINCE NO TRACE OF HIS PASSAGE INTO THE FUTURE HAS BEEN MANIFESTED, IT IS BELIEVED THAT HE IS RETURNING BY A DIFFERENT MEANS THAN HE WENT FORWARD. HE IS ALIVE IN OUR PRESENT. OUR PAST IS HIS FUTURE AND OUR FUTURE IS HIS PAST. THE TIME OF HIS APPEARANCES IS SHIFTING GRADUALLY IN SOLAR TIME TO CONVERGE ON THE MOMENT OF 1153.6, ON MAY 2, 1989 OLD STYLE, OR DAY ZERO.

THE EXPLOSION WHICH ACCOMPANIED HIS RETURN TO HIS OWN TIME AND PLACE MAY HAVE OCCURRED WHEN SOME ELEMENTS OF THE PAST INSTANTS OF HIS COURSE WERE CARRIED WITH HIM INTO THEIR OWN PRIOR EXISTENCE. IT IS CERTAIN THAT THIS EXPLOSION

PRECIPITATED THE WORLDWIDE HOLOCAUST WHICH
ENDED FOREVER THE AGE OF HARDSCIENCE.

—He was falling, losing control, falling in his fight against the terrible
momentum he had gained, fighting with his human legs shaking in the
inhuman stiffness of his armor, his soles charred, not gripping well now,
not enough traction to break, battling, thrusting as the flashes came, the
punishing alternation of light, dark, light, dark, which he had borne so
long, the claps of air thickening and thinning against his armor as he skidded
through space which was time, desperately braking as the flickers of Earth
hammered against his feet—only his feet mattered now, only to slow and
stay on course—and the pull, the beacon was getting slacker; as he came
near home it was fanning out, hard to stay centered; he was becoming, he
supposed, more probable; the wound he had punched in time was healing
itself. In the beginning it had been so tight—a single ray of light in a closing
tunnel—he had hurled himself after it like an electron flying to the anode,
aimed surely along that exquisitely complex single vector of possibility of
life, shot and been shot like a squeezed pip into the last chink in that rejecting
and rejected nowhere through which he, John Delgano, could conceivably
continue to exist, the hole leading to home—had pounded down it across
time, across space, pumping with desperate legs as the real Earth of that
unreal time came under him, his course as certain as the twisting dash of
an animal down its burrow, he a cosmic mouse on an interstellar,
intertemporal race for his nest with the wrongness of everything closing
round the rightness of that one course, the atoms of his heart, his blood, his
every cell crying Home—HOME!—as he drove himself after that fading
breath-hole, each step faster, surer, stronger, until he raced with invincible
momentum upon the rolling flickers of Earth as a man might race a rolling
log in a torrent. Only the stars stayed constant around him from flash to
flash, he looking down past his feet at a million strobes of Crux, of
Triangulum; once at the height of his stride he had risked a century's glance
upward and seen the Bears weirdly strung out from Polaris—but a Polaris
not the Pole Star now, he realized, jerking his eyes back to his racing feet,
thinking, I am walking home to Polaris, home! to the strobing beat. He
had ceased to remember where he had been, the beings, people or aliens or
things, he had glimpsed in the impossible moment of being where he could

not be; had ceased to see the flashes of worlds around him, each flash different, the jumble of bodies, shapes, walls, colors, landscapes—some lasting a breath, some changing pell-mell—the faces, limbs, things poking at him; the nights he had pounded through, dark or lit by strange lamps, roofed or unroofed; the days flashing sunlight, gales, dust, snow, interiors innumerable, strobe after strobe into night again; he was in daylight now, a hall of some kind; I am getting closer at last, he thought, the feel is changing—but he had to slow down, to check; and that stone near his feet, it had stayed there some time now, he wanted to risk a look but he did not dare, he was so tired, and he was sliding, was going out of control, fighting to kill the merciless velocity that would not let him slow down; he was hurt, too, something had hit him back there, they had done something, he didn't know what, back somewhere in the kaleidoscope of faces, arms, hooks, beams, centuries of creatures grabbing at him—and his oxygen was going, never mind, it would last—it had to last, he was going home, home! And he had forgotten now the message he had tried to shout, hoping it could be picked up somehow, the important thing he had repeated; and the thing he had carried, it was gone now, his camera was gone too, something had torn it away but he was coming home! Home! If only he could kill this momentum, could stay on the failing course, could slip, scramble, slide, somehow ride this avalanche down to haze, to home—and his throat said Home!—called Kate, Kate! And his heart shouted, his lungs almost gone now, as his legs fought, fought and failed, as his feet gripped and skidded and held and slid, as he pitched, flailed, pushed, strove in the gale of time-rush across space, across time, at the end of the longest path ever: the path of John Delgano, coming home.

ABOUT THE EDITOR

Editor of the World Fantasy Award-nominated *Narrow Houses* anthology series for Little, Brown (UK), Peter is also coeditor of *Heaven Sent* (with Martin H. Greenberg) for DAW Books and, with Ed Kramer, of the White Wolf anthologies *Tombs* and *Dante's Disciples*. His latest all-new anthology—*Destination Unknown*—appears from White Wolf this year. Pete's short stories, articles and reviews appear regularly on both sides of the Atlantic and *Escardy Gap* (a novel written in collaboration with James Lovegrove) was published by Tor Books last fall.

THREE IN TIME

Novels written by Chad Oliver, Wilson Tucker & Poul Anderson Edited by Jack Dann, Pamela Sargent, George Zebrowski Time travel waits as a powerful, unrealized dream, inspiring some of our most spectacular science fiction. Here are three such novels, each extraordinary in its own way, in White Wolf Publishing's first

Science Fiction

Trade paperback

omnibus

ISBN 1-56504-985-3

WW 10041

$14.99 US

$19.99 CAN

REDISCOVERY TRIO. This exciting new series is dedicated to bringing enduring classics of science fiction to a new generation of readers. Foreword by Arthur C. Clarke.

THE WINDS OF TIME by Chad Oliver
"Oliver is a prime contender for the Heinlein-Clarke front rank of genuine science fiction, in which the science is as accurately absorbing as the fiction is richly human."
—The New York Times

THE YEAR OF THE QUIET SUN by Wilson Tucker
Winner of the John W. Campbell Award for Best Novel
"An H. G. Wells-type time machine takes this chilling story's anti-hero into a nightmare only-a-few-years-from-now future. This highly entertaining realistic novel is a Hugo contender..."
—A. E. van Vogt, Nebula Award Grand Master

THERE WILL BE TIME by Poul Anderson
Hugo and Nebula Award-winner
"Poul Anderson has made time travel more plausible and rational than anyone since H. G. Wells invented it...and makes it all new."
—Analog

*D*estination *U*nknown

Fantasy
Trade paperback anthology
ISBN 1-56504-941-1
WW 11941
US $12.99/CAN $17.99

Edited by Peter Crowther
Cover Photograph by Douglas Winter

"Here are haunted rooms, elevators and mazes, and towns where strange insect life holds sway or office buildings seem reluctant to let people go home. Here, too, are off-beat worlds which exist beneath the risers of a staircase or deep in the bowels of the earth, and alien landscapes where one might invoke the power of the angels, discover long-lost magicians or simply commune with deceased relatives...locations rich and strange and bizarre, and all yours for the taking."

Climb aboard and join Charles de Lint, Alan Dean Foster, Lisa Tuttle, James Lovegrove, Ramsey Campbell, Storm Constantine, R.A. Lafferty, and nine others for an unforgettable ride into realms above and beyond your wildest imagination.

Includes a special introduction by Anne McCaffrey.